The Conjure Man

by

Peter Damian Bellis

*For Leilani
All my best!*

River Boat Books

Printed in the United States of America.
Published by River Boat Books, St. Paul, MN.
First printing May 27, 2010.
Second printing January 22, 2022.

ISBN: 978-1-955823-12-8

Praise for *The Conjure Man*

"I couldn't put the book down. At times I would get lost in the action, but I was so overwhelmed by the lyrical beauty of the images and the prose that this did not bother me. I began to let the images and the action wash over me. The whole book was like a song. Would I like to read this book again? Most definitely yes!

—Mary Eschet, Book Reviewer,
Times Union, Jacksonville, Florida

"*The Conjure Man* moved me because of the beauty of the language, and the world of characters the author created."

—Andrei Codrescu, winner
of the Ovid Prize for poetry

"Peter Damian Bellis' novel *The Conjure Man* is unusual, sprightly, adventersome, and risk-taking. More importantly, it succeeds in doing what it sets out to do—it establishes a world of primitive, elemental, natural creatures, one with their environment and in time themselves. On a more ambitious level, it establishes a creation myth and a semi-mythic figure in the conjure man."

—Richard Rupp, author of
Celebration in Postwar American Fiction
as well as the novel *Unity*

"This novel is a fantastic, challenging read, and an experience to take part in."

—*The Columbia Books Examiner*

A Brief Introduction
by Quentin Brand

Set in the deep bigoted South of revival meetings, alligator hunts, Spanish moss and bible bashing lynch mobs, *The Conjure Man* occupies a similar fictional territory to Faulkner and Peter Mathiessen's *Shadow Country*. It consists of two intertwined and alternating narratives, that of Thaddeus, a man of no origin, an outcast, a loner who is his own sort of conjure man, who comes to live on the edge of a small community; and a boy who forms an uneasy friendship or alliance with him. The connections between these two characters is teased out over the course of the novel until gradually their relationship becomes clear to the reader. Interleaved with these two narratives is a third narrative describing the vanquishing of a (possibly mythic) alligator by a huntsman: this fable illustrates themes of 'nature red in tooth and claw' in which man establishes primacy over nature through cunning and cruelty.

Mr. Bellis is a marvelous, sure-footed stylist, employing a breathtaking range of totally different styles and voices for the two main narratives. The first person voice for the boy reproduces with marvelous accuracy the rhythms of Southern rural dialect, the kind of ungrammatical word-salad the woefully

undereducated produce (this voice is highly
infectious, and I found myself 'speaking' it
for several days while reading the novel). The
author achieves here a kind of beauty and
sincerity which seems to elude most contem-
porary American novelists who 'do the police in
different voices' and who usually only achieve
pastiche.

> *Time we up to the square, the*
> *festival lights they already on. The parade*
> *it done with and most the folks they done*
> *circle back to the tables. I aint see Mama*
> *or either Tramsee for too many folks, but*
> *there Willie in front of the barbecue, and*
> *he smoke-shouting for everybody step on*
> *up and get some...*

The third-person voice for Thaddeus
is quite different although recognizably
from the same locale, modernistic, stream of
consciousness, in turn split between two voices,
that of the narrator and that of the internal
monologue of Thaddeus's memory, this voice
tumbling on unbroken by sentence boundaries:

> *...the good Reverend now*
> *forgotten, him in his black church boots*
> *standing once more in front of the now*
> *smoke black tent beneath the quaking*
> *aspen, the Reverend watching the tent*

burn to the ground, the bible still in
his hand, a dream of what was to come,
perhaps, or what was, or what might have
been, or so it seemed...

    The Conjure Man is hugely atmospheric: one can feel the mosquitos biting and the crabs tugging, and there is an almost unbearable sense of menace and threat hanging over everything, occasionally erupting into shocking scenes of violence which seem to arise out of the landscape itself. Bellis is himself a conjure man, able to bring to our eyes and senses a very realistic depiction of a specific milieu.

    The novel contains a number of brilliant set-pieces, one of which is extracted in the excellent short story collection: *One Last Dance with Lawrence Welk*, in which this writer's ability to conjure up a range of settings, voices and characters is also displayed to the full.

—Quentin Brand, June 20, 2018

The Conjure Man

This novel is dedicated to my father.

when the world was first born, the swamps like
the one here they was all bigger then they is now,
everything was, the pines they was knocking they
blackgreen heads up against the sky, look like they
knock down some cloud every once and a while, and
they was hundreds of blue snapflies fly about, some
days couldnt see or either hear nothing else, and
mosquito too, and long as a mans arm, and there
was all kind of hawks and buzzards and crows circle
this way and that maybe looking for something eat
up like a dead hog, and every one of them birds big
as a horse is now, and the water it was full up with
snake, mostly cotton mouth and black snake, but
some rattler too, and they was all maybe fifty foot
long slither this way and that in the black-green
water, in the grass too, and they was looking for
eat up something same as them birds, but the king
of that there swamp he was as big as all the rest of
them animals put together, and more hungry too,
and what he was was a bluegreen alligator . . .

The Island

I been living on this here island my whole life long and aint never been off, which it dont bother me like some cause there plenty to do. Seems like every day me and Jonas Lee Porter we is stretching out for somewhere, maybe one day is a hog killing and we grabbing a ham hock right off the table, and the next we down to the dock even there aint nothing but tins and wire and pieces of wood stuck down in the grass, but maybe we find we a old boat and head on up the coast, so we down there all the same, and every now and then we be slipping out to the backwater come night, we eyes set on witches, cause Jonas Lee his brother say how there plenty of witches what roam about the wood, them out looking for something to eat.

Today aint no different. Jonas Lee he come along he saying say let we head on out to the tidewater no telling what we might find floating in the shallows, so thats what we done, and is there we seen old man Thaddeus napping in the sand. He look most dead the way he stretch out white as he is, and he must of been that way a while cause there a flock of white gull fish-fighting back of his head a bit, and then a couple them fat gull they come up to the old man hisself and look him dead to his eye, and

with that we done bust ourself laughing, and
then they all fly off. The old man he dont look
so bad close up, nothing like people say, but
Jonas and me we quiet up and steady ourself
just the same. My mama she tell me say I ever
see the old man coming up the road I should
keep my eyes to myself and pass on by without
saying a word. I use to think he been the devil
hisself the way she be talking on and on, and
there wunt too many peoples argue the other
way. Only thing was, when me and Jonas Lee
come along, the old man he wunt on no road at
all.

"What you think he doing," Jonas Lee say.

"What you think," I say.

"Maybe he dead," Jonas Lee say.

"Maybe he aint," I say.

Jonas he done know about the old man same
as me, but he wunt thinking past his stomach.
The old man he had hisself nine or ten string
tied round some fish heads or maybe chicken
heads, them heads mud-flapping back and forth
in the yellow-green water. Aint a crab in the
world pass up a meal like that. They go nibble
on them heads no matter the time of day and
then all you do you just net em. It looked like
the old man done netted hisself a few cause he
had a cutacoo basket full of some big old blues
and all of them pile up claw on claw see which
one get to the top. Jonas Lee he saying say it a
shame the old man is died like he done, only

no sense let all that sweet blue crab meat go to waste, and with that then he flash me a smile like it been his basket all along, but before he even think to grab it he down on his knees and he pointing at something move in the water.

"You see em there, Kilby," he say.

I seen em just the same. Four big blues nibble on a head down in that yellow-green water. Jonas Lee then he saying say they just enough room in that cutacoo basket for maybe four more, and he smiling with his whole stomach now, and before I know whats what I down in the sand, and I pulling them heads into the shallows, and them crabs they right behind, and Jonas Lee all he can do he saying say hurry up hurry up, and the more he talking the more I thinking four more they bound to cost we something, but I aint know what just yet. Then the crabs so close I can maybe catch em with my hands, but all the same I is spitting out sand for where the net where it at and Jonas Lee he say he looking he find it, only just like that it aint Jonas Lee talking at all, it the old man, and he sure aint sound dead the way he cussing and spitting and kicking hisself awake, and look like Jonas he done come to the same conclude, cause he running away like he bleed to death. Well with that there aint nothing else to do but follow his tracks, only my feet they catch a hold of that cutacoo basket, and then me and that basket we both rolling in the sand.

My mama she like to say to me time trouble
fall it fall. I knows right then aint nothing more
to do but watch them crabs come bubble up out
of that basket. They is heading for the wet of
the yellow-green water fast as they can go, and
I wishing I was with them, only the wishing it
dont do no good, and then this net come crash
down a top of my head. The next thing I know
I see the old man face it hover up above, and
it white white like the moon, except it pitted
with dirt and grease, and then the old man he
bending down close and closer, and then the
white white it gone and all I see is his red-devil
eyes.

"You see what you done, boy," he say.
"They is all gone, every last one of them."

I is pretty much froze by now and watching
after them crabs and not saying a word.

"Just what do you think I oughta do?"

Then the old man he shaking that net at
them long-gone crabs and then he fling it to
the water. Then he do the same thing with that
cutacoo basket. Then he look down at me some
more.

"Get up," he say.

I aint move nothing, except maybe my eyes,
cause they watching that basket sink low in the
yellow-green water, and seem like it aint never
go under, only it does, and then it gone, and all
the while I watching, the old man he watching
me. It have the feeling like I go under the same.

"Get up," he say again, so I does, and then he grab a hold of my arms and he dragging me along.

By and by we moving through the long grass along the edge of the marsh, which I dont want to cause the marsh it full of snake, only there nothing much I can do. My mama she say ifn you has to choose youself between a alligator and a snake you best choose the alligator, cause you cant see or either hear the snake before it come to strike. The old man he dont seem to know about snakes, or maybe he do and dont mind none on account of he the devil and been a snake hisself what just as bad. Either way Im is holding my breath to see what what, only nothing happen, and then pretty soon we leaving the tall grass and coming up a rise. There some black-green oaks up top with they branches sagging to the ground, and up past that theres a dirt-white clapboard cabin with a tintop roof cover up with rust, and three blackeye window looking out to a porch. The old man he drag me up the porch and open the door, and then he chuck me inside leave me pile up on the floor.

Next thing I doing I telling myself aint nothing be scare about, but I crawling up to the window all the same see what the old man he doing, and there he is sitting hunch over on a old Co-Cola crate in front of the door, and he holding a alligator knife in his hand like so. The

knife it bother me some, on account of a knife
it big big trouble, but then it come to me how it
aint the knife I has to worry about. The old man
he whittling down a piece of hickory, and every
now and then a dark dark look come to his eyes
like all he can do is grab a hold of that stick
and laugh, but the only sound be the cut of that
knife on wood, which it mean the old man he
making up a switch and soon as he done he go
beat me good. It then I looking to the door, like
maybe I go bolt on through, but the old man he
in the way, and with that then I waiting on him
he do his worst and talking to myself the while
I saying say I the one all right aint no one else
done trip up on that basket aint no one else lock
up in the old man cabin but me and that the
truth, and then I saying say maybe it aint go be
that bad, maybe it aint, cause it only a stick.

The old man cabin it aint like people say, it
like every other clapboard cabin I ever been. Is
a threelegged table and a couple of chair push
up against the wall, and this yellowglass lantern
resting easy top of the table, only it aint lit up
so the room pretty dark, and there some kind a
barrel in one corner and a couple bag of beans
on top of that, and in the other corner there a
fat old blackbelly stove, and a bucket of charcoal
and a can of kerosene to one side, and a big
black pot on top with a mess of beans inside
been cooked and hardly ate and left cold, and
with that it have the feeling like Im go be the

next thing go into that pot, cause them beans is why the old man done went crabbing in the first place. I just standing there looking at that pot, and all the while Im is wishing some more I was with them crabs, so hard it feel like praying, only the wishing it dont do no good this time neither.

Then the old man he slap open the door and step inside. I can see the last line of red in the sky go black with that, and the old mans face look like it going black the same, and then he slap that door shut and turn around give a look around the room. Seem like he waiting on me make a move, only I dont. Then he step over to the lantern and he fire it up and hang it on a hook. Then he turn to stare me down, he holding that switch in one hand, and the light from that lantern washing yellow over his face and his eyes and his teeth, seem like he starting to burn and smoke, and he looking more and more like the devil in that yellow light than the devil ever been.

"You move yourself over this way, boy," he say.

Before I knows what what I moving up from the table just like he say, and then he grab a hold of my pants and he give em a yank like so, and with that I is looking down at the floor, my pants they wrap loose round my ankles, and it have the feeling like the old man he grinning.

"Time we settle up."

The old man he wet that switch on the tip of
his tongue and he bring it across my rear with
a whack couple time like he done gone butcher
up a hog, and it seem like I gone numb all over,
except for I can feel two raw welt breaking
through my skin. Then the old man he lay that
hickory on the table, like maybe he done change
his mind, but I aint one test the devil neither,
so Im is keeping my eyes to myself and waiting
what come.

Nothing more happen. And by and by I
looking around some and there the old man he
over at the stove and grumbling low to hisself
about beans for supper how he done had his fill
of beans and bread and not even a bit of ham
he should of dumped the mess out back for the
crows, and then he bending down in front of
that blackbelly stove and looking through the
grate. Look like maybe he go toss in a couple
three more piece of charcoal, only he dont.

"Say boy," he say. "You hungry? Hell,
you gonna have to be hungry eat some of this
goddamn mess."

I aint guess what the old man about to do,
maybe he laughing to hisself and then give me
a plate or either take up that hickory a second
time. But the old man he dont even look up, he
just keep on talking into that stove.

"Whyunt you just pull up them pants and sit
yourself down. I aint gonna eat these goddamn
beans all by myself. I dont like em that much."

It dont sound like the old man he like much
of anything the way he talking, but the next
thing I knows Im is sitting at the table and the
old man he bringing two plate heap high with
beans and some bread, and he sit down and say
dig in, so we does, and all the while we eating
Im is looking at the old man see what he go
do next, only I aint exactly sure I want to find
out. Then we both done, and the old man he
pushing hisself way back in his chair and take
out a pipe, and then he smoking some, and Im
is watching the smoke curl up to the ceiling
with one eye, but I still got the other one on the
old man, and he looking at me now like he dont
know what to say or either do, like maybe he
still thinking on that hickory. Then he lean some
closer and start talking.

"Boy, you let me tell you something, on
this here earth aint hardly nobody been born
who ain't afraid of one thing or another, and
most folks got a list. Most folks is so afraid of
living they cant wait to go to war. And they is
so afraid of dying they cant pass up a church
without going inside. Hell, boy, most folks
they's afraid of just about everything there is.
And that's God's own truth talking."

I looking at him and nodding, only what
exactly he talking about I dont know cause aint
nobody afraid of everything, not even Jonas
Lee Porter his little sister. Im is looking and
nodding, and waiting on him say some more,

but the old man he done talking. All he do he
lean back in his chair, and he seem pretty please
with hisself now and looking out the window,
and then by and by that pipe slip from his
hand, and he sleeping like a mule. I aint move
for a minute, just to be sure. Then the next thing
happen Im is heading for the door, I aint fool
enough wait around see if he go wake up, and
then Im is across the porch and past them black-
green oaks, and them beans and the bread and
that blackbelly stove, they all been left behind.

-2-

The next couple three weeks I aint doing
much. I just laying around the house and
thinking about the old man. Mama she dont
know what to do with me. I aint tell her about
them crabs and the cabin, and I aint going to
neither. I figure to let the whole thing lie where
it is. But mama she figure there something
peculiar going on inside my head, and if I wont
talk to her, maybe I go talk to God, so thats
when she start taking me to church. I dont tell
her I is almost thirteen and aint been to church
in maybe two year. I figure maybe it a better
thing to go to church and have her praying over
me than have her worry about some crazy old
man. Besides, there aint no telling what she❂d
do if she found out about me and old man

Thaddeus. She is a pretty big woman, packs
a pretty big wallop. There aint no sense even
taking a chance.

Church is like its always been. And after its
over, me and mama we sitting down by a few
womens resting in the shade of a scrub pine,
and they all waving they fans like thats all they
know how to do, and then there come Delilah,
she the fat one in the fade yellow dress, and a
fade yellow hat too on top of her head, and she
has this I-a-beauty-queen-was-once kind of net
hanging down to hide her face, which it all right
by me cause her face enough to bust up a piece
of granite. The next thing she do she leaning
herself up against that pine tree, cause she cant
sit herself down on the ground if she want to
get back up, and all the while she be fanning
herself and cussing out the bugs and the hot
and this island and even God hisself, and that
scrub pine be about to bust from under. Then
she see me and mama sitting there and she start
in with the question. The same question she say
every time she see me. Like she stuck up in a
movie.

"That you boy there Isabelle? He such a fine
looking boy for his age?"

Mama she nodding her head and give me
a nudge, and with that Im is standing up so
Delilah can see, and Delilah she clucking to
herself now like she some kind of hen. Then
she grab hold of my arm, and it feel like a claw.

Delilah she one of the reasons I stopped going
to church.

"He sure is. He as fine a looking boy as I
ever seen."

"You tell her Delilah," say a voice from
the flock, and they all getting into it now they
laughing and flapping they wings, and mama
she just nod her head some more.

"What you plan on doing with him," say
Delilah. "Better have something special in mind
the way he look."

Then Tramsee come along, she wearing
a slinky red dress and waving a skinny red
umbrella in the air, and you should see the rest
of them womens struggling to they feet and
their arms flapping and they all of them cluck
cluck clucking, and then they all fly off, even
Delilah, like Tramsee was some kind of crazy,
dirty dog looking to get herself a chicken. Then
it just me and my mama and Tramsee, and she
saying Ty he still in the church, he be coming
along in a minute. Then she look at me and
wink at my mama and then she saying say now
who is this, all the girls they gonna go crazy
over him, remind me the next time she throw
a party, he go be the guest of honor, then she
wink at my mama a second time and give me a
smile.

My mama she the only one have anything
to do with Ty and Tramsee when they aint
having a party. Most peoples talk like them two

been live under some kind of hoodoo spell, like
maybe she done witch him or he witch her, so
most times wont nobody have nothing to do
with them. Part of it cause they living out the
beach in a shack gets blowd over every time
a storm come along. When that happen Ty he
race into town let everybody know he need
some help put it up again, and everybody go
even they aint want to cause when they done
they know they go have one hoodoo of a time.
There something about Ty and Tramsee bring
everyone together, and that the truth. Pretty
soon there all kind of people out the beach and
they hammering at boards and hanging up
windows and sweeping out the kitchen where
Tramsee she cook up her peach pies and such,
and Ty and Tramsee they watching everything,
and every now and then Ty he say how he want
a couple more nail in this board or that board so
it wont get blowd off so easy the next time, and
before he even done speaking there a couple
more nail in it, and then he saying he want six
layer of tarpaper on the roof he dont want to
get wet when it rain, and there it is just like Ty
done said, and by and by the work it done and
the peoples they all dancing and drinking and
eating and laughing, and Ty and Tramsee they
doing the same, only they aint have to shell out
a single dime.

Mama she been friends with Tramsee since
before I was born, and she say Ty the best thing

ever happen to that girl. I cant see it, but thats
what she say. She say before Ty that girl didnt
know the sky was up. Everybody figure she
go walk into the ocean sea and drown herself,
or fling herself at some alligator get eat up, or
something else just as crazy, and then one day
she say she was go head up to Charleston, and
she was go walk all the way too, and right then
everybody figure this was it. Now Tramsee she
didnt know nobody there, but all the same she
started walking and walking, and pretty soon
she found herself up along the East Side. She
was five-day hungry, only there wunt no place
to eat, and she was tire too, looked like some
raggedy old hoodoo doll, and she was thinking
how she want to lie down, and was just about
to stretch out in a alley when she seen this two
story brick church, and before she knew what
what she was walking through the doors and
sitting down in the back, and by and by she
done fell asleep.

Tramsee she didnt know but she was sitting
in back of the Fourth Baptist Church of Saints
and Sinners, which it was the Reverend Otis
C. Pettigrew in charge. The Reverend he said
he had hisself a church where saint and sinner
they was the same, though wunt any saints ever
come through the doors, and there was some
said how the Reverend Pettigrew he was the
worst sinner of them all, though no one seem to
mind. Well, time the Reverend he saw Tramsee

in the back of his church he done start to shake,
look like he was about to shake right out of his
skin, which was saying something cause he was
a big big man, but he let Tramsee be a while
thinking she go need her strength, and then
come the morning he done slid on up to her
and tap tap her arm light like so, and Tramsee,
well she must of been dreaming cause she jump
straight up and grab a hold of the Reverend
round his collar and she was saying say she
aint had herself a cooked chicken in a month or
more and ifn she couldnt break this fat chicken
neck then where was the butcher knife, and
then all of a sudden Tramsee she open her eyes
and she seen how there wunt no chicken in
her hands, it was a Reverend instead, and with
that she done slid herself back, and her hands
they was letting go of the Reverend collar and
sliding down into her lap, and her jaw bone was
sliding down the same till her mouth open up
look like she go speak, only there wunt a single
word come out. It was then Tramsee she start
to cry, the water rushing down her face like the
tide, and every now and then she was saying
say she sorry she sorry, and the Reverend he
was smiling more and more like he was looking
at a chicken dinner hisself, and pretty soon he
was chewing like he already some in his mouth.
Tramsee she couldnt hardly see she was crying
so much, and when she did look to that smiling,
chewing mouth all she could see was some

raggedy yellow teeth look like they about to fall
out.

The Reverend he was a older man, and so
fat he had trouble grab hold of his own hands,
but when he seen that girl crying like she was,
he done squeeze them hands together and then
he start to talking, careful and slow at first, and
then faster and faster and faster. All Tramsee
done heard was noise, wunt no sense to it, but
all the same she was nodding her head like so,
and the Reverend was saying he was the world
renown Otis C. Pettigrew, and this was his very
own church, and she was welcome to stay on
for long as she like, only she have to help out
in the chow line and with the USO dances on
account of there was plenty of boys coming
home. Then the Reverend he was done with his
talk, but he was still looking at Tramsee with
them chicken-hungry eyes, and almost bite off
his tongue. And Tramsee she was done with her
cry, but she wunt looking at the Reverend at all.
Her eyes was turned in and she was thinking on
them coming-home boys.

Tramsee she done stayed with that church
for almost a year. Evenings she help the
Reverend Otis maybe serve up some rice soup,
or maybe stew and cornbread, and then some
shrivel-up fruit, and come every Friday night
she be dancing with some soldier boy done
come home. Wunt none of them what she
expect, but Tramsee she wunt about to give up

cause them boys they was all pressing her to dance, and wunt no better way she say to find herself a man. The Reverend Otis C. he wunt about to give up neither on account of he could still taste that chicken-dinner, and he be smiling at Tramsee and wouldnt she help out in the kitchen tonight clean them pots, and then he be smiling some more, and Tramsee she do enough pots keep him smiling, but every Friday night she be off to the dancing floor all the same, and the Reverend Otis he be left with a couple three dozen empty pot on his hands.

Then one night Tramsee she met up with a fellow call hisself Icebox Pete. Wunt no one full up his belly like Pete, didnt matter what, and he told Tramsee all about it too, how he been eat up more than all the boys in his squad put together, how one night they come down to Charleston on a weekend pass, they was most of them from there but it was Pete's first time, and Pete he been eat five stack of rib in ten minute and there been room for maybe five stack more. Then Icebox Pete and Tramsee they was both laughing and dancing across the floor, and when the dancing was done they both went off.

The next day Tramsee she come to the church by two, and she was wearing a cream-color picture hat with black trim, and a cream-color dress hang down to her knees, and some square-heel pumps was black like the trim, and the first thing she done she tug on the Reverend arm and she was saying say how she was full up with gratitude the way he done let her stay on but she was heading out with Pete he had hisself a horse farm down Florida and she hadnt even been out of South Carolina fore this but it wouldnt be long she was stretch out in the sun or riding bareback, and with that she done pick up a little black string purse she been dangling, and she give a hiccup she mean for a laugh, and she run out wait on the steps, cause her Pete done said he was coming round three o'clock.

The Reverend Otis he knew what she was saying even he didnt hear all the words, and he was feeling sorry for hisself on account of he wunt go have no chicken dinner now, but he didnt know exactly what to do neither time she run through the church door, so he just stood there a while, watching her words where they was hanging in the air, and then the words they was gone and the Reverend he give a heavy, slow rolling slouch with his shoulders like that, and then he head on back to the kitchen to wash what was left of them three dozen pot.

Tramsee she wait on Icebox Pete past three o'clock and moving on to four, but didnt nobody show up except a fellow what come with Pete the first time she seen him. This fellow he didnt bother none about his name, and he didnt smile neither except to say evening, and then he was saying say how Pete he sure was sorry, he been down working the docks most of the day, and he was still there too, even he barely move his arms, but he said he go be a drowning man soon as he seen her and wouldnt she wait on him and Florida till three o'clock the next day. She was frown and sore-hip from sitting on them steps, but she like the part about drowning, even it didnt make no sense, and time that fellow he say Florida she was saying say fine that'd be fine, and moving like she a suitcase to pack, and that fellow he just tip his hat and off he went.

The next day was the same thing, only Pete he hadnt been to the docks, he been hoofing it through the Battery. Tramsee she want to ask just what it was Pete been doing he couldnt do with her, but before she could say a word that fellow he just tip his hat like so, and off he went again.

Well, by and by it come on seven day of Tramsee waiting on Icebox Pete, and she done give him up already, but she know she want the truth, so time that fellow come strolling up the street, and he was singing to hisself about some girl wearing one red shoe, Tramsee she almost tackle him before he reach the steps. Seem like she too skinny, but time she jump she grab a hold of him with both her arm and both her leg like she some kind of crab, and with that he felt hisself falling, and then he land a heavy thwack on the sun- burn brick, and he was hoping he aint broke his back.

"What you mean by coming here every day this week with that same beat-up story coming from out you mouth? How long you think I a fool?"

Tramsee she was sitting square on that fellow chest and looking like she go beat on his face but good if only she could find a loose brick to hit him with, and that fellow he was looking up to her and blinking and he didnt know just what to do cause his back it was pretty sore even it wunt broke, so he allow a what-ever-you-say-I-do smile come creep across his face and he hope for the best.

"You be telling me now."

"Yessum, I is."

"And none of you lies, you hear, aint nothing but the truth come from out you mouth today."

"Yessum, I hear you."

"That better."

"What it is you want to know?"

Mama she say that there how Tramsee done met up with Ty, and he wunt but a bigknuckle tarbaby look like he lost his hat, but Tramsee she done took to him all the same.

-3-

Now the truth is that going to church didnt do no good. God he didnt need no telling. And I still thinking about the old man and that

piece of hickory and wondering if he go come
after me again, cause a couple of whacks dont
seem enough for losing him a crab dinner. I been
thinking on him so much it seem like he living
up inside my head. Maybe he is. I told Jonas Lee
about it, but he just laugh.

"You been sitting in the dark of your own
room for too, too long. What you need is to get
out have a little fun. Why dont we head on down
to the dock, maybe wait on the ferry boat come
in."

And just like that I aint thinking on the old
man no more, and me and Jonas Lee we out the
door.

The ferry boat been coming to this island two
or three time a day for more than twenty year,
and that mean there all kinds of junk been left,
but aint nobody never done nothing about it, so it
just pile up all over the dock, but mostly around
the ferry boat company office. There three or four
empty barrel out front of a couple mud-dusty
window and five maybe six tire from some old
Fords roll up against the washroom side, a old
buoy out front what rust and crack and look
like it nail down to the dock, three or four sign
what say Co-Cola shove back in the grass where
the road come up and another one nail to the
washroom door, and there one more sign say
United States Post Office, it hanging from a hook.
Is a fine fine place to be out the dock, even you
just sitting on two barrel halve look out at the

water and the yellowtail jumping, or maybe some mullet, and theres no other place in the world you want to be, and thats just the way it is now.

One time someone from the ferry boat company he come on out to the island and he was saying say the dock was a absolute disgrace there was so much junk laying out, and fill up the office too, and where was the man in charge he want to see him right away. The man in charge was Hugo Brown, he about seventy year old then, and he come out the washroom and wiping his hands on his pants and who was it want to see him what it about cant a man have some peace and quiet he was trying to think. That company man he fire Hugo right on the spot. Then he tried to hire someone else but wunt nobody want the job, even for eighty-cent a day, and so pretty soon he give it back to Hugo. Aint no one from the ferry boat company been back since.

Hugo he have a battery radio turn on to some ballgame, only he aint listening too hard cause his feet they prop up on top his desk and his head it flop over on his shoulder. But me and Jonas we listening. We sitting down the end of the dock and looking out at the water and listen to that game. We aint even mind the heat. Then about the eighth inning Jonas he have a idea. First thing he looking at me with one of his sly eyes and then he nodding his head over at the washroom door and he saying say pretty soon the ferry boat go be in and peoples getting off

and some of them go want to use the toilet and
wouldnt it be something if we done took a wrench
to the drop pipes leading down to them toilets
and loose up the joints and soon as anybody pull
on them chains why there be water spray all over
the place.

I have to say it a pretty good idea, and the
next thing I know Im is sliding in back of Hugo
I go rummage around his office see what I can
find, and Jonas Lee he scrunch down waiting by
the door and he telling me say they has to be up
under the desk and is they there and whyunt
I just grab em now and run, and I sure is glad
Hugo he a hard sleeper cause Jonas he have the
kind of voice cut through a wall, and he dont shut
up neither, he just talking and talking, and Im is
looking where he say, but there only three or four
box of bent nail and some metal scrap, and then I
sliding past the window and then up along some
shelves, only aint nothing but some empty coffee
cans there, and Jonas Lee he talking so loud he
almost drown out the radio, and Im is saying say
Jonas I dont know where they is I aint seen em
yet, only just then I does, and with that I is out
the door with two green monkey wrench in my
hands.

The ballgame it over by now but Hugo he still
stretch out, he even snoring some, and there a
old song call *I Be Seeing You* come on the radio,
which it almost make me laugh, only I dont. Then
me and Jonas Lee we in the washroom, and first

thing he do he point out a black pipe run down
along the white tile wall to the toilets, and then
he give me a wrench and he say lets we do it, so
we does, only I aint exactly sure just what it is
we suppose to do so I looking on over to Jonas
watch him work. He standing up on one of
them toilets, and he having some time of it with
his wrench hook around the pipe and he pulling
and pulling and pulling, but then the joint come
loose and some water come crawl down the
pipe, and then the water stop. Then Jonas he off
to the next one and he pulling and pulling some
more, and I up there next to him and pulling
the same, aint go be long now, and then all of
a sudden we is blast from them toilets by the
ferry boat whistle, and it sound like it pretty
close, too close for me. Then Jonas he give me
a flat-lip smile and he saying say there nothing
more we can do now but wait and see, and then
he pitch that monkey wrench into a bluegreen
waste-can and he busting out the door, and I is
right there with him.

Hugo he almost kick his radio off a that
table there come a second whistle, and then
he fall to the floor, and his legs they so tangle
up with his feet, by the time he make it to the
edge of the dock, me and Jonas Lee we sitting
on them barrel halves like we been there the
whole day. We both looking up at the sky, there
some black black clouds a ways off, and there
a sick, green color under that, and it seem like

the sky it saying say these here the ones, these
boys, they the ones done it, but Hugo he dont
hear nothing, it dont even seem like he know
we there, he just standing on the end of the
dock and mumble some about a storm coming
in and he glad it aint now cause he aint have
his supper. Then he see the ferry boat and he
waving his hat, and somebody wave back.

The ferry boat it aint a big boat, it barely
hold fifteen maybe twenty people, and every
time out the peoples they wondering if it gonna
sink, but it aint sunk yet, and every time it pull
up to the dock the peoples they waving they
hats. They all waving they hats now, and some
they laughing, and the wheelman he standing
up and waving his hat like the rest, and then he
crow-squawking some, and then two boys they
toss down a couple three tires keep the ferry
boat from smash itself up against the dock, and
then they jumping down theyselves with these
raggedy old ropes go tie that ferry boat down,
only fore they even take a breath, the peoples
they all of them already on the dock, and some
they shaking mill dust from they shirts or either
wiping down they faces and then they off, and
some they in all kind of hurry they talking it
look like rain just look at that black black sky
coming in it go be some storm, and then they
off the same, and some they smoking from they
pipes and talk about the chickens or the hams
or the soup they go eat up at Capn Calloway

come supper, and maybe some peach pie, and some they hardly looking where they going cause they just tire as they can be. But they all walking right past the washroom and heading into town, and me and Jonas Lee aint nothing we can do we watching them go, and then it just the wheelman and his boys, and then they heading into town the same as everyone else have a little supper before they go back.

Look like we done loose up them pipe joints for nothing, and we just about to head into town ourself maybe go home when we see a couple three marine they still on the dock. We aint see them get off or either where they been, but there they is now, they standing there all spit and polish in they Sam Browne belts and they flash a couple three leatherneck smiles, it look like they waiting have they picture taken. Then they talking to Hugo up alongside that rust-out buoy, and we cant hardly hear them, except every now and then they up and laugh, and one he step up a foot to that buoy and he pull out some smokes and then they all smoking, except for Hugo, and then they laughing some more.

Then Hugo he locking up the office and he saying say he see them at the Capns and then he gone. But them marines they just waiting around, smoking some more, and talking some, only it aint so many words it mostly just hmmming and such, and then they toss they smokestubs to the dock and give them stubs

a twist like so, look like they just one black
shoe doing it, and then they heading off to the
washroom.

Jonas he clap his hand over his face to keep
hisself quiet the while we watching, and time
they inside, Jonas he say how we best be gone
fore they come out again cause they be ready
to bust some heads time they does, so me and
Jonas we up fast as we can climb on board that
ferry boat, and then we both ducking down
low in back of the rail. All we doing then we
listening, and then we hears some shouting
from the washroom and one of them marines he
cussing all up and down and then the door it
bust wide open and they all come race out onto
the dock. Jonas he wave for me have a look and
see whats going on, and I shaking my head slow
slow like does he think I crazy, only the next
thing I know my eyes they up over the rail.

Them marines sure is angry. They done
come out wet and they shirt tails hanging out
and they stomping around the dock like they
three knockabout alligator, and one of them he
waving a wrench in the air and he shouting out
how he go loose up some joints hisself, and the
other two they poking through them barrels and
roll up tires and shoving at them Co-Cola signs,
and they all turning they eyes this way and that
look for something to have at, only they aint see
nothing but the dock and the ferry boat and the
water and them two barrel halve.

Jonas Lee he say again say what going on,
and I wave him up have a look for hisself, and
then we both eyes up over the rail, but it too too
hard not to bust up laughing, so we back down
again, we go wait on them marines give up
they search. Seem like we waiting and waiting
and waiting. Dont know how long, except by
and by them black clouds they straight up over
the boat. And then Jonas he cant wait no more
he up again looking over the rail and then he
laughing out loud he saying they been long
gone, and with that he climbing over the side
of the boat, only he aint have a good grip, and
then all a sudden he give a short yell and he
waving his hand in the air and then he land on
the dock with a heavy thumpump like that.

Well Im is up with that and wondering
what what, and I calls out to Jonas, only he
just answer with a low moan, so I climbing
down have myself a look, and there he is, he all
spread out with his leg twist up one side of his
head. He look just like some of the junk been
left around the dock the last twenty year. But I
talking to him anyway.

"Say, Jonas, what you done to youself," I
say.

Jonas he just roll his head at me and moan
some more. He sure pick a fine time break a
leg. Hugo office it been lock up, and aint no one
come down from the backwater wood or either
up along the road, so I grab hold of him myself

and drag him across the dock set him up against
that rust-out buoy, and then I saying say how I
going to town for help and dont he be worrying
none cause somebody go know what to do, but
Jonas he just roll his head around some more.
All the way into town Im is thinking say what
if that storm break and Jonas still out there,
maybe it go wash him away, or maybe it aint
go be the storm that get him, maybe it go be the
witches, cause witches they always out before a
big big blow, and even when it blowing, what
if they go stick Jonas Lee in a pot, what he go
do then, and then it have the feeling like I is
the one stuck up in that pot, only it more than
a pot now, it a big big cooking kettle, and there
a pack of witches standing round and they
waiting to eat me up, and with that Im is trying
to shake them witches out of my head, I is too
too old believe in such truck, but they up in my
head all the same. Then there some yellow lights
up ahead, and just like that them eating witches
is gone from my mind and Im is thinking say it
aint go be long now Jonas Lee, you hold on, it
aint go be long.

The first place I come is Capn Calloway Bait
Shop and Grill, only why he call hisself Capn
aint no one know cause he never been foot on a
boat his whole life long. The people they dont
bother none about me when I open the door so
I go on in. Some they is sitting at the counter
and eating on they fried chickens and rice or

they ham and biscuits and beans or maybe some
hog pudding, and they all drinking Co-Cola,
and some they sitting in the booths up front and
eating and drinking on some of the same, and
theres a girl name Shirley working the counter,
only there aint nothing for her to be doing till
the people they done, so she just sitting up front
on this three-legged stool and humming and
scraping the dirt from up under her fingernails,
and the Capn he standing off in the corner and
he arguing with little Fergie Wallace about the
best way go catch sheepshead, and hard to say
who winning cause they both waving they arms
like they reeling in fish. I open my mouth to tell
em all what what only there aint no sound come
out at first except this rasphuhrasphuhrasphuh,
and with that then some they turning they
heads so they can see what making that kind
of noise, and then they see me stand in the
doorway cover up with a pasty, wet dust from
running. Some they asking me then if I all right,
and I just nod my head and they nod back, and
some they asking if I was running and what I
running for or either from, and I nods my head
some more, and all the while I breathing in
and out, in and out, and soon as I done steady
myself, I open my mouth again and I saying
say how Jonas Lee Porter he done fell from the
ferry boat to the dock and broke his leg upside
his head, and with that then the peoples they all
up talking fast like fire, only that about all they

doing, which Jonas Lee he needing more than that cause he still up at the dock.

Is then I hears these voices come from one of the tall red booth near the back and them voices they saying how they knows just about everything there is to know about broken bones and how they better get up to that boy fast as they can fore he done gone into shock, and I just about to turn around lead the way when I see who talking, it them three marines we was laughing at, only they aint wet no more.

"It all right boy," say one. "We know what we doing."

Then the one who closest he shaking me some, get a move on boy, and aint no telling how long he do that, but then he aint shaking me no more cause Im is moving through the door and out, and them marines they following close behind, and the rest of them peoples what been eat at the Capns, and Shirley and little Fergie Wallace, and even the Capn hisself, they all following the same and talking on and on about poor little Jonas Lee what was he doing top of that ferry boat he wunt suppose to been up there and that a fact, only they voices is soft as the wind.

By the time we up to the dock, them black black clouds they everywhere, look like the storm go break in a minute. And Jonas he still leaning up against that rust-out buoy, only it look like he slip down some, and he moaning

and shivering like the rain it already coming
down. Soon as them marines see that, one he
taking off his jacket throw it over Jonas Lee,
and then they checking him up one side and
down the other and pull on his leg a bit, and
Jonas he moaning some more and roll his head
this way and that, and all the while the peoples
they is all crowd around on the dock to look,
and then Hugo he break off from the rest and
into his office and he flick on a couple of light
so every one can see more better, and some they
stretching out they brown rooster-necks cause
they aint seen a bust-up leg before, and some
they is shaking they heads they saying say poor
little Jonas he dying for sure what he must of
done for the good Lord to come down on him
like that they didnt know but they glad it wunt
them, and little Fergie Wallace he saying how he
wouldnt trade places with that there boy for a
pot of Chinee tea, and the Capn he aint saying
nothing at all, he just trying to stand away from
that black black channel water, far as he can,
keep hisself from falling in.

Is just then the rain coming down, and Jonas
he moaning again, only not so loud now, and
pretty soon he looking like a half-drown cat,
and all Im is doing I standing there like Jonas he
is died already, and why it aint my leg bust-up
I dont know, and Jonas he roll up his head look
at me like he ask the same question. Then the
marines they done wrapping his leg and they

pick him up, and the light from Hugo office it
been put out and the door shut and lock up.
Then everybody they thumping across the dock,
and Jonas he be swinging side to side in the
arms of them marines, and his head it bobbing
as he go. Then the thumping and the peoples
and Jonas Lee and his bust-up leg they is all
gone, and I is left there standing in the rain.

-4-

The storm it was a big big blow, bigger than
what anyone off the ferry boat been talk about,
and by the time it done blow itself out it done
lay flat most everything from the trees below
the bluff to some of the stores down along
Front Street. The next day me and mama we out
stacking some pieces of board what blowd up
onto the porch, and is then Ty he come on up,
and he looking like he a blowd-up board hisself.
Then he catch his wind and look to mama and
me, and then he saying say how Tramsee and he
they been working on fix up they cabin, and it
be scatter all over the beach and back along the
dunes, and how Tramsee she done look for her
silks and her fine hats and such and she done
hike up into the dunes she scrounging about,
and then she down in the marsh flats, maybe
she find something there, and wunt too long
after that Ty hear something wail and wail and

wail, and he head off see what it is and it was
poor old Tramsee, only she aint find no silks
or either hats, she just find herself stuck up
in the middle of one of them bogs back there,
she floating in muck up to her neck, and there
all kind of flies buzzing by her nose, and she
swinging her arms out above her head like she
have at them flies, only all that do it make her
stuck the more, and all the while she yelling for
Ty to get her out, only Ty he say he cant help
just hisself, and that why he come running.

Mama she nodding like she cant decide
on pray or either laugh, cause she know how
Ty he all exaggeration, and then she say for
me she say to go on with Ty and keep he and
Tramsee company how she be coming there by
and by with some people help poor Tramsee out
before she sink to the bottom and how I best
mind my manners and wait till she come. Ty
then he say he oblige, and then he saying say
for mama be sure she bring along something to
drink cause it be hot out the bog and Tramsee
she must be near to spitting foam her mouth
so dry, and then Ty he smile hisself and he say
how Tramsee she like that sweet rye liquor they
selling down at Willies and she could probably
do with as many of them bottles as Willie go
give up cause it getting hotter and hotter by the
minute. Mama look like she smiling inside out
cause she know who them bottles for, and then
she turn sharp on her heel and head into town.

Well, I wishing my Mama she hadnt up
and volunteer me like she done, but she done
it anyway, and then Ty he clap me hard on
the back and he say for me to get a move on
cause Tramsee she been waiting, and so I does
what he say, and pretty soon me and Ty we
walking out the beach. Now most people they
hear the name Ty what come to they mind is a
man lost in the desert. Ty he always looking for
something to drink, so much so people saying
he done drink up more than the devil hisself.
Mama she wont never say why Ty he drink
so much, and I aint about to ask her cause she
a big big women, but I knows it something
to do with womens cause soon as Ty he see
a pretty one, and he aint like most mens they
talking heat soon as a pretty girl come round
the corner, no Ty he quiet up like he bite off a
piece of kerosene charcoal, and then he looking
around for something wash it down, and then
pretty soon he a bottle in his hands, sometimes
two. Ever since I know him he been drinking
most near all the time. Mama she say people
just oughta humor him along. What she mean
by that she mean people oughta give Ty all the
sweet rye liquor he can hold.

The next thing I knows we walking through
the dunes and the air it full up with a screechy,
whining sound, give me some kind of shiver,
but Ty he saying say it only Tramsee, and
aint she sounding some sore thirst, and then

a slow-rye smile come creep across his face.
All I can think of is Tramsee and I cant hardly
believe that her she aint sound human and on
and on like that.

Then I aint thinking of nothing.

Then we coming down a sandy ridge, and
there a sandy, grassy place at the bottom,
and on one side of that there a thin stand of
red-brown sycamore, and on the other theres
the bog, look like a kettle bog, and Tramsee she
sure enough stuck up in the middle, she maybe
twelve foot out, only she dont know we coming.
She sure is something to see. She cover up in
all that black, black muck, look like she a frog,
and all she doing she looking out at the world
with two frog eye, and it them eyes what get
to me the way they blinking and the mud drip
down, and before I know what what I bust up
laughing.

Ty he give me a what-you-crazy look, only
then he looking out to Tramsee, and she looking
back, and then she open up her big blue mouth
again, only now she angry more than tire, and
she saying say what the both of you fools doing
there standing there laugh like some kind of
hyena, and she flinging some of that black muck
with every word she say, look like a sawtooth
windmill, and me and Ty we both ducking
down in back of them red- brown sycamores,
and then we looking to the middle of the bog.

"He aint mean it," Ty say.

"Well what he laughing for then?" Tramsee
say.

"He aint laughing at you," Ty say, and then
he looking to hush me up. "Tell her you aint
laughing at her."

"I aint laughing at you," I say.

"Well what he laughing at?"

"What you laughing at," Ty say, and he
talking hush to me some more, only I aint know
what to say, and then Ty he aint give me no
time to think about it he just call on out. "He
laughing at his poor old self, how he done walk
all the way out here only he just now see he aint
wearing shoes," and then Ty he looking at me
some more he want me to kick off my shoes.

"It . . . it just like Ty done said," I say, and
I leaving my shoes up under them red-brown
sycamores, and then we both hush up. Aint
nobody talk or either move, like there aint
no such thing as a clock to live by, and then
Tramsee she open her mouth again.

"Well, all right then."

And with that, me and Ty we up from them
red-brown sycamores and walk across the grass,
only it hard to leave them shoes, and then Ty
he give me a shove with one of his bigknuckle
hands send me a couple step out ahead of him,
and there I face up with them two frog-eye
again. This time I aint letting out a sound, and
Tramsee she asking me say I always go around
scream like they is witches riding my back every

time I meet up with peoples floating in a bog
is that how my mama raise me, and I saying
say no maam no it aint it wunt her it was the
shoes that all and then would she like for me to
get her something what she want anything at
all and then my mama she be coming by pretty
soon with some help to haul her out. Tramsee
she aint all the way satisfy, and she give me a
look like she aiming a gun, and then she asking
me say I think it a proper set of circumstance a
girl like herself she stuck in the middle of a bog
without even a towel to wipe her face or either
a ribbon pretty up her hair what she go do now
there people coming by for a visit.

I aint much of a choice so I saying say no
maam that aint right of course she needing a
towel I aint blind, only I thinking say what
she need a towel for when all them peoples
be coming for is pull her out of the muck, and
then she asking me say maybe I hike on out to
the beach to her place maybe rummage around
till I find everything she want and then bring it
back so she can fix up her face, cause she want
to look good them peoples show up, and Im is
nodding my head say a whole lot of yes maam
I do just that, only I thinking say aint nothing
go help her show off her mud-cover face less it
a dip in the ocean, and then Tramsee she give
me a thick slice of peach-pie smile, and before
I know what what I up over the ridge and then
out the beach, and pretty soon Im is wishing on

my shoes some more, cause the sand it sure is
hot.

The storm it done a pretty good job on
that shack. But all the same I poking around,
scraping through the sand, shoving through
some of the wood pile up, and all the while I
poking and scraping and shoving, Im is thinking
on how Tramsee she got herself stuck in that
muddy black bog in the first place, cause she in
there pretty deep, and aint no way she could of
just walk on out cause a bog dont hold nothing
up that long, and maybe she done jump in, but
why anybody do that I aint even guess, and the
more Im is thinking the more and more it seem
like the only way for Tramsee be stuck like she
is is to get herself throwd in, and the only one
throw her in like that be Ty. I almost laugh out
loud for picture Ty holding Tramsee up above
his head and Tramsee kicking in the air and
calling him some kind of foolishness and then
Ty he letting her sail, but I done lost my shoes
for laughing at Tramsee the first time and I aint
looking to lose anything else, so I keep it inside.
Then Im is ready to go back. I been pretty much
over the whole beach with a pine-wood crate
in my hands, and it full up with ribbons and
small yellow soaps and a crack-handle mirror,
but there aint no towel, there a small white
bowl with the word candy carve in, or maybe it
a dish, and a red lace hat with a button on top,
and all kind of Tramsee stuff like that, but there

aint no towel, and with that then Im is walking
through the dunes to the ridge and whistling all
the way.

I is almost to the ridge when I hears a
grumbling come from in back of me, and I twist
myself around almost drop the crate, cause it
old man Thaddeus standing there, he has hisself
a empty pail in one hand and some sticks in
the other, and he looking at me with his white
white devil face and his red devil eyes. First
thing he do he scratch the stubble on his chin
some and close one eye to the sun, and then he
done poke at my crate with them sticks. Then he
one big grin.

"Say, boy, what you got in there," he say.

I aint say a word cause all I can think about
is them long- gone crabs and wondering if
the old man come to give me a couple more
whacks, and there aint nobody around go help
me get away, just a couple green heron looking
for something to eat in the grass, and then they
flying off. But the old man he aint have a piece
of hickory. Then he talking some more.

"Aint any crabs, is it?" he say.

But I still aint saying a word. Then the
old man he put them sticks in his pail and he
leaning some closer have a better look see into
that crate, and seems like he have a hungry
look about hisself, like maybe he aint been eat
since them beans, so I telling him say I aint any
crabs I sorry about the last time too but like my

mama she say what done is done only you want
me net some more and give em you I do just
that only not now just now Im is bringing this
here crate it for Tramsee Singleton she down on
the far side of that ridge only she stuck in the
middle of a bog which is why she aint up here
get it for herself. And all the while I talking,
the old man he nodding like so and chewing
something I aint know what it is, maybe it his
tongue, and then I done and the old man he
saying say he know a bit about bogs and not to
worry none, and then he tap my shoulder with
his stick he saying say we best be moving along,
and so we does.

Time we to the top of the ridge, the old
man he stop and look to the bottom, and I stop
right alongside. Ty he sleeping up under them
red-brown sycamores, and he using my shoes
for a pillow too, and he look almost like he a
dead man the way the flies they be crawling
down around his face, and every now and then
he give a snort from his nose it blow them flies
clear, and the flies they humming up above
his head a while, but then they come on back.
It almost too hot to do anything. The bog it
spitting up muck this way and that, it almost
bubbling over with the heat. And poor old
Tramsee look like she a shrivel up raisin been
chew up and spit out herself, like maybe we too
late, but just then Tramsee she look up, and she
give a hollow-out cry for hello and something it

look like a wave, and then she watching while
we climbing down. Soon as we step to the
grass then she waving her hands like so, and
the words they come muck-spitting out of her
mouth, and she saying say how glad she is she
see some peoples and did I go like she done ask
and where her things where is they and when
we go help her out of this bog and on and on
and on, and I saying say yessum we glad too
we is and this here the crate and dont she worry
none we go get her out, but the old man he dont
say a word, and then we standing up along the
edge and Tramsee she all smile and relief.

The first thing the old man do he give me his
pail and take hold of that crate and he empty it
to the ground, and there go all the ribbons and
the yellow soaps and the crack- handle mirror
and the rest. Then he sitting down on top of it,
and when Tramsee see that her smile it gone
and she flinging some more of that muck, only
she pretty tire now from flinging it at me and
Ty from before, so it all falling short. The old
man he dont pay her no mind anyways, he just
reach down to a strap on his leg and he pull
out that big big alligator knife of his, and he
checking the blade, and then he look around
some, everywhere but where Tramsee at, and
she still flinging muck. Well, it hard to say if
the old man he know what he doing, how he
go get Tramsee out with a knife anyways, but
then is like he know my mind cause he pointing

his knife over to where Ty asleep under them
red-brown sycamores, and the old man he
saying say he go cut hisself a mess of sycamore
branches, see which one long enough, and that
how he go drag her out.

The moment he say that, the muck stop
flying, and I looks out to the bog and Tramsee
she aint doing nothing but sit up quiet like
some kind of rock, and if you didnt know she
was there you be thinking the same with all
the muck cover her up from the spitting-up
heat and the way she been flinging it about,
nothing but her two frog-eye staring out at
the world, and even they is pretty hard to see
now, except every now and then Tramsee she
mud-blinking. Then the old man he step over
Ty and he hacking at them sycamores. It sure
a lot of work. Aint none of them twenty foot
high yet, and they mostly just saplings even
they look dead, but a knife it aint the best thing
hack at any tree, dead or not. But by and by
the old man he cut hisself down a whole mess
of red-brown branches, only aint none of them
long enough, and he sour and disgust with that
so he throw em all away, and Tramsee when
she see him do that, she blink back a cry, but
the old man he dont notice, he just staring at
them trees. Then he grab hold of one it only
twelve foot tall and give it a shake maybe loose
it up, and then he down to his knees digging
and cutting at them shallow roots and cursing,

and then he up and trunk- twisting and then
he down some more, and then he calling me
to grab hold and help, which I aint thinking
I just does, and he call out for Ty, only Ty he
aint move nothing but his lungs they blowing
them flies about, and it seem like we been at it
a couple three hour, only it aint been that long,
and then the old man he put his knife away,
and then he dragging that twelve-foot sycamore
over to the bog.

Tramsee she almost drown herself she crying
so hard, but she try to shut it off she see the
old man with that tree, and then the old man
he holding it out for her to grab a hold, only it
a foot short, and Tramsee she about to drown
herself some more, only the old man he move
some closer and reach out again, and Tramsee
look like she wishing she had longer arms she
strain and strain, only then she catch hold of the
tip of that tree, and with that her frog eyes they
almost pop, and then she clutching hard with
both her hands, and then the old man he haul
her in.

For a moment or two Tramsee she stretch
out along the edge like she been dead a month,
but then she up on her feet, she slow and
tremble, and she dripping wet with that black,
black muck, and then she smile at the old man,
he back on the crate, and she smile at me sitting
in the grass, and is then she spy old Ty asleep
up under them red-brown sycamore. Tramsee

she aint smile none at Ty, but she give him a
look like she go be smiling soon, and then she
take a hold of his legs drag him to the bog and
let go of his feet, and they go plopopp into the
black muck like that. Then she settle herself
down in the yellowgreen grass and she give her
sleeping Ty a sharp sharp shove with both her
heel. Aint a thing old Ty can do but roll in face
first, and then Tramsee she standing up casual
and collect, except she smiling at Ty now, and
then she heading to the top of the ridge and then
she gone.

The old man he laughing to hisself with that,
and then Ty he waking up all cough and surprise
and sput sput sputtering he trying to catch his
breath, and he wiping the muck from his eyes
and nose, and then he up from the edge he
crawling through the grass, and then he sitting
hunch over and sour and he give a look see what
what. The first thing he see is them ribbons and
them small yellow soaps scatter round in the
grass, and then his eye turn on me and the old
man, and Im is wondering if Ty think me and
the old man done roll him in, how long we go
be in the bog before someone drag us out, and
then Ty he grabbing me up around my arm, and
I almost feel myself sail through the air, but all
Ty do he ask me where his Tramsee done gone.
I cant hardly look in his eyes Im is thinking how
good it feel my feet on the ground, but then Im
is saying say I aint know exactly where she gone

she just gone that all, and with that Ty he let go
of my arm, and then he running up the ridge,
and then he gone the same.

-5-

The sun it almost down now, except for
some red burn through the tops of the trees a
ways off, and I aint know exactly what Im is
go do just me and the old man sitting in the
dark, but my mama she told me to wait, so I
waiting. The old man he hunch over that crate
and grumbling some about his appetite, and
every now and then he look over at me, and
Im is thinking maybe he want his pail back or
either want to talk about them crabs some more,
but he dont say a word, and then he pull out
his pipe and by and by he blowing smoke. Is
then I hears a shout come from the top of the
ridge, and then some peoples laughing, and
then another shout, and then I sees a couple
three yellow ball lantern float down through
the shadow, and then there some peoples
float down the same, and most they load up
with boxes and crates and talking about how
much they go drink, and someone he singing
bout a couple three fellow what climb up on
a roadhouse fence like they straddle up on a
girl name Annie Rose, only what happen after
that he aint sing about, and then I hears Willie

his voice he saying they all come too late for
Tramsee, too late cause she done sunk to the
bottom of the bog, and why they haul up all
these box for someone what knocking on Peter
gate this very moment, well he cant say, only
they here the same and someone better dig
down and pay for all this liquor he brung and
the time he done spent carry it all the way out
here cause he a man making a living, and is
then my mama voice she cut through all that
Willie talk for shut his mouth and what he need
to blow his hot air up and down people neck,
it hot enough, and she know Tramsee wunt in
no bog at all, it just Ty talking cause he lonely
want someone to fix up his cabin and give him
a hoodoo jump, it dont matter who paying for it
cause we all in need. Willie he look around like
maybe he want to kick something, only he dont,
and he saying say he aint a Christian charity
give away his liquor unrepent, only mama she
act like she aint quite hear him so she saying
what, and Willie he aint say another word to
that, he just keep walking with the rest of them
peoples down the ridge.

By and by all the peoples they be down
from the ridge, and the yellow of them lanterns
swinging this way and that, and I saying say we
over here right here, and the next thing I knows
they all gather up around the old man and me
and setting they boxes and crates in the grass,
and everybody smiling, except for Willie, he

looking to the bog like he looking into his own
grave, and his eyes they roll up into his bald
rumple head, and then he shouting and stomp
around the grass and waving his hand in the air,
and he asking if any give a thought to Tramsee
and why it was they aint and the answer he
say it the devil cause only the devil he take you
thought, and some of the peoples they looking
shift and unease with that like maybe the devil
he done stole they thoughts that very minute,
and Willie he keep right on about Tramsee and
how she aint to blame cause she didnt know
more better, but she down at the bottom of the
bog now she waiting on the devil come eat her
up cause that what the devil do he find a dead
body aint been bury by the church, and time the
devil he done, well what we think we doing here,
cause they aint ever been one body keep the devil
he hungry and we all know that, and some of
the peoples they aint been hear that kind of talk
before, and they surprise and worry, and some
they saying the devil he been work that way ever
since Elijah born so you just better watch youself,
and some they just looking around this way and
that over they shoulders, and aint nothing come
yet, but all the same they about to run.

The old man he aint bother too much about
Willie he just be smoking on his pipe. Mama she
crossing her arms and she saying say it too dark
we working on anybody⊚s house and anyways
it look like Tramsee she got out she ever was in

so might as well set up the food and the liquor
and have ourself one hoodoo of a time dont
nobody worry none cause everyone know Ty
he be along soon as he smell that liquor even
he ten mile off, and Tramsee she aint be far
behind, and with that the peoples they mostly
forget about Willie and they slicing up cold
chickens and ham hocks and laying out all kind
of pie and bread and some they reaching for
them bottles of rye and opening them up and
drinking and laughing and going on, and some
they done make up a circle with them lanterns
set shallow in the long grass for maybe some
dancing or either some hey-de-hey, and then
a couple three start up kind of low and steady
with they voices while the rest of the peoples
they all eating and talking, and every now and
then someone laugh, and then someone he
singing about that sweet and pretty sorghum
Sal, and by and by everyone singing or either
dancing, and the light from the lanterns it
dancing the same.

Most everybody they is having a good time,
even old man Thaddeus. He sitting on that crate
at the edge of the circle and tapping his feet and
laughing to hisself and smoking some more on
his pipe. The only somebody aint have a good
time is Willie. He standing outside the circle
of them yellow lanterns and looking at the bog
and back at the singing and the dancing, and
every time someone cry out, Willie he look like

he go jump up out of his ownself. Then a little
while later he watching the old man, and the
more he watch, the more his eyes they fulling
up with blood and pulling him do something,
and the next thing he know he find hisself face
up with the old man even he aint want to be,
and with that Willie his two eye they bust wide
open, seems like there blood pouring out all over
the place, and then he stumble into the light
and shouting some more and the dancing and
singing and drinking and eating it stop right
there, and everybody they looking to Willie like
they all one trouble eye.

Willie he still scare, only aint so bad with
people watching, and then his voice come flash
through the lantern light and it saying how we
been live with the old man ever since he come
to this island only what we know about him
we aint know nothing just like we aint know
nothing about Tramsee why we aint even see
her pull from the bog so how we know she
aint there yet and how we know the old man
aint the devil hisself and waiting he work up a
hoodoo of a appetite and even he did pull her
from the bog maybe it just to eat her up some
other day cause once the devil he a hold of you
he aint let go, and all the while Willie his voice
it rant and rattle, and the peoples they looking
from Willie to the old man and back again, and
then that rattling voice it saying how the devil
he aint never sleep he looking to eat we all up,

everybody he can find, and that just what go
happen we stay here tonight.

Old man Thaddeus he looking more and
more now like maybe he really is the devil,
what with the light from them lanterns dancing
all across his face and the smoke from his
pipe, and the peoples they all backing off just
a step, they wondering maybe Willie he right,
and Im is wondering right along with them,
Im is thinking back to me and Jonas Lee and
that basket of crabs, and it sure seem like the
old man was asleep in the sand, but maybe he
was just waiting there try to catch two for one
only he didn©t cause Jonas Lee run away, and
Jonas would of knowd he was the devil for sure
I didnt come home, which the devil aint want
nobody pin him down, so he let me go.

Well just then there come a scream from up
the ridge, it hanging up there in the air, and the
longer it hang, the louder and louder it get. Aint
nobody know what to do. Some they looking
up and up, but aint nothing to see just yet, and
some they looking at the old man see if he have
a hand in it, but he just smoking his pipe, and
some they looking at Willie see what he go do,
but he just standing there like a harness-up
mule, with the sweat bead up on top of his bald
rumple head like it is and then down his back,
and all the while he be looking to crawl into
one of them empty box or either run off into
the backwater wood, only he aint decide which.

Then somebody say look, and everybody does,
and there something up there, look like a ghost
fall out of the sky the way it screaming all blue
in the face, but the closer that ghost get, the
more it looking like Tramsee herself, and then
someone he say how she screaming like that
cause the devil done eat her up, bones and all,
and how we next we give the devil a chance.

Soon as Willie hear that he give a yelp like
he done swallow his tongue, and then he run
off into the woods, and a couple three more
they run off the same, but most they aint run
or either hide cause they just aint sure. Some
they edge up close to the old man, only he aint
bother about nothing, he chewing some on his
pipe and then smoking some more, and some
they eyes on Tramsee, her whole face it blue
from screaming, only what exactly she trying
to say aint no one tell. But soon as Tramsee at
the bottom, people see how she wunt floating
at all, it was Ty carry her down, he holding her
up above his head, he heading straight for the
bog, and Tramsee she screaming and kicking
cause she already been once and she dont want
to go again. Then Ty he feel the eyes of all them
peoples stand in the shadows, and with that he
dont know what to do so he stop, and Tramsee
she stop her screaming at the same time, only
she still up in the air.

It then the voices start up for agitation
and confusion, like they crabs in a basket they

trying to claw they way to the top, and they is all
talking about Willie, cause he gone now.

"What we listen him for," say Joe Heywood.
"We always been listen him about this or that."

"He sure do like to talk," say another. "Aint
a family with twenty female talk more an he do.
And that a fact."

"Aint his fault, T-Bone," say Mose Heywood.
"It the devil fault."

"How that?"

"I heard it say Willie he born with a lock jaw,
and his mama and papa they didnt know what
to do they was praying and praying, only wunt
nobody listening except the devil."

"So what that mean?"

"It dont mean nothing," say Mattie Simmons.

"It do too," say Mose. "The devil he come for
Willie a couple night later, but soon as he Willie
in his arms, he trip over his own tail send Willie
to the floor. Done broke Willie jaw in two place,
and then you aint never heard such a wailing
in your life. The devil he cover up his ears he
like to run out the door, he aint like a surprise,
and Willie he been talking worry and cajole ever
since."

"Well he sure do breathe worry just to look at
him," say someone else.

And a couple three more voice they chime in
with agreement.

"How you think he lost his hair," say Mose
Heywood.

And there some laughing from the shadow.

"He a damn fool," say his brother Joe.

"You right about that," say another voice.

"He aint no right talking about folks being dead if they aint," say Joe. "That kind of talk just asking for trouble."

"You right about that too," come a couple three echo.

"What I aint like about him," say T-Bone, "is the way he puff hisself up before he speak, and then aint no one say a word till he done. It like we all scare."

"We is scare," say Joe. "That what I talking about."

"Well, I aint scare Joe Heywood," say Mattie Simmons. "Willie he just words. People hear him talking it like the wind come blow through a pile of dry-up leaves. Before you know it you up in the air and toss about a while. But then the wind it gone and you is back on the ground."

"That aint scare you be blowing around like that?" say Joe. "Well it sure scare the hell out of me. I likes my feet where I knows where they is. Man, you remember the time Willie he talk about we should get off the island before them Nazi Germans come? I so scare then I almost kill a man he come along the beach, and he only come from Georgia."

"That more an ten year ago," say T-Bone. "Willie he aint against Germans no more."

"That right, Joe," say Mose.

"Well, he has to be against someone," say Joe. "That the way he is."

Then the voices they hush up like they all thinking about Willie some more but they afraid to say, and then mama she move into the circle and break it up.

"What's the matter with you all," she say. "Willie he just Willie. What you doing? We come for something more than scare ourself with a bunch of Willie stories so you all just hush up. Ty, you put that girl down. She been up there long enough. Come on now. This here suppose to be a party."

And with that the peoples they done with they Willie talk, and aint long before they dancing and singing and drinking like they was before Willie open up his mouth, and Ty he done with Tramsee the same and looking for a bottle, and soon as he taste a drop he laughing and hollering and dancing, and every now and then he knock down a lantern, only he aint notice, and Tramsee she all peacock and expectation and she laughing and dancing the same as Ty, only she aint bother with him, she has herself a couple three young mens they pressing up against her one for another, and they all talking how pretty she is and was she a movie star actress, and Tramsee she laugh and laugh and then look to them some more, and every time she do them mens they more

and more want to press up against her, and
then the first two they rolling about in the long
grass they fighting each other now, they saying
say she mine she aint she mine she aint, and
Tramsee she laugh some more with that and
take to the third one, and by and by it seem like
everyone press up against everyone else, except
for Thaddeus sitting there on that crate and
watching what goes.

The next thing I know I is walking through
the woods down along the backwater and
wondering where Willie run off to, and then I
aint wondering a thing cause it too too dark, I
has to watch the way I is going. Im is climbing
over logs now and brush on past the moss
hanging low and kicking up chips and rock, and
the air it full-up with marsh frogs singing and
the wind it come crisp and warm through the
grass, and every now and then a bellow come
from out the black, sound like a alligator. Then
I sees a tiny ball of fire up ahead, it glowing
like the devil◉s own eye, and next to the fire
there a shadow all hunch over and mumble low
like a hoodoo conjure man. I aint never seen
no hoodoo conjure man before this, so I edge
up a little more closer to a couple three water
oak, and Im is pretty quiet and restrain cause
I aint need a hoodoo spell cast my way just
yet, only then it come to me this shadow it aint
no hoodoo man at all, it just Willie, and he all
huddle up like he scare or maybe tire.

Soon as I see that I moving up to the fire,
and Willie he look up he mumbling like he hear
or either see me come, only he dont, and then
he hunch back down, and then Im is sitting by
his side, and he still aint see me so I say hey
like that and Willie he jump ten or twelve foot
back and land up against a tree. Im is looking
direct into his eye then, only he still aint see
me, and then his voice come shaking through
the air and it saying how it aint his time not
yet not yet take them at the bog only leave him
be. I crawling to Willie now and leaning close
to his face maybe ask him what the matter but
he keep on saying it aint his time it aint, and I
just about to shout in his ear hope to shut him
up, only is then he look down across the top of
his nose and he see me crouch in the grass, and
with that he aint talking no more, he just caught
in a stare, and his eyes they burning a bright
bright orange from the fire. Then he nod like
so and ask me say what you doing here how
come how come didnt you know, only before I
say a word, Willie he going on about old man
Thaddeus how he really is the devil and there
a lot of people know the same even they aint
say a word but Willie he tire of waiting it time
everyone know, and with that he clear his throat
and hunch over real low, and the orange glow
from that fire it spread out from his eyes to his
face to the top of his bald, rumply head and
then up to the black branch of that tree behind

him, and all of a sudden I looking at him in
that orange orange glow and it have the feeling
like Willie he been right about the old man all
along, and with that Im is thinking say I in for a
whole lot of trouble, cause there something that
old man want with me ever since that basket of
crabs, only we aint got to it just yet. But I knows
now we going to. Once the devil he put his eye
on you there aint no where to hide. And that the
truth. Then the feeling it gone, and Willie he tell
his story.

Willie he saying how old man Thaddeus
like to been going the three four mile up the
backwater to Pappa Toms when he first come to
the island, and Willie he say it the same kind of
place then it is now, drinking and dancing and
people coming across from the coast in any kind
of old boat they lay hands to, and there any
kind of girl a man want up at Pappa Toms even
he short of cash, a boy too, if he big enough.
The old man he use to been drinking every
night, only he didnt look like he ever drunk a
drop, and most the peoples they done took him
for the devil on account of that, and Willie he
come to the same conclude, only didnt no one
say a word they was waiting on Pappa Tom
see what he do. Pappa Tom he wunt thinking
on supernatural cause he was a drinking man
hisself, and he done figure to let the old man
be even he hadnt paid a nickel yet cause he was
sure to pay something sometime soon so long

as he wunt bother. The rest of the peoples they
went along, and by and by everybody done
forgot the old man and the devil was one and
the same. That was just what he wanted. Every
night he done come in he drink some beer, and
maybe he leave a dollar on the table and maybe
he didnt, and time he was done drinking he find
hisself a girl nineteen maybe twenty year old,
and if she had on a pair of black nylon stockings
he done take her upstairs, and if she didnt
he done take her out back in the grass, and
sometime it be the same girl ten or twelve night
in a row, and sometime it wunt, and every now
and then he find hisself a girl with coffee cream
skin and pale blue eyes and he take her on up to
his cabin for a month or maybe more.

The girls he done took to his cabin they
wunt never the same again, and time he done
with them they come on back to Pappa Toms,
only they eyes was like bits of blue glass glue
to they heads, wunt none of them recognize a
thing, and some they didnt know what to do
and by and by they was walking off the edge of
the dock they go drown theyself or maybe up
into the backwater be eat up by a alligator, and
some they daddys done come catch them up
and bring them home, only they was brood and
resist like mules so they daddys have to knock
them out and slop them over they shoulders,
and then theyød carry them off, and some they
was angry or either scare, they didnt say which,

and then they was on the next ferry boat for the
coast. Willie he say it use to been like that for
ten or twenty year, and there been plenty of talk
too how the old man he done witch them girls
with his red devil eyes, only not to his face,
and then Willie he hush up a moment he look
around like maybe he hear the old man creeping
up from behind, only it aint nothing but the
crack of that orange ball of fire, and when he
satisfy we alone, he hunch over again and tell
some more.

Willie he say the last girl the old man done
took to his cabin her name was Kiri Girl, and
she was the softest coffee cream color anybody
ever seen, and her eyes was a pale pale blue,
and she had herself a long black braid of hair
down the middle of her back. The first night she
come to Pappa Toms, the old man he come in
and he sit next to her. The whole place it was
jumping and the peoples they was drinking and
shouting and some they was dancing, and there
was a big old boy name of Sam Henry he was
wearing hisself out on a old upright Conover
piano, and there was a fat-hip woman in a
yellow slip, she was sliding up and down the
frame of that piano while she singing a song,
but the old man he didnt see none of that, he
was watching them two blue eye floating free in
the dark. Kiri Girl she wunt hardly looking at
the old man cause she was singing along with
that fat-hip woman, but the old man he didnt

say a word yet, he was just listening to Kiri Girl
singing to herself the words, and then the song
it was done, and that fat-hip woman she was
done the same, and then the old man he was
asking Kiri Girl where she from. She didnt say
nothing right away cause she was looking over
her fingernail first one hand then the other, and
then she said she was nineteen and didnt have
to answer to no one even they was white. The
old man he done swallow some of his beer she
say that, seemed like maybe this here one girl he
wunt go have for hisself, but it wunt long before
they was both swallowing they beer, and the
old man he was laughing, and Kiri Girl she was
laughing the same even she didnt want to, and
then come the next morning she was hanging on
the old man arm and playing with his shirt and
they was heading on up to his cabin.

Kiri Girl she done took to living with old
man Thaddeus after that, and every night they
be coming to Pappa Toms and dancing and
drinking and walk along back by the backwater,
only it seemed like she was more and more
tire, and maybe even scare, only what it was
about nobody knew. Then Kiri Girl she just stop
coming to Pappa Toms, and the old man he was
carrying on like she never been, and with that
some was saying how Kiri Girl she been try to
burn his cabin down or either poison what he
eat, so he done tie her up from hand to toe and
left her back of the cabin for she soften up a bit,

and some they was saying how she done run
off to the backwater scrub to hide, only the old
man he done catch her up in his hands and he
eat her only two bite, even the bones, and some
they was saying how she wunt but a she-devil
herself and the old man he done call her up for
a while and then he have to let her go back, and
there was all kind of story like that, only no one
knew for sure what was what, and wunt no one
fool enough to find out neither.

The truth come out one night. The old man
he was running into Pappa Toms and he was
waving his two arm in front of his face like he
was some kind of windmill and shouting out
for someone to fetch up a couple old woman
midwife cause his Kiri Girl she was about to
give birth, and with that the peoples they was
moving fast as rain, and the girls they was
jumping out of laps and knocking they bottles
of beer to the floor, and big old Sam Henry
he done bust up his toe against the leg of that
piano he move so fast, and must of been ten
or twenty other what running around like a
flock of hen, only they didnt know where to
run. Then the old man he was out the door and
running through the backwater wood, and the
peoples they was out the door and running the
same, and pretty soon they was coming up the
rise to the old man cabin, and they could hear
poor Kiri Girl she was a bellowing away like
she a alligator been stuck by a knife, and the old

man he could hear her same as the rest, so he
was moving hisself faster and faster, and then
he was through the door, and the rest of the
peoples they was right behind him.

Kiri Girl she was spread out across the old
mans bed, a red-check blanket thrown across
her legs, and she was breathing pain and resist,
and with every breath her brown- ball stomach
it bubbled up and then down and then up and
then down again, and the peoples they was
looking at her, though mostly her stomach, and
the old man he was looking the same. Wunt
none of them knew what to do. But was then
old Mara Higgins come through the door, and
she was hallow and portend even she wunt but
five foot tall in her shoes, and she done press
her teeth together she see Kiri Girl in the bed,
and then she took off her scarf. She didnt even
show the mens the porch, they went out on
they own for refuge, and maybe a smoke, and
then the girls they was getting out sheets and
boil up some water, and all the while they was
humming and hover up around the bed, and old
Mara she didnt say a word, she was just holding
on to Kiri Girl arm.

Kiri Girl she was bellowing most of the
night, and old Mara she was with her all the
way, and the old man he was standing off to
one side of the porch and smoking on his pipe,
and every now and then he was up have a
look through the window, his eyes they was

burning red, and then he was talking to hisself,
only there wunt no sense to the words coming
out, sound like the old man he was coughing
up some kind of hoodoo spell only the devil
could know. The rest they was huddle up the
other side of the porch, and they wunt saying
a word while the old man grumble, and then
they was betting on what that baby was go look
like down to the size of it peanut, and then one
he was saying by the sound of that Kiri Girl cry
it go be the size of a barrel, and then they was
all laughing, and all the while Kiri Girl she was
bellowing louder and louder, like she was ready
eat up the whole world for breakfast when she
done, and by and by it was hard to tell she
even catch her breath, and then that bellowing
done stop altogether, and Kiri Girl she give a
hollow-out gasp seem like it come straight up
out of the ground, and then the air was still.

The old man he done looked to the door
with that, only wunt no one coming out just yet
so he tapped on his pipe some and took a puff
or two.   The rest of the mens they was looking
to the door the same with eyes what was saying
get you money out that one big boy or either no
it aint, and then the door it open up slow and
old Mara she come waddle out, and she done
look to the old man like she had something to
say, only she wunt able to open her mouth,
and then she stepped to the side, and it looked
like the old man give her a wicked smile, like

the devil does when he done what he come for. Then he went inside, and the rest of the mens they was all crowding in behind, and Kiri Girl she was laying curl up on her side with her arm pull in and that red-check blanket pull up around her neck, and she was all perspire and exhaust, and the girls they was cleaning up the blood, it was all over the place, only they wunt humming no more, and up alongside the bed there was a cutacoo basket and a thin cotton blanket, and there was the child, but it didnt look like a child, no sir, its skin was all a blueblack kind of pebbly color, it looked more like a dried up frog than anything else, and it wunt moving at all. But the old man it didnt bother him none, he touched that little blueblack child, and then he done pick it up and bring it close to his grizzle up face a while like he was trying to tell it something. Then the old man he was moving stiff and slow like he was having trouble even think what he go do, and then he done walk out of that cabin and into the shadow.

Willie he stop a bit, take hisself a breath of air, and then he start saying how a child born blueblack like that one was is a sign of the devil sure as we sitting here only the devil take up such a child in his arms and then how no one know what the old man he done with that blueblack child, only some say he done bury it up along the backwater, and some say he done

toss it in the water for some alligator eat it up,
and some saying he done eat it up hisself. Most
the peoples they pretty much give up talking
about the old man after that even they thought
he was the devil, and the old man he didnt
bother come into town no more neither, so it
squared both ways, but every now and then the
name Kiri Girl come up, and what done happen
to her, cause no one seen her since that devil
baby born, and she sure was a pretty girl, and
then theyod all shake they heads.

Then one day five or six year later, Kiri Girl
she come to town, only no one asked her where
she been or where she was going on account
of they all took her for some kind of ghost.
She was wearing a bright blue dress and a pair
of white glove, and a pretty blue hat done up
with bits of white lace, and looked like she was
going to church, only she was heading the other
way, and dragging a black leather suitcase as
she went. She walked down through the square
and down along Front Street, and then up past
the firehouse, was like she saying goodbye to
the whole town, only she wunt saying a single
word or either nodding her head at anybody she
knew, and then she was out the edge of town
and then down to the dock, only she wunt alone
cause by that time must of been half the town
done turn and follow her see what what. All she
did she pull up her suitcase and sit down on top
of it, and then she was looking out out across

the channel. The peoples then they was hanging
back and talk some, and then they wunt talking,
and then some was looking out out across the
channel same as Kiri Girl, but most was looking
at her on that suitcase. It looked like a picture
with the sunlight bounce off a Kiri Girl bright
blue hat, and the wind it come crisp and warm
through the channel grass and up across the
dock, and a crowd of heads looking on, wunt
none of them move or even breathe, and it
looked like that for two whole hour till the ferry
boat came chugging up the grassgreen channel
and blow its whistle a couple three time and
then it stopped alongside the dock to pick up a
couple of passenger.

Aint no one know exactly what happen after
that. Kiri Girl she was still waiting, and the
peoples they was still waiting the same, only
she didnt move to get on the boat, and maybe
fifteen, twenty minute later, the ferry boat it
give a quick, sharp whistle, and then it done
pulled away from the dock, and then it was
gone, and everybody was talking with that they
was saying what a fool they been come wait on
a ferry boat for a pickle-head girl get on like she
suppose to, and they done lost two whole hour,
and what she go do about that, just look at her,
only Kiri Girl, with her coffee cream color, and
her pale pale blue eyes, and that long black
braid of hair stretch down the middle of her
back, well she was gone the same as that ferry

boat, and time the people see that, didnt none
of them say another word, and then they was all
heading home.

-6-

The next thing I know, Willie he asleep. The
fire it almost burn out, aint nothing but a small
ball of orange it glowing from the black of the
ash, and that ball it getting smaller and smaller,
and then it gone, and then something it telling
me move along, so I does just that.

It too dark to see or either hear a thing, like I
done been swallow up, and every now and then
a piece of moss come rap me in the face, but
before I know what what Im is back at the bog
and looking at the ring of yellow lanterns, only
they mostly been knock over or kick in, and
there aint but a few strings of light sliding up
through the grass like they snakes.Everybody
there must of had some time of it. There all
kind of empty bottle toss about, and a couple
three empty box floating in the bog instead of
Tramsee, and shoes and shirts every which way
you look.

Ty he done sack hisself out by them red-
brown sycamores again, and he using my shoes
some more, and he clutching a couple of empty
bottle like he done married them instead of
Tramsee, and Tramsee she all twist up in the

middle of them three young men, only two of
them look like they went down fighting the
way they all cover up with blood, but they
holding her ankles all the same. Then it have
the strangest feeling like everyone done fell
dead from dancing the way they stretch out and
tangle up in the grass, like all it take is a nudge
to roll them into they graves, and the more Im
is looking at all them peoples, the more Im is
thinking they really is dead, and with that then
I aint know what to think.

I only been face up to death just one time
before this, and that was when the Widow
Mrs. Baxter her husband die, and his name was
Mister. My mama she been knowing Mister and
the Widow a long time, since I born at least,
and so we was over early and she was helping
with the grief- talk. Wunt much but wait around
the house, and Mister he was stretch out on the
dining room table, so I was having a look. His
skin look to been stretch up over his face look
like he was a red face hog, and I was tapping on
his face like so a couple three time, and then my
mama she come up behind.

"Aint nothing anybody can do now," she
said. "When death come swooping down most
he ever left been a long, white feather."

My mama she was quiet with that five
maybe ten minute, and I didnt know just what
to say so I didnt say nothing, and then I was
heading out maybe sit on the front stoop, but

all the while I was thinking about that feather
and wondering where it was, only I didnt see it,
and then there come some voices gum-greasing
through the gate and up the walk past the
Widow Mrs. Baxter her chinaberry tree, and
they was saying say how you do son this here
a time we all grief and perspective but we get
over it by and by, only I wunt but nodding my
head the while they talk, and then them voices
they was up the steps and into the house have
a look they ownself and maybe shake on Mister
his hand, and then some they was saying say
he aint look any more better then when he was
alive, and laughing to theyself, and some they
was a pasty white and maybe perplex, like
Mister he owed them money only they just then
thinking how they wunt go see it, but by and by
the voices they was gone, and it was just me on
the stoop, and I wunt thinking on a single thing
except about that feather.

It the same thing up at the bog. Im is looking
up and down that tangle of arms and legs and
bottles and shoes and boxes, and it hardly seem
coincidence how death done swoop on down
get all of them peoples and he aint even left one
white feather, not a one, but that how it is, and
then Im is looking up to the trees and the dark
of the ridge and the sky maybe catch me a sight
of death his wing when all of a sudden a voice
reach down through the dark and grab me from
behind.

"Say boy, what you doing there in the
middle of all them folks?"

I looking around, only I aint see where
it coming from, and I ready to run off to the
wood, only it grab me again.

"You thinking maybe they all dead, aint you,
boy?"

Is then I see the voice it coming from the old
man. He been sitting hunch over on top of his
crate and smoking his pipe, and he have his pail
back now but he aint bother with it, and then
he straighten hisself up and he telling me to sit
alongside him in the grass. Well aint nothing to
do but run, all this Willie-talk about death and
the devil and them peoples tangle up by the
bog, that the smart money, but for some reason
I aint move except to do just like the old man
said.

What go happen then I dont know. The old
man he just smoke some more, and then there
a flicker from one of them kick-in lantern come
snake across his face, it just enough to give his
face a hollow-out look against the dark. Then
he saying aint nobody dead, not all them folks,
not hisself, and me neither, and then he poke
me with his pipe stem just to prove hisself,
only he aint have to prove about me, and then
he smoking some more. I aint say a word but
rub my side with that, and I aint move none
neither, Im is just watching the old man what he
do next, only he aint do nothing but smoke on

that pipe, and by and by there so much smoke
snaking up around his head I thinking if he aint
the devil then there no such thing.

Then the old man he look at me like he
reading my mind, but all he do he ask me where
I been, and before I know what what my mouth
it open up and Im is saying how I been up in
the backwater wood, only I aint say a word
about Willie how he been saying the old man
the devil and eat up his own children, instead
Im is saying how I been hunting alligator, only
they all must of been asleep or it too too dark
cause I aint seen any.

The old man he a knowing look in his eyes
now, like he knowd wunt nothing for me to
do but lie and now he done caught me, but he
aint do nothing about it, all he do he wait till I
done, and then he saying say a alligator he aint
asleep when most people think, he like to move
about in the cool of the dark, but even he look
asleep in the middle of the day, he one eye open
for whatever come along maybe a wild pig or a
heron or even a mule come down to the water
take itself a drink, and that all she wrote.

Then the old man he smoking on his pipe
some more, it look like his eyes they lost in the
smoke, and then he telling me about the first
time he ever went hunting a alligator.

This here the story.

The old man was traveling with a flock of
them evandalistic preachers, he was just a boy

then, and everyone call him Tad. The time he
talking about they done set up they tents in this
narrow wedge of a field maybe three mile from
a town call Barclayville somewhere down along
the Yamahatchie river, and Tad he was waiting
for the show to start around seven o'clock so
he was thinking he head on into town and see
the sights. Before he done gone five step he met
up with Henry Jacobs and Henry cousin Oliver
walking out of a tent. Henry he wunt as big as
a raccoon his ownself, and he look like one too
he wearing a pair of wire-rim eye-glasses, but
he was the only son of the Reverend Samuel T.
Jacobs, so wunt nobody go put him in his place.
Oliver he was bigger than Henry, but that wunt
saying much, and he was down for the summer
from Charleston cause his folks they was hoping
a traveling preacher show do him good, wunt
nothing work so far. Tad he said how he was
going into town, and Henry and Oliver they
done fell in behind, and off they went.

By the time Tad and them other two boys
hit town they seen wunt much for them to do.
They walked by row after row of white-wash
buildings, and some was shops and some wunt,
and the peoples they was dress up with they
parasol and they hats and walking in and out
of the shops, and they was all talking about
the revival coming up. They wunt asking for
any miracle, but it couldnt hurt none to pray
for some, and wouldnt it be nice see them

Everets get that plow horse and plow they been
wishing on, maybe if the whole town went out
the Lord would see fit to bless them people.
But the boys they wunt paying no mind to the
talk. The only folks they'd ever seen blessed was
them gang of preachers, maybe a girl or two
come the morning, but wunt nobody suppose to
know about that. So they kept on walking and
walking, and by and by the town wunt nothing
but a ball of road dust.

Was maybe a couple more mile and Tad
he stopped, and the other two they stopped
the same, and Tad he was dog-sniffing at the
air, and then he wet his lip with the tip of his
tongue like so, like maybe he hungry, and then
he was saying say he done smell the saltpeter
of a backwater wood, and wherever it smell like
that was bound to be a alligator or two, maybe
more, and wouldnt it be something they done
found theyself a ten-footer they kill it dead,
and Oliver he wunt saying a word, he was
thinking on them alligators, but little Henry he
was saying how the meeting was go start up
soon and shouldnt they be getting back and
what they go do if they late, his daddy have
something to say about that, only before Henry
he said another word, Tad he just pointed to
a black black clump of wood up by the river,
and he was saying over there it over there that
the place, and then off they went, with Tad he
leading the way.

The boys they must of been walking through
the woods of that backwater for close to a hour,
they was following the black, slow-moving
water of the Yamahatchie, and they was passing
by river birch tangle up on the banks, and
sweet gum, and water oak stretch out low to
the ground and the branches rustle this way
and that, and every now and then they heard
a bobwhite or some other bird, and always the
hum of the flies, and they was walking and
walking and walking, only there wunt no sign
of a alligator anywhere they walked. Wunt long
after that little Henry Jacobs he was fed up to
here, and he said so too, he was saying say how
he was go head back to camp it didnt matter
if he was going alone or not on account of he
was sure the meeting done start up already,
and wunt nothing anybody could do about that
even they did find a alligator, and Oliver he was
nodding his head like wunt nothing he could
say against his cousin. Tad he didnt hardly miss
a step he was saying say the reason they aint
seen no alligator was the alligator he the one
been hunting them all along and maybe the best
thing they could do was to split up head on
back to camp that way the alligator only get one
of them instead of two or even all three. Little
Henry he done shut his mouth with that, and
he was looking around like maybe there been a
alligator behind every tree, or maybe just down
along the bank, and Oliver he was nodding his

head some more, but he didnt say a word, and
the boys they just kept walking.

Then they done come to a bend in the river,
and Tad he done stepped out to the edge, only
then he rush back and hush, and the other
two they hush the same, and then Tad he was
pointing to the far side of the river, and the boys
they was twisting they heads for a look. What it
was they done seen these knock-knee cypress rise
up black out of the water, and up on the bank
in back of them cypress they seen this big old
alligator. Tad he was saying he aint never seen a
alligator long as that why it must of been twenty
thirty foot long, and the other two they wunt
saying a word. Then Tad he have a idea, he was
looking to the other two and saying how they
was go swim that river and sneak on up to that
alligator from both sides, and Oliver and Henry
they was go jump on his back, keep him from
rolling into the water, and then Tad he was go
hack away with his knife and kill that alligator
dead.

Well, the boys they done swim the river like
Tad he said, and they come out by them cypress,
with Tad on one side and Henry and Oliver on
the other, and then Tad he done give the sign,
was only a flick of his chin, down like this, on
account of there wunt time for more, and with
that the boys they done jump on a twenty thirty
foot alligator. Mostly they was just hollering, at
least at first, and little Henry he was hollering

the loudest, and that alligator he done wake
hisself up all in a rush and he was trying to
shake hisself from the three of them boys,
only he wunt able to just yet, and then he was
twisting this way and that, and he was looking
all hunger and revelation. It wunt pretty. Oliver
he was hanging on to that alligator head and
his arms was wrap tight around that big old
mouth keep it from open up, and Tad he was
straddle back of that alligator's eyes and he was
pulling out a sawtooth hunting knife, and little
Henry he done grab a hold of that alligator tail,
only he was so little that alligator hardly knowd
there was a boy hanging on the tip, and Tad he
was just about to bring his knife down, only just
then that alligator he done give a big big belly-
shake all the way from his tail to his head, and
with that then little Henry he was flying off all
ball up like he shot out of some kind of cannon,
and then he was gone, and Oliver he done lost
his grip around that alligator mouth and before
he knowd what was what he was sliding down
the bank and into the water of the Yamahatchie,
and Tad he was knock up his heels where his
head suppose to be, and when he come down
he seen that alligator mouth open wide go eat
him up one bite, only Tad he was too quick, he
roll hisself up under that alligator and he was
swinging that knife up and then into the soft
part of the neck and grunt some and grind and
twist and turn, and then the alligator his eyes

was popping out, and then just like that he fell
dead to the warm black earth of the river-bank.

It was something to see how big that
alligator was, and Tad he was resting a moment
on the bank and looking awhile make sure that
alligator wunt just playing dead on account
of he done heard plenty of story, and he was
thinking on how close he done come to lose
his head, and then he heard Oliver climbing
up the bank, and Oliver he was breathing
heavy, but he still wunt saying a word, and
then they was both resting they heads in they
hands and looking at that alligator, they was
both retire and relief. They didnt know exactly
what to do next they'd never been that close to
a deaded alligator before, and maybe they'd of
been there the rest of the day except they heard
some shouting from off in the distance, and it
sounded like little Henry hisself and he was
saying over here over here over here, only he
wouldnt say exactly where here was.

Both Tad and Oliver they was looking up
and around, only they had no idea, and then
Tad he was moving hisself along the tangle of
the bank and he was calling out little Henry
name, and Oliver he was moving along the
same, and every so often Henry he'd answer
up, only he was sounding weak and confuse
and didnt even know what day it was, but Tad
and Oliver they was coming closer with every
step, and then they seen little Henry, he was up

in a big black oak maybe a quarter mile down
the Yamahatchie river, but this oak was maybe
forty foot high, and there was little Henry up
at the top. When Tad and Oliver seen that they
wunt able to move nothing except they open up
they mouths let em fall to like that, and all they
could do they was wonder how little Henry he
done got hisself all the way up there, and then
why he wunt climbing back down, and little
Henry he was saying say was something wrong
with his arm, like maybe he done broke it, and
with that then Tad he was saying how he and
Oliver they'd be coming right up. It done took
the both of them two whole hour for they done
carry little Henry down from that tree, and
little Henry he been talking the whole way
about wunt that alligator something to see, only
he mostly seen it from the air, and did they get
him or did he get away, and wunt he lucky he
only done broke his arm and not his neck, and
is they hunting up some more before they go
cause there just has to be a couple three more
alligator lay around here hiding in the weeds
in the grass this being the saltpeter backwater
like Tad done said, and maybe all they need is
a bag of pig feet sprinkle some out along the
bank and watch them alligator come rushing up,
and little Henry he was looking up and around
like maybe he was go tackle some more of them
alligator by the tail, and by and by, Tad and
Oliver they done carry him all the way from the

top of that big black oak all the way back to the
alligator, and little Henry he could see the knife
how it was stuck up in the neck and the blood
all around, and with that little Henry he done
shut his mouth.

It was then Oliver he done open up his
mouth and he was saying say what we go do
now, meaning the alligator, and Tad he was
saying how they was go knock out some of
them alligator teeth, one for each of them there,
cause a alligator tooth it close to the most
prestige charm on the face of this here earth,
and then they was go set that alligator on fire
burn him to ash and bone, and all the while that
alligator was burning, they was go say how they
was the ones kill him dead, just so there wunt
no mistake about who done it.

Then Tad he reached up under that alligator
head and pull out his knife, and it was scrape
up with blood, only Tad didnt mind, and then
he was knocking out them alligator teeth, just
like he said he would, and there was one for
Henry and one for Oliver and one for hisself,
and then he was telling the other two to wear
they teeth up around they necks till the day
they died or the charms wouldnt work at all,
only with that Oliver he was asking just how
them charms knowd if a fellow go take it off
tomorrow if he wearing it today, but Tad he was
saying that just how charms work, and damn
if they didnt always guess right too, and then

he was telling how one fellow he done heard
about he had hisself a alligator charm only it
wouldnt work and it wouldnt work and damn
if that fellow didnt throw that charm away,
what only went to prove it for the real thing
all along, and then Tad he was up gathering
some wood and dry brush for the fire, and
Oliver he was doing the same, and Henry he
was looking from the alligator to the tooth in
his hand and then back again. Then Oliver and
Tad they was ready, and Oliver he done pick
up his cousin from the black, black earth, and
Tad he done set the wood and the brush on fire,
and then the three young boys they stepped
back from that alligator to watch it burn on a
bank above the Yamahatchie river, and the fire
it was burning bright and then brighter, and the
smell of alligator meat it was rising up with the
smoke through the black-green of the trees and
swirling around the branches and into the night
sky, and then the alligator it was gone, wunt
nothing left but some black ash and some bone,
and little Henry he jump down from Oliver to
have a closer look, his broke arm dangling by
his side, and then he was saying how that there
alligator he done gone up like old Elijah hisself,
and the other two they didnt say nothing they
was nodding they heads just so and watching
the smoke some more, and then the smoke it
was gone, and the three boys they turned they
heels and they was heading on back to camp.

With that then the old man he done with his
story and he arch up his back give it a stretch.
Then he smoking some more on his pipe, and
the smoke its curling up around the old mans
head, and Im is thinking on a alligator charm,
how it the most prestige there is, and then I
trying to see around the old mans neck if he
wearing his like he done said, only there too
much smoke to see and too much dark. Then the
old man he saying when it his time he want to
go up just like old Elijah, how there aint nothing
like watch what a fire can do when it catch a
hold of a body, it the hand of God hisself come
down to take up the dead, and then the old man
he aint paying me no mind at all, which it all
right by me, even if maybe he aint the devil.

The next thing I know I is heading for home.
It so late now it almost early, which means
there aint nothing more to do anyway. Let all
them dead folks be even they aint dead. And by
and by I is coming through the dunes and then
down along the beach, and the sky it kind of a
pale blue by now and spreading itself thin along
the water, and then the sun it coming up. The
beach it cover up with a pack of fish stretch out
dead on the sand from the storm, and some they
been half eat up, and some they aint, and there
a couple three shark belly up the same, and
plenty of seagull walking in and around them
fish, they fighting among theyself over a scrap
of fishmeat. I aint never been up a whole night

before this, and maybe that why, but I aint tire
or confuse a bit, at least not yet, and then Im is
laugh and laugh, and chasing them gulls back
to the sea, only soon as I pass by they back at
them fish and I chasing them some more, and
then Im is walking down along the shore, and
the waves they coming in gentle and lap lap
lapping up over my toes, and there must be ten,
twenty fiddler crab running in and out of the
waves and up over the sand and the shells and
the fishes and the seagrass and then back again,
and then Im is thinking some more on the
old man, and maybe there aint nobody know
for sure what he is or what he aint, not even
Willie, but maybe that aint nothing to worry
about, and then Im is thinking on old Elijah and
cutting out them teeth and it sure would be nice
have a alligator charm like the old man, aint
nothing I wouldnt do have me one, and then I
aint thinking no more, there aint nothing more
to think about, the sun been up a couple three
hour, and I is just now heading home.

. . . now this here bluegreen alligator he know'd he was the most powerful animal ever come out of the swamp, and the rest of the animals they done know'd it the same, and ifn they done got too close why he'd just gobble them up, so the alligator he done set hisself up on a big old black stump of a log stick up from the blackgreen muck, and every morning he'd be sunning hisself his eyes half close like he asleep, only he'd be waiting on one of them animals, and sure enough, down come a coon or maybe a pig get hisself a drink of water, only before they done open they mouth that alligator he'd just gobble them up, and wunt nothing nobody do about it neither, and then that alligator he'd look up from his log to the rest of the swamp, and his head it'd be rolling up and around, and then he'd give a roar come rumbling all the way from his belly, and he'd be saying say just me and my world, and with every word come out of that alligator mouth, the rest of them animals they'd be scrambling through the long grass and hiding up in the trees, they was plenty of cover what with all the moss hang about, and they was doing like that for the longest time, but all the while they was wondering say just what was they go do cause they was getting awful damn sore and tire of living up in them trees . . .

Ghosts

-1-

A young man squatted stiffly in the damp grass in front of a small, canvas tent, the flap of the tent tied back and the just-rising sun flashing against the exposed corner of a small wooden cot, and a pair of roughed, brown workboots underneath the cot. There was a strange stillness about the camp this morning, a waiting kind of silence which filled the air like wind-blown ash, making it difficult to breathe, and which suggested, among other things, the unblinking vigilance of God.

The young man's name was Thaddeus Jacobs, and he was thinking about the past few days and a girl he'd only just come to know, only now he was wishing he hadn't, and all the while he was thinking his grayish-blue eyes were flashing about, impatiently, aggressively, like fish flashing about in the cool of a river. What the hell had he been thinking. It was one thing to head off down by the river. Maybe go for a swim. But to go back to her tent in the middle of the night. Then again it was only supposed to be the two of them. How the hell was he supposed to know. Then he thought of a few other things he should've done or should've thought and he became angry and his mouth filled with a bitter, coppery taste, and then a

few minutes later the taste was gone. He did
not see the older man approach, stand to one
side of the small, canvas tent, elbows hanging at
odd angles, and a prayerful uncertainty etched
in a thin, weather-worn, oblong face. He did
not hear the words angling down, quiet words,
almost subdued in the morning blue, lingering.

"Thaddeus, hey Thaddeus, you okay?
They're ready for you. They're up in the tent.
Come on Thaddeus, you know aint nothing else
you can do, come on."

The young man said nothing. And the older
man, having delivered his message, smacked
his lips together, a look now of almost prayerful
anticipation spreading across his thin, oblong
face, then stuffed a wad of tobacco into his
mouth and chewed, chewed, looked to the
young man and chewed some more, and then
headed back across the field through the wet,
wet grass, the young Thaddeus watching,
thinking, watching, remembering,

*the revival meeting a couple of nights before and
the sheriff and the main tent collapsing and him and
her ignoring the commotion and heading down to the
river for a while. but not to swim, the two of them
talking softly, a lazy kind of talking, the commotion
of the camp a distant echo, her moving closer, asking
him if he really loved her and when did he know
and him not knowing what to say at first but then
the words rolling out his mouth of course he loved
her he had loved her since the moment she and her*

*father had joined the Reverend, since that very first
day they rolled in and he saw her there sitting up in
the front of the wagon with a red-letter bible plopped
in her lap and her father on the one side and the
good Reverend Jacobs on the other, and she smiled at
that, and all Thaddeus could look at was the brown-
ish-pink color of her face, and every now and then a
flash of something white when her skirt caught up
above her knee, and then she was asking him to say
it again, and he did, and now he was smiling also,
he had never thought they'd even get to talking,
she troubled him too much for that, every time he
got near her he couldn't seem to get his mouth to
work right, her giggling at that and telling him his
mouth was just fine, and then the two of them not
talking, and then the commotion of the camp had
quieted and they headed off to her tent, the soft, hazy
light of a single lantern on a hook, the girl slipping
inside, slipping out of her dress, her soft lace girdle,
the pink of her skin budding up and the arc of her
hips flashing in the lamp light, and then she was
stretched out on the cot, her clothes scattered about
the ground, motioning for him to join her, which
he had done, losing himself in the emotion of the
moment and the nakedness of both of them, like
losing his entire soul, he had thought, which was
all right by him, but then the flap of the tent had
blown open suddenly, or been thrust open, and the
two of them had looked up to see what it was, the
warm dark shell of the night exposed, a warm wind
then blowing through the opening, and there they*

saw the Reverend Jacobs himself in the dark of the
opening, a large black hat on his perspiring, balding
head, an oil lamp in his hand, the yellowish, oily
light mixing with the light of the other oil lamp,
the light too much now, the girl and the young
man blinking in the sudden glare, but as the good
Reverend stepped into the tent he was unaware of the
two on the cot, or so it seemed, the canvas flap still
flap flap flapping with the wind of his presence and
the Reverend trying to grab hold and pull it shut but
unable to and then setting his lantern on the ground
and getting a firmer grip and then tying the flap
securely, and still unaware, for he wasn't looking
directly at the cot even then but past it to the heap
of the girl's clothing on the ground, the girl herself
only half- recognized in her nakedness, and the
young man seeming a part of the girl, the Reverend
flinging his own coat onto the pile, then loosening
his tie, his shirt, his pants, and all the while the
Reverend's mouth was flap flap flapping also, how
he knew it was late, he'd have been there sooner but
the tent was down on account of that blithering,
bumbling fool of a young sheriff, still down as it
turned out, but he'd given up on it for the night,

Then the memory faded and Thaddeus
put on his boots and followed the other, older
man across the sunny, dew-grassy, tent-dotted
field towards the waiting reverends, towards a
long, black table and a narrow white tent. He
could almost see them. The Reverend Jacobs
and two other ministers of the camp walking

slowly towards the long white tent, the day
just breaking, the good Reverend mumbling to
himself about wagging tongues, the other two
a step or so behind, their tongues wagging in
agreement, and then they would be through
the white canvas flap and inside, the interior
strangely dark with the sudden morning blue
breaking full across the field outside, and within
the dark dark tent the loamy, earth smell of
brushed leather and Castile soap, and then the
Reverend Jacobs sitting down behind a long,
black table, the other two following, still a step
or so behind, lighting the lanterns on either side
of the table and then sitting down also, and
the darkness inside somehow darkening in the
lamp light, deepening, the three talking amongst
themselves for a moment then stopping, looking
up at the open flap, the brightening triangle
of morning blue outside but not entering this
place of the long long table, the three waiting
reverends, each rigid in his silence, each
burning with the self-righteous infallibility of
men who see with the eyes of God.

Thaddeus walked into the tent and was
instructed to kneel, which he did, his body
swaying slightly on the uneven earth, and then
he looked up at the waiting reverends, at the
light of infallibility shining from the shadows.
He asked the good Reverend and the others
what it was he had done that they wanted to see
him. The others looked to the Reverend, and the

Reverend said he knew the moment he'd laid
eyes on the boy, from the moment Thaddeus
first came into his care, he'd known the boy
was no good, but he had turned a blind eye, so
to speak, in the fragile hope he could mold the
boy, tear him loose from the rigid, inexorable
grip of the devil, but to no avail, he could see
that clearly now, there is no excuse for your
behavior, such a wild and utter disregard for
the sanctity of the laws we live by, I will not
tolerate it any more, I will not tolerate such
moral turpitude, what did you think you were
doing with this girl, good Lord, son, to shame
her so beneath the umbrella of my care, the
umbrella of this ministry, my ministry, and her
father, the good Reverend Fillmore, a witness
to this shame, what you have done Thaddeus,
you have committed an unspeakable, an unpar-
donable sin, and I am sorry for you, I truly am,
but I suspected all along this day would come,
and here it is, I have no choice now but to see
that you never set foot in this camp again.

On and on he went, his words flickering
in the tentshadow like the yellowish, gloomy
light of the oil lamps, and every now and then
the other two would nod in instinctive, tacit,
simultaneous agreement, particularly the girl's
father, the good Reverend Martin Fillmore.
And the young man heard the words, or so
it seemed, but they had little effect. He was
beyond the angry incoherence of this man who

was not his father. Him thinking again, remembering again,

how the good Reverend had moved towards the cot and then stopped, a black shadow against the light of two lanterns, the blackness deepening with rage, and then a moment of inarticulate, gurgling sounds, as of someone being strangled, and then a rush of anger, you harlot, you harlot, the words rushing also, the young girl squirming out from beneath the young man and then up from the cot, screaming, then running past the shadow, past the words, struggling with the flap then into the night, and the young man after the girl, but the shadow grappling with him, grip of the devil it seemed, then the young man breaking the grip, the rage, you harlot, you harlot, then the shadow stumbling into the side of the tent and the tent falling and the lanterns falling also and the fire scattering upon the ground, spreading, the canvas beginning to smoke, and the young man looked to the fire and then to the shadow of the Reverend, which was not moving, then to the fire again, the fire speaking, leave him be he belongs to me his bone his flesh his soul are mine they are not yours you do not need him alive you do not want him alive to save him would be a mistake you know that you must know that he will not thank you so go and leave him to me go and the girl is yours no one will ever know, then the fire burst into laughter, a taunting, eviscerating laughter, the flames becoming brighter and brighter, but in spite of the warning, the young man grabbed hold of the

*Reverend's arms and pulled him free of the burning
tent, the glint of the fire showing itself on the dry
dry grass and the two of them there and no one
else, not even the girl, and him thinking why, why
had he done it, why had he pulled him out, maybe
he could put him back, but the moment had already
passed and the next thing he knew a crowd of men
and women stood in a ragged half- circle behind him,
behind the Reverend, the tent fire burning just a
few yards away and the cinders showing themselves
orange against the sky, and then the men and
women moved closer, wondering at the young man's
nakedness, wondering at the heavy, unmoving heap
of the Reverend, also naked but seeming clothed, the
impenetrable shadow of righteousness blurring the
line between faith and reality, or so it seemed, and
then slowly, even painfully, with an almost theat-
rical flourish, the Reverend opened his eyes and
looked at the wondering men and women, some of
the men shaking their heads and slipping off into
the crowd, but the rest crowding closer and offering
the Reverend a chew of tobacco or a snort from a
jug, and the women crowded around too, pushing
the men aside and sneering at their offerings and
wiping the Reverend's brow with aprons or scarves
and their voices piping up with awe and indignation,
what happened, was he all right, how did the fire
start, was it Thaddeus, what's the matter with that
boy, no wonder you was in shock Reverend, here
let me get you something, Lord a mercy, what got
into that boy's head do you think, and as the voices*

merged with the cinder-filled dark, the Reverend
turned his eyes from the crowd to the young man,
the eyes of the crowd following, then falling upon his
naked young skin, and Thaddeus looked first at the
grim-standing crowd assembled there, the yellowish
glow of the fire showing itself on their faces, and
then he looked into the face of the silent, raging,
recuperating Reverend, the fire showing itself there
also, but only in the eyes, for the Reverend's face was
strangely obscured by shadow, and in that instant,
the young man knew that the fire had spoken the
truth,

Again the memory faded, the Reverend still
speaking, the others still nodding, have you
nothing to say, your actions alone are reprehen-
sible, but that you have nothing to say is surely
cause for concern, the devil himself could boast
no greater apathy for good than you, Thaddeus,
are showing now by your silence, well I am
done with you, I've done my best, but it is no
use.   Then he stopped speaking, sat back in
his chair, arms folded across his chest, and
he stared at the young man from the glinting
shadows, the young man nodding now, but
indifferently.

Then the other two leaned forward, a head
on either side of the good Reverend Jacobs.
They looked to the young man and then spoke,
quietly, almost inaudibly, first one, the good
Reverend Fillmore, having returned from Jasper
county the evening before and only then finding

out about his daughter, first the Reverend
Fillmore, and then the other filling in.

"Son, you must know you're heading down
the road of the Devil."

"Yes, Thaddeus, you must know that."

"And you must stop."

"Yes, you must stop."

"Turn back to the Lord."

"Yes, turn back."

The voices stopped a moment, waited for
the young man to respond, and when the young
man said nothing, the voices continued.

"Thaddeus, I'm not blaming you for what
you did, only God knows I've a right. She is,
after all, my only daughter. But I am not a
vengeful man. What's done is done. All I ask is
that you repent of your sinful ways."

"Yes, Thaddeus. Repent."

"Do not mistake me, son. Think on this
carefully. It is not too late. Though you may
no longer remain here, and I agree with your
father, the Reverend, on this, it is not too late to
save your immortal soul."

"Yes, Thaddeus. We are all concerned with
your salvation. Your father most of all. But listen
now to what the good Reverend Fillmore has to
say. Who better to instruct you than the father
of the very girl you have tried to corrupt?"

The young man looked up at the men who
were speaking to him, the dim, dark, heavy light
of the lamps burning on either side of the table

but now the light was not shining beyond even
the glass, or so it seemed, the waiting reverend
faces obscured by the darkening darkness of the
tent, and all the young man could think was he
is not my father, this one, you have mixed it up,
and so he said nothing.

"Do you think he understands what is
happening here?" "Yes, Martin. I think he does."

"Then there is nothing more we can do. Is
there?" "There is nothing."

So the voices stopped again, and the two
men sat back in their chairs and folded their
arms and stared out from the shadows. Still
Thaddeus said nothing. There was nothing to
say. Always he has been against this one who
was not his father, but up until the last few
days it had been an unexpressed, groping sort
of opposition, something felt but not known,
as a small child feels, but now he knew, they
both knew, they had both been in the girl's
tent, and they both knew why, but nobody else
knew, you would've thought different with the
Reverend laid out on the ground as naked as he
was, but nobody would ever know, you couldn't
say anything against the man, not so anyone
would believe you, so why would they believe
their own eyes, and then the young man looked
up at the unblinking face of this one who was
not his father, could not really see the face in
the oily gleaming obscurity of the lamp light,
but he could have tried to make them see the

truth, yes, he could have, but then he hadn't, and then the young man was filled with a rage and a longing and an emptiness and fear all at once, but still he said nothing.

Then the meeting was over, and Thaddeus walked from the tent of his banishment and he was thinking of nothing in particular, not even where he might like to go. The strange, watchful silence from before had given way to the shock of a morning already there, the men and women now stumbling from their tents, the grumble of put-upon voices, a "where's the wood" and a "hurry up with that there water there's coffee needs making," and the cookfires smoking with the smell of side meat and bread. But Thaddeus was not hungry. And he had nothing to pack.

So he left.

-2-

A small white child was born in the spring of the year a thin caul across his face and the mother and the father of the child removed the caul and cleaned the child as best they could and then they kissed the child and looked into his eyes and they asked themselves what name they could give the child but they could not agree on a proper name so they decided to bring the child to a preacher a minister a man of the cloth and ask the good Lord to name their

child then they wrapped the child in an old blanket
for there was still a chill in the air then carried him
through the alleys of the town to the edge of the
town and into a large green field and in the center
of the field a large white tent had been raised a tent
that housed the word of the Lord and there were
many wagons gathered around the tent and many
horses pawing at the ground and some snorting
and some eating grass and there were many people
gathered around the tent also some standing outside
in the evening light for the service had not yet
begun some talking the last time they had a minister
come preaching in town half the congregation came
drunk started throwing empty bottles at the podium
then some laughing some just nodding their heads
some smoking then a man dressed in black stepping
outside calling to the people waving then inside and
the mother and the father smiled and walked across
the field and they were not the last ones inside the
tent and then they sat themselves down on a bench
near the back the child in the mother's arms and
they let the music and the words of the service wash
over them and they did not try to understand what
they heard and saw they did not sing or pray as if
just coming to the tent and sitting on the bench
was enough to cleanse their simple souls and so
they sat with unconscious acceptance as the people
around them sang and prayed then the Reverend a
man of the cloth stepped to the podium and raised
his hands and spoke and he spoke with the voice of
God or so it seemed to the people gathered before him

and the mother and the father of the child felt the
power of his words and so they listened to him and
the Reverend called out to the men to the women
to the children and he asked if any were in need
of the Lord and some did say they were and their
voices were heard save me Lord save me Lord save
me from myself and the Reverend then asked them
to come up to the platform and bow down before the
Lord and one by one the voices with need became
men and women and children and one by one they
stood up and walked to the platform and bowed
down before the Lord and the mother and the father
stood up also and they walked down the aisle with
their child in their arms and they stopped before the
platform then they laid the child upon the platform
and bowed their heads and the Reverend looked down
upon the men and women and children before him
and he called to the Lord to save his people and the
people called out also and the air was filled with the
cries of intolerable suffering and some were rolling
about on the platform and some even on the ground
their holy roller arms and legs flailing in the air and
some were moaning and speaking gibberish their
words rising from the black of their souls and some
fell down upon the earth and prayed in silence their
suffering caving in on itself and when the frenzy
had passed the Reverend raised his arms a second
time and blessed the people gathered in the tent and
he said the Lord is surely among us then the people
on the platform walked back to their benches some
shaking their heads some smiling many more not

smiling then the Revered looked down and saw the
child on the platform and he picked up the child and
looked to the people before him and he asked whose
child was this and he held the child up in the air but
no one answered for the mother and the father of the
child had left the tent and were walking across the
field to the town where they lived and the Reverend
asked a second time and a third time and still no
one answered so the Reverend lowered the child and
looked out to the crowd and he said he would claim
this child in the name of the Lord and then the spirit
of the Lord descended upon the child and the people
gathered in the tent were witness to that spirit and
they cried out hallelujah Lord hallelujah and with
that the child with no name opened his eyes and
looked first to the people gathered below him and
then to the Reverend looking down upon his face and
the child's eyes shone with the fire of God a white
fire a too-hot fire and the Reverend recognized the
fire for a moment and he was afraid but then the fear
passed for it was only a newborn child before him
and so the Reverend left the platform with the child
in his arms and gave the child to his wife and told
her the child was a gift from God, and thereafter the
child with no name was called Thaddeus.

Thaddeus sat in the rear of the lead
wagon, looked from the morning blue fields,
the morning blue woods to the Reverend, the
Reverend smiling, sitting next to a young girl,
the young girl smiling also, then the Reverend

expounding upon his virtuous mission to bring
the word of God to the poor people of South
Carolina, his arms pointing randomly to the
fields and the woods passing by on either side
of the wagons as if the poor of South Carolina
were hiding in the grass or behind the black line
of the trees, the Reverend going on and on, his
voice deepening with every word, the voice of
God, or so he seemed to think, and the young
girl listened to his words, not quite believing
he was God but willing to try anything once,
had tried, perhaps, hallelujah then hallelujah
again, and the young Thaddeus wondered why
she was carrying on like that, what hold did
the Reverend have on her, he didn't understand, he didn't want to understand, and for
a moment he imagined the Reverend and the
young girl sitting naked in the front of the
wagon, the driver whwhwhipping his wrists,
the horses clopclopclopping, and the young girl
wrapping her legs around the Reverend, the
Reverend nibbling on her arms, her breasts, her
neck, taking all of her in a single breath, the
girl wrapping her legs tighter and tighter, the
good Reverend nibbling faster and faster, and
then the Reverend was gone and in his place
was the young man name of Thaddeus, the two,
the girl and the young man, clipclopclipping,
their naked bodies moving faster and faster and
faster, and then hallelujah one final time, and
then the vision was gone, and the wagons were

off to the side of the road down in a shallow
gully, the horses tied down, the wagons empty,
the men squatting in the shade of the wheels in
twos and threes, some chewing on grass, some
talking, some listening, seems like folks aint
showing much interest in religion these days,
not like they used to, aint enough faces to fill
a tent, sure aint, aint enough pockets to fill a
plate neither, sure aint, seems like folks have
turned their backs on the Lord, seems like, and
the women cooking soup in a shallow gully,
same old scene, same old same old, three black
pots each hanging from an iron rack, a large
fire underneath, the women watching over the
pots and the pots boiling anyway, the women
talking, also talking all at once, hope we fare
some better up in Barclayville, we always do
well there, sure hope so, we aint made enough
to buy a ham, to buy a goose, seems like folks
have turned to buy a new blue dress have
turned their backs to a new white hat seems like
seems like the same old scene, and then a single
woman's voice, soups on soups on, then a single
line, the men and the women and the children
each with a bowl and a spoon, then sitting
down in the grass, the men in the shade of the
wheels, the women by the pots, the children
scattered here and there like stones, and the
young man name of Thaddeus sitting away
from the rest, sitting with his back to the road,
then the young girl sitting in the grass beside

him, not quite smiling, then warm and wet her
blue blue eyes looking at him as if she thought
he might know God, or so it seemed to him,
and he fell in love with those blue blue eyes,
and then the two of them eating their soup,
the young man looking into his bowl, almost
thoughtfully, the young girl's eyes looking still,
then the bowls empty and the young man and
the young girl walking through the grass to the
wagons, talking softly, quietly, and that was the
first time they talked, and then later they talked
some more, and the next night also, and then
they were in Barclayville and the tents were
set up and the big tent and the show was over
but they didn't care, arm and arm they walked
through the dark wet grass, dark wet smiles
spreading across their faces, the huddled clump
of ghost white tents sinking into the ground
behind them, and then they were into the trees,
pine, oak, some redbud mixed in, dark wet
smiles and warm wet wood, a moonless night,
then sitting down along the root-worked bank
of a slow- moving river, the black sky mixing
with black water, the two staring into the
blackness, not daring to look at each other just
yet, listening vaguely to the wash and ripple of
the current, and then the young girl spoke and
the young man answered, back and forth, and
back and forth again, their voices drifting down
and across the black, black river,

       why did we have to go so far from camp

you afraid
no im not afraid I just wondered why
i don't know you want to head back
no not yet I just wondered thats all
      i wasnt really thinking about where just
wanted to get away from all the tents and the
voices and the people moving in and out and
the shouting and the lanterns and the horses
and the trucks i didn't say nothing before but
i was standing outside the big tent when the
trucks pulled up i saw the sheriff come down
with his men the sheriff he even come up to me
ask me what i seen but i didn't say nothing i
was just standing there on the outside looking
in but i didn't say a word
      the young girl moving closer now, looking
with blue blue eyes at the young man staring
at the river, the young girl pulling his arms
around hers
      is that why you brought me here
      the young man still absorbed in the ripple
throb of the river thinking of an answer perhaps
the girl repeating herself softly now a ripple
throb herself
      is it
      the young man shifting now moving his free
arm to rub some warmth into his suddenly cold
hands then the warmth returning spreading
      no that's not why i didnt think so
      the young girl rippling some more her dress
pulled up to her knees and then a little higher

the young man noticing pretending not to but
wanting to see more then the sound of the river
flooding his thoughts the wash of the water
along the bank sucking surging damping the
black black earth the young man standing up
moving to the edge the darkness of the river
flowing past his boots sliding into the wet
    do you love me
    the young girl's eyes now swimming with
the wet of the river
    do you love me
    the young man climbing back up the bank,
falling into those blue blue eyes once again
    do you love me
    her thoughts now swimming with his
thoughts

and then their thoughts became a dream revealed,
the very same recurring dream that had plagued
the good Reverend Jacobs from the first moment
he had looked into the eyes of young Thaddeus, a
dream that would wake him in the middle of the
night in a cold sweat or a hot sweat and the flies
swarming and the mosquitoes, unable to get back
to sleep, sometimes for days, and he told no one
about the dream, it became a dark, private, hidden
thing, but not from Thaddeus, for it was his dream
as well, or so it seemed to the good Reverend, the
dream taking root deep within the boy, too deep
to root out, a dream of becoming, a too hot night,
profoundly hot, everyone awake could see the steam

rising off of their own skin, which was everyone
in camp, there wasn't anything to do but toss and
turn on their cots, maybe walk through the dry, hot
grass a while, maybe down to the river, then head
on back to bed, and then, as if on cue, a respectful
silence descended upon the camp and the men and
women bowed knee and prayed for deliverance from
the all too oppressive and yet potentially edifying
heat, their bodies bent in stiff homage before their
God, wouldn't He send them a nice cool breeze off
the river, give them a chance to get some sleep, and
of course their prayer was answered, and quickly
too, in twenty-five minutes a cool breeze was indeed
blowing through the camp, but along with their
prayer- provoked breeze came the largest bluegreen
alligator ever seen in South Carolina, the alligator
also prayer-provoked, and particular too, for it spent
a good hour moving from tent to tent, stopping, then
sniffing at the air, then moving on to the next tent,
then, finally, coming to a smaller tent set up under
three shaking aspen, the only tent in the camp with
the soft yellow light of a lantern burning through
the canvas, through the black-green branches of the
shaking aspen, the soft yellow glow somehow making
the whole night seem darker, blacker, even hotter,
and the alligator stopping, then sniffing, almost
tasting the air around the tent, then snorting at
the flap, its head a shadow stuffed up against the
white- yellow glow of the canvas skin, and then the
alligator gave a prayer-provoked bellow, the alliga-
tor's prayer answered now, burst into the tent with

*an almost religious fervor, bellowing, bellowing some
more, the two inside up and bellowing, also with an
almost religious fervor, two chasing one then one
chasing two, the alligator knocking a lantern on its
side with a thrust of its tail, the white-yellow light
spilling out, catching hold of the grassy floor, the
white canvas cloth, then a bellow of voices gathered
round outside the tent, the voices saying whats
going on who's in that tent aint sound like nothing
human do it, then the voices circling closer, stepping
over one another, moving to the front of the tent to
get a better look, then the whole of the canvas-skin
etched with flame, smoke curling out from under the
flap and then up, the Reverend running from the
midst of this unforeseen conflagration into the midst
of a waiting, intent- around-the-tent congregation,
also unforeseen, a bible in his hand, of course, the
Reverend waving it in the air like he might wave
a weapon and calling out to the alligator in the
tent stand back demon stand back, the word of God
stands before you, the word of God in the naked
flesh, and quite literally too, for the good Reverend
was dressed only in a pair of black church boots, and
then he was running from the tent, from the crowd,
a pretty young girl running out the tent and after,
a step or two behind him, without even the black
church boots, and then the bluegreen alligator, jaws
snapping at high-stepping heels, then the awestruck
congregation giving chase, some running to their
tents for guns then off into the wood, every now
and then a shot ringing out, then a couple more,*

then a whole rattle of shot, the woods smoke-full of
shotgun revivalists hunting alligator, the alligator
hungry for the tang of girlmeat, or so it seemed, the
girl just running for her life, the good Reverend now
forgotten, him in his black church boots standing
once more in front of the now smoke black tent
beneath the quaking aspen, the Reverend watching
the tent burn to the ground, the bible still in his
hand, a dream of what was to come, perhaps, or what
was, or what might have been, or so it seemed.

-3-

It is hot, he thinks. Going to get hotter, too.
He is in shirt sleeves, brown pants, the brown
workboots from under the cot. He has been
walking long enough for the fields to pass by
one into the next, the same sun-burned grass
growing in clumps, thick like the bristles of
brooms, the same small white stones scattered
here, there, the same live oaks, their giant black
limbs stretching up to the sky, black silhouettes
against a pale arc of blue. He has been walking
the back country roads of Barclay county for
hours, or so it seems, a couple of cars dusting
past now and then, an old black woman in bib
overalls and a mule and a cart and the mule
with an ear lopped off, a prison chain-gang
working up ahead and then the trucks and
wagons moving on. But these country roads

offer young Thaddeus no comfort from the
suddenness of his banishment, and no escape
into the future either. He suddenly wonders
where he is going and what he is going to do,
and then it occurs to him that the only life he
knows is back among those Saturday night
penitents and the small, canvas tents and eating
soup in a ditch by the side of the road and then
moving on to the next town, maybe he'd have to
go back, maybe there wasn't anywhere else to
be, and this thought leaves him with a burning
sensation in his stomach and again the bitter
taste of copper in his mouth. But he does not
turn around, and then in the heat of his bewilderment he hears a wagon coming up the dry
dry road, coming up behind him, the steady
clop clop clopping of two horses, the wagon
slowing, stopping, and the ghost of the present
becomes the past.

"You need a lift, son?" He was a skinny
man, unshaven, his face twisted into a kind
of perpetual snarl, but he seemed unaware of
his disfigurement. When he spoke the words
seemed to roll out of the side of his mouth.
"You're more than welcome. I've plenty of room.
Besides, I could use the company."

For the longest time neither man spoke.
The brownish green of the fields on either side
soaking up the heat of the day, the black line
of uncut woods shimmering in the distance,
always in the distance, it seemed. Every now

and then the skinny man would lean forward, soberly, earnestly, give the reins a jerk and yell at the two browns to giddyap there and get a move on, but the two browns ignored him, clop clop clopping steadily, unimpatiently, as if the only time were now, the only place here. So the wagon moved on, past the fields on either side, past the unattainable woods, the skinny man not quite in control.

Then a disfigured face turned towards Thaddeus. "Just like women they are."

The young man nodded, looked to the horses.

"Worsen being married."

The young man nodded again. He had never been married.

"I knowd this fellow once, wasnt much older than you is now, and this fellow had hisself a wife just wouldnt stop talking, jabbing like a jaybird about what she done that day what she hadnt done what she shouldve done when was they going to visit her mother when was he going to buy her that silk scarf from out the catalogue her mother had told her about marrying a fellow like him and on and on and on."

The skinny man started laughing and spitting through his teeth.

"Of course it come to this fellow that if he stayed around much longer his ears was going to be hanging down to his knees, so one night,

had to been around midnight cause that women
she wouldnt shut up till most everyone was
asleep, so one night this young fellow packs
up heading he dont know where he dont care,
and by and by he come on some railroad tracks,
so he figures to wait on a train. He didnt wait
more an twenty thirty minutes fore one swing
into sight, and then this young fellow he was
running long side it, and then he hopped on
board. He stayed on that train for three whole
nights and three whole days before he even
thought to get off. He figured he wunt the
marrying kind."

The skinny man stopped speaking a
moment, his wrists jerking the reins, a giddyap
here and a get a move on, the two browns
ignoring his efforts, then a shrug of his
shoulders and a settling back into his seat.

Then he continued.

"Well, wunt but a month went by and he
found hisself with a quiet boarding house room.
Found hisself with a job hauling bricks. And
then he found hisself with another wife. He
didnt remember how it happened, but it did just
the same, and this second one was worse than
the first. She⊙d talk and talk until her head
would just sort of pop off and fall to the floor,
and then she'd pick her head up, wipe it clean
with a damp towel, set it back on her shoulders,
and then she'd start talking all over again. Wunt
long before this young fellow he figures it time

to go, so early one morning, had to been just
after dawn this time cause that second one she
liked to watch the sun come up, he packs up,
leaves his room and his job hauling bricks and
his matrimonial bliss, and heads out into the
woods, and by and by he come on some more
railroad tracks, and before he even think on a
train one come swinging into sight, and this
young fellow he was running not a thought in
his head, and then he hopped on board."

Again the skinny man stopped speaking. He
jerked the reins a little bit harder and cursed
the browns under his breath. Then he winked at
Thaddeus and went on with the rest of his story.

"Well that fellow he stayed on that second
train for seven nights and seven days. Wanted
to leave his second wife even further behind
than the first one. Which he did. Found hisself
another room like before, only it wunt as quiet.
Found hisself another job too, only it wunt
bricks. And then he found hisself another wife.
Or just about. There they was standing at the
altar, and this one was worse than the first and
the second tied together. Took her ten minutes
just to say „I do.◎ She◎d just about talked his
ears off before they even got out of the church,
so he left her on the steps. She didnt even see
him go she was so busy talking about how hot it
was in her wedding dress she was soaked clean
through hoped he didnt mind none but she was
going to peel it off soon as she could hang it up

to dry, and then she was laughing and talking and talking some more. By the time she seen she was talking to herself, he was already down the road to the train yard, and the next thing he found hisself an empty boxcar on a train heading south. Folks they say his ghost is riding that train to this day. Only way he ever found some peace and quiet."

And with that the skinny man stopped speaking altogether and his disfigured face twisted itself into a smile. The young man returned the smile. He wondered what life in an empty boxcar might be like. A life of unending freedom, he thought, a life where who you were and where you were going was never a question, a life of going and going and never returning. It wouldn't matter then his parents had left him in the tent of a traveling preacher show the day he was born. The Reverend Jacobs used to tell him how lucky he was not to been thrown in a ditch. But it wouldn't matter any more. He'd be out on his own and no one to say a word, and then the Reverend Jacobs and what he used to say, and everything that had happened with the girl in the tent, none of it would matter.

"We almost there."

"Where?"

"Up ahead there."

A skinny arm hung in the air, wavering, pointing, a couple of side-rail trucks in the

heat-shimmering distance, and also some
wagons, and Thaddeus could see a group of
men, some squatting along the side of the road,
looked to be black, looked to be eating from tin
plates and drinking from tin cups, then some
standing in the ditch, some on the road by the
trucks, some in back of the wagons a ways down
from the squatters, looked to be white, well-fed,
finished with their own plates, looked to be
holding shotguns, arms cocked, ready, vigilant,
watching the squatters eat. The skinny man
pulled in his arm, and Thaddeus caught the glint
of a deputies badge on his shirt, which he had
not noticed before.

"Hey, Hurly. What been keeping you?"

The voice came from a burly sort, reddish
beard, belly lapped over his belt, a shotgun
dangling from his hand. The man stepped to
the side as the wagon slowed, stopped. Hurly
nodded. The young man name of Thaddeus
looked to the reddish beard, the shotgun cradled
in the burly man's arms.

"Hey Bill."

"Hurly, you sure the slowest sombitch I ever
know. Them browns still giving you trouble?"

Hurly smacked his lips together and grinned.
"Worsen being married."

"Who you brung along?"

"He didn't say. Just some fellow I give a ride
to."

"Where's he going?"

"He didn't say about that neither."

Then the men drew closer and spoke in low, guttural voices and looking over to Thaddeus and then a burst of gruff laughter. And beyond the laughter of these two Thaddeus could hear the guarded almost inaudible murmurings of the blacks, like the sound of a river at night, and there was laughter too, but softer, almost like sighing. Then the heads drew apart and the one named Bill motioned to Thaddeus with his gun.

"Say, boy. You hungry?"

Thaddeus smiled weakly, nodded, his eyes on the seemingly poised shotgun. Then the gun pulled back and another burst of gruff laughter.

"Hell, boy, I wasn't gonna shoot you. Just wanted to know if you really was hungry, that's all. Go on, get something to eat if you've a mind. It wont kill you. Long as you dont mind eating after all them niggers."

So Thaddeus climbed down from the wagon and made his way past the squatting blacks to the back of the dinner wagon and a plate of beans and a scrap of pork and some cornbread and a tin cup of water. He was mostly thinking how hungry he was, but he was also aware of the black squatters watching him, silent now, uneasy, wary, waiting until he had moved on with his plate before they continued eating and drinking and talking and laughing, as if he alone were responsible for putting the chains on their feet. He sat down in the dry dry grass and began to eat, far enough away, and again there was the quiet murmur of black voices. Then one voice swelled above the rest and began to tell a story.

This was the story.

"Seems dere was dis convic wokin on dis here chain gang some years pas only he wunt so happy like we all is about all de tasks dem bosses had fuh him to do an de whippins dey done give out when dem tasks wunt done de way dey wanted. One time he come in and dey axed him how much cottin he done picked and when he tole em dey said dat wunt good enough so dey laid him flat across a table whip him bloody wid a strop. Dere was so much blood seem like Noah an his ark be coming long any minute, an dem bosses dey was lookin roun fuh ol Noah like maybe dat nigger he was gonna climb on board get away."

The other blacks started laughing to themselves with that, but Thaddeus wasn't sure what they were laughing about. The whites with the shotguns weren't listening.

"Anyhows dis here nigger he wunt so happy about all dat like i said an he started talkin to hisself bout what he was gonna do. First one side of his mouth open up like so, an den de other side, an de first side sayin was about time he done scape from dis here prison farm an de second sayin how he gonna do dat and de first sayin de nex time dey wokin out de swamp

he gonna take off an de second sayin what he
gonna do bout dem chains round his feet and
de first sayin dat once he done reach dat swamp
de bosses and de hounds dey wunt never gonna
fine his trail so he take his time about dem
chains and de second sayin how if he done
met up wid some hungry ol gator and de first
sayin he be better off dead in de belly of some
gator den wokin de res of dis here life wid dem
chains on his feet an de second he sayin he dont
know about all dat but he willin give it a try, an
den dey was both grinnin at each other cause
dats what dey decided to do."

And the voice stopped a moment, the blacks
nodding, some looking to the long grass of the
field like they were trying to gauge the distance
to the nearest swamp, not at all bothered by the
possibility of meeting up with an alligator, or so
it seemed.

Then the voice continued.

"Well de nex time dat chain gang was wokin
out de swamp dis here nigger he was ready to
go. Come time fuh dinner dem niggers gather
roun de kettle den eatin an all de bosses dey
standin roun an hardly watchin what goes so
dis here nigger he done slip away easy as pie
an den he was runnin fuh de swamp. Wunt
long he done foun hisself smack in de middle
of some black water an dere wunt much to see
cept some black green trees risin from de muck
an some moss hang down from de branches and

a couple heron poking dis way an dat trough de
grass, and den dey fly off. Well wid dat dis here
nigger he done set hisself down on a big ol log
and he start a talkin to hisself again about what
he was gonna do nex.

"First voice sayin he tired of runnin so he
jus gonna rest up a spell on dis here log an de
second voice sayin de middle of a swamp aint
no place to be restin and de first sayin dere aint
nothin he can do he feel de need to shut his eyes
dey gonna shut jus like dat an de second he was
about to answer somethin smart when a black-
green gator come bustin up trough de grass its
mouth wide open its teeth sparkle in de black
black of dat niggers eyes, an he give one look an
he shut dem eyes he hopin dat gator wunt after
him, only it was, an de nex thing happen dat
gator come chomp down wid dem teeth.

"It was sure some lucky day fuh dat nigger
cause all dat gator done was bite trough dem
chains.   But when dat nigger he open his eyes,
he wunt thinkin bout chains or no chains, no
sir, wunt no time fuh thinkin at all cause when
he open his eyes, all he see was dat gator open
up his mouth take a second bite, and wid dat
de nigger he was gone running fas as he could
go, so fas he done lef a trail of fire burn trough
de grass, and it wunt long fuh de whole swamp
was burnin, an dat gator he wunt able to see
from all de smoke, so he let dat nigger go, but
dat nigger he aint know dat, so he runnin an

runnin an runnin, an fuh he know what what he done run all de way back to de chain gang. De rest of de niggers dey was done eatin by den, an de bosses dey was roundin em up send em back to wok. Poor ol nigger. He foun hisself wokin right along wid de rest. Had to wok on a empty stomach too. Dem bosses never did fine out he done run off. An he never tole em neither. But dey did see how his chains was broke, an by de by dey done slap some new ones on his feet fuh he took another step. Aint nothin like a new set of chains on a niggers feet keep him in one place. And dat de truth."

And with that the one voice stopped, the hum of the words suspended in the air, and some of the blacks were nodding their heads some more, and some were laughing to themselves or maybe talking softly, and some were rubbing where their own chains cut into their ankles.

The story was over.

"Thats enough of that now. You niggers back to work."

"Yes boss."

"Get them kettles and them plates and all back on the wagons."

"Yes boss."

"You niggers get a move on."

"Yes boss."

"We gonna work a field down the road a piece."

"Yes boss."

And the young man name of Thaddeus
looked to the road, to the two trucks moving
out, to the wagons moving slowly from the
ditch, kettles bouncing about in the back, to
the blacks moving along, slowly also, steadily,
moving but unmoved, a thin black line wavering
in the heat of the day, chains dragging in the
dust, and then to the whites, some walking
alongside the blacks, shotguns lowered, waiting
for one or two to make a break for it, perhaps,
and some walking a step or so to the rear, not so
eager, laughing softly, and some not laughing,
and then the trucks and the wagons and the
blacks and the whites were gone.

-4-

And then he was moving again. He had
spent two days holed up in a barn, sucking
down a few pilfered eggs in the shadow of a
loft, but mostly sleeping, for in the excitement
of the girl and the raid and the first day of his
banishment he had not slept at all. But now he
was moving again. In his gray-blue, unblinking,
eyes there was something fierce, obsessive,
inevitable, a madness in the sense that youth
was a madness, all this urging him on. He
wouldn't go back. Not that he was afraid. He
just had to move on. Like that fellow running
away from his wives. Or that other one trying

to escape the chain-gang. Hell, he'd rather
get his head caved in by a lop-eared mule,
and he laughed grimly at the thought. So he
left the road, a dusty reminder of everything
his life had been, and abandoned himself to
the dark, steaming, shimmering woods, deeper
and deeper through the pine and oak and the
clutching undergrowth. By late evening he
had come upon some old railroad tracks. He
sat down on the ground below the tracks and
decided to wait for the next train to come down
the line and then hop on board and be on his
way. Going and going and never returning.
A life of relentless freedom. Then evening
became night. In the distance he heard the low
rumbling of wheel on rail, a lonely sound in the
cool of the evening, but a welcome sound, also.
He stood up, and a moment later he could see
a train, a smoky blue ghost of a train rattling
its chains in the dark, a yellow, unblinking eye,
the rush of a thousand tons of iron straining as
it slowed to round a curve. He caught his own
breath at the sight and sound and stumbled up
the dusty embankment with arms outstretched,
his hands ready, the blue of the train now
moving slowly past, and then he saw an empty
box car, the door half open, caught hold of an
iron side-rail near the door, his two legs rattling
against the side of the car. Again he caught his
breath, sure that he could not hold on for long,
sure that he was not sure how to swing from

the rail to the door, the blue of his face blending
in with the color of the train. He would have
fallen had not an arm reached out from the
half-open door, a bony arm, half hidden in the
blue shadows of the empty car. He reached out
to the arm with his nearest hand, then hand
clasped hand, and when he felt the strength
of this one-arm grip he forgot that his legs
were rattling against the side of the train and
he reached out with his other hand. Almost
immediately his legs bounced off the gravel
of the embankment below, but before they
bounced a second time he grabbed hold of the
bony half- hidden arm and tried to pull himself
into the car, hand over hand, slowly, but the
bony arm straining, his hands slipping, then his
legs bouncing off the gravel once again. Then a
second bony arm reached out from the shadows
and hauled him inside.

Slowly the two arms released him, pulled
back into the blue-black shadows of the no
longer empty car. The young man name of
Thaddeus stumbled away from the door to the
opposite corner of the box car and sat down,
the hard wood floor a welcome support. He
felt the light of the moon wash across his face,
the light drifting through the cracks in the roof
of the car, drifting downward, mingling with
the shadows. He looked to where the two arms
had been, but saw nothing, as if those arms
had reached out from some other world into

this one, for a moment. He looked again, and
he thought he heard the sound of laughter, a
hollow sound, a faraway sound, as if it came
from another world, also. And then the laughter
began to swell, no longer otherworldly, a
sound from this world now, an ungentle sound,
slightly mocking. Then the laughter stopped
and Thaddeus could see a man standing in the
middle of the boxcar, the man looking down at
him now, close then closer, the white moonlight
washing across his face also, black eyes sunken
like craters.

"What you doin here?"

The young man did not know what to say.
He was sitting there. That was all he was doing.

"I said what you doin here? You hear me?"

"I heard you."

"You aint so good at catchin trains. Is you?"

And the caricature came closer still.

"No. No I aint."

Thaddeus readied his arms to swing at the
man with the crater-like eyes, then remembered
the strength of those two bony arms and relaxed
his fist.

"I didnt think so. Didnt think so."

And with that the man stopped talking and
squatted down next to Thaddeus, slowly, still
grinning. He reached into his pocket and pulled
out a small black bag full of nuts and began
eating. He was an older man, graying hair
cropped close behind his ears, a bit of stubble

growing on his chin, narrow shoulders flattened
by age, narrow hands, narrow fingers, shaking
slightly as he brought each nut to his mouth, as
if he were curious about what was inside, but
also slightly worried. Then he turned and fixed
his eyes on the young man.

"What you doing here?"

Again the young man did not know what to
say, so he said nothing.

"I been riding in this here car for more years
than I care to count on account of these chains
on my feet. I been riding round hope to come
across someone help me break free." Then the
older man paused, leaned closer, the black of
his sunken eyes deepening, swelling. Thaddeus
could smell the bone-rot of his breath. "Is that
what you doin here? Is you the one?"

Thaddeus blinked stupidly at the question,
but then he was strangely alert, for it suddenly
seemed that he'd been asking himself the very
same thing his whole life long. "Is you the one?"
Maybe not in those words exactly. But toss in a
why and you were close enough. Why is you the
one? Or just a plain old "why you?" Growing up
in the Reverend's tent and always the Reverend
shunting him aside and then Little Henry was
born and it only got worse. He was the one
all right. The one got shunted aside. But why
the good Reverend had picked him out with
his almost biblical hatred he never knew. Not
exactly. Not the why of it. It was like he'd come

direct from God himself just to keep an eye on
the old bastard. At least that's how the good
Reverend took his being there. Or seemed to.
Yeah, he was the one all right. And now he was
out on his own, sitting in a railroad car going
he didn't know where, but then again maybe he
didn't care neither, and there it was, the same
goddamn question getting in his way.

"Is you the one?"

His face almost caved in with uncertainty.
He didn't know what to think. Then he looked
down at the feet of the older man and saw
they were bound by chains. He touched the
chains lightly with one hand, and the older
man nodded, so he took a firm grip with both
hands and then, with a growing sense of rage
and despair that surprised and frightened him,
he tried to tear the links apart. But they did not
break. He tore at the chains a second time, and
then a third, and still they did not break, and
he was about to try again when the older man
grunted, shook his head, slowly, purposefully,
his eyes no longer grinning.

"That aint the way to break them chains
son." The older man carefully regarded the
younger man. "Them chains was forged by the
hand of the devil. And they gonna bind me to
this here earth till I find me someone with the
fire of God in his eyes. You aint got that fire.
Has you? You got that fire son? Is you ... is you
the. . ."

And then the older man suddenly stopped speaking and a seething, wild look came to his eyes. "You better be. You goddamn better be." And in that instant he reached for Thaddeus, two bony white hands shining in the heavy boxcar dark, the younger man stumbling to his feet, his eyes focused on the black of the half-open door, then a step, then the older man grabbing hold of the younger by the shoulders and spinning him into the corner. For a moment the two men stared at each other, the older man with stern, unmoving eyes fixed on the young man's face, and the younger man blinking his gray-blue eyes in bewilderment, but also he seemed strangely willing to accept whatever the older man dished out. But then a second change came over the older man. An unearthly calmness settled about his stern, hawkish features, a look of satisfaction, as a dead man is satisfied. Then he stepped away from the corner and squatted down in the center of the box car and went back to eating nuts.

But Thaddeus was not satisfied. He could still feel the bony, determined grip of the older man and trembled slightly from it, and then the way he broke it off, Thaddeus wasn't sure what had happened there, but it left him with an unsettled feeling, like trembling on the inside instead of the other way with that bony grip. He looked at the older man and took a couple of deep breaths and slowly his trembling stopped.

But still he didn't know what to think about
the older man's sudden transformations. Too
much like the lunacy of a madman. Then again,
he'd go crazy too if he had to wear chains like
that. And it must get cold living in a box car
all the time. In the winter. Freeze your balls
off when you take a piss. Yeah, he had to be
crazy. And then suddenly Thaddeus saw this
ghost of a man as an older version of himself.
He rested his head against the side of the car
and tried to comprehend this thought. The hum
of the wheels on the rail echoed beneath him.
The warmth of the night air began closing in.
And then Thaddeus closed his eyes, the image
of this older version of himself fading into the
darkness. Swirling. Mixing with the swirl of box
car shadows.

And then nothingness.

How long Thaddeus slept on the floor of the
boxcar, his idiot companion eating nuts in the
corner, he did not know. Perhaps time did not
matter here. Perhaps time had ceased to exist. At
least this it how it seemed. Perhaps Thaddeus,
in coming aboard, had entered a myth of his
own making, a place outside of time where he
could reshape the riddle of his past. Here he
would either come to terms with the impulsive
delirium of his young manhood and take
strength from that and move on, or he would
be abandoned, as had happened to his idiot

companion, to the bewildering isolation of an old age without end.

"We here now. We here."

Thaddeus woke suddenly, painfully, to the almost gleeful words of the older man.

"We here. We here."

"Where's here?"

There was no further explanation. The older man grabbed hold of the young man's shoulders and started dragging him towards the black of the half-open door. Thaddeus tried to move, to maybe twist himself free, but his groggy-from-sleep self did not respond. Then the older man paused in his dragging and wiped his brow and Thaddeus broke loose and stumbled back to the corner. But the older man followed, and grabbed him from behind once again.

"We here. We here."

Again the young man heard the words, again they meant nothing.

"What do you mean we here?"

This time the older man grunted impatiently as he picked up the young man, a firmer grip this time, carried him towards the half-open door, his chains rattling with each step, and he stopped in the doorway, a knowledge of time and place burning in his eyes. Or so it seemed. Then he looked to the young man and grinned. "I mean we here." And before the young man could reply, the older man tossed him from the train, the young man bouncing down the

gravel of the embankment, and then the older
man followed the younger, bouncing down
the embankment also, and when the two men
stopped bouncing they found themselves sitting
on the cold ground below the now empty tracks,
sitting and then staring after the blue blur of the
train vanishing in the distance, blue into black,
the thin wail of a banshee hanging in the air,
and then silence.

The two men sat at the bottom of the
embankment for a time but did not look at each
other. The young man moved his legs back and
forth, sliding them along the ground, his hands
massaging the ache of being tossed, brushing
away the dirt. He wondered what the older
man meant to do next and what could he do
to stop him, for he remembered the strength
of those bony hands. Maybe he could hit him
over the head with a rock, if he could find
one, a piece of granite maybe, or a crowbar,
but he didn't really think that would stop this
one, hell, his head its probably made of stone
itself. The only comfort, he supposed, was there
wasn't a train to get tossed from now, he'd just
wait and see and maybe run if he had to, if he
only had a crowbar, come on you old bastard,
he thought, what are you gonna do next. And
in the very next instant, as if in response to
this silent and bitter question, the older man
unfolded, got to his feet, shook the dust from
his clothes, looked up to the black of the trees

edging up to the embankment, and again there was that unearthly calm about his face, again the satisfied look of a dead man. Then this older man of the disquieting face disappeared into the blackness of the wood, only the sound of chains rattling in the dark to suggest where he was.

Of course the young man followed, but not at first. He looked to the cold white of the moon and then to the black iron of the tracks shining in that light and he listened to the sound of those chains echoing softly through the wood. *Them chains was forged by the hand of the devil.* He heard the words distinctly, the words of a madman. Yet he couldn't rid himself of the idea that he and this lunatic were mirror images of each other. Again and again he heard the words, and the bitterness and rage he had felt only moments before emptied into the loamy soil beneath him. Even the physical hurt from being tossed from the train was gone.

He started up after that, walking through the woods, the branches slapping at his face and the midges and mosquitoes swarming, and he wondered what had become of the older man, for even the sound of the chains rattling had faded into nothingness. Then the trees parted and a white square of moonlight broke through and he saw the older man standing on a ridge over-looking the black of a river. On the other side of the river he saw a backwater honky-tonk, a couple three cars parked in the tall grass to

the side, some bright blue lights strung around
the outside of the building, clapboard walls,
unpainted, some of the planks rotten, giving
way, a tin roof, rusted, holes here and there, the
wood and the tin and the wire shaking with the
sounds of music and laughter. The younger man
stepped to the ridge. The older man looked on
in silence for a moment. Then he turned to the
young man and nodded.

"This here where we gonna begin."

Before the young man could reply, the older
man raised his arms, and with that they were
both standing in the back of that honky-tonk by
the river.

"This here what happened."

The older man nodded to the younger, then
to the swirling memory of smoke and laughter
and music. The younger man nodded also,
absently, his eyes following the older man's
tacit direction. Everywhere he looked he saw
men and women, black ones mostly, silk ties
and satin shoes, like they had just stepped off
the streets of Charleston instead of wading
through the muck of a swamp, the men eyeing
the women, eyes up and down and up again
looking to get a closer look, the women knowing
just how far to let those eyes wander. The young
man found his eyes wandering, also, and he
took a step as if to follow his eyes, but the older
man put a hand to his shoulder and the young
man stopped. Then the older man pointed to

a fellow in a checkered vest playing a piano,
a fellow with fat fingers plucking on an old
bass, the rest of him fat also, a snake- hipped
girl sitting on top of the piano, the girl singing
somewhat hoarsely about some Charleston gals
how they danced with holes in their stockings,
the men and women listening to the music,
singing along, some talking and smoking and
talking some more, some on the floor dancing,
most drinking. One woman took her shoes from
her feet and said she had a hole in her stocking
just like the girls in the song. The men sitting by
her snickered at that, and one said he know'd
her take off more than her shoes and he'd bet
five dollar cash too she'd do it again before
they went home for the night, and then they
all laughed. Then the song was over, and a tall
man in a red hat and a red bow tie walked to
the middle of the floor and waved the men and
women to silence, for he had something to say.
"I is gonna introduce y'all to a man I knows was
born with a horn in his mouth and been blowin
dat horn ever since, a man I knows been in most
all de juke joints from here to Chattanooga, and
he done blow'd de roof off a every one of dem
places too, and now he done come here tonight
see if he can do de same, a man y'all know by
de name of Gabriel Dupree."

With that the men and women clapped and
shouted the roof the roof and the man in the red
hat and red bow tie smiled like he knew he was

going to do a brisk business that night, at least enough to buy a new roof, and then he walked from the floor. The older man looked to the young man and nodded, his face etched with thoughtful expectation, and then he spoke.

"This here's the first mistake."

The young man stared blankly at the words as they fell from the older man's mouth. They were the words of a man who can see the train coming but cant jump off the tracks. Like he'd seen that train coming a thousand times. Then the older man nodded in the direction of the band and the young man followed the nod. A small man stepped from the blue shadows of the corner, a square jaw grinning in the swirl of smoke and light and laughter, a smartly polished brass horn in his hands. Then he stepped to one side of the piano with the girl on top and began to blow, narrow hands holding the horn as if it were a part of his bone his flesh, narrow fingers tapping out the rhythm of the notes. The men and women sitting at the tables jumped up with the first note, silk ties and satin shoes shouted, play on Gabriel play on.

And so the man name of Gabriel blew on his horn with every breath in his body, and when his breath was gone he blew some more. Play on, Gabriel, play on. And the men and women shouted some more. And some clapped their hands. And some danced on the floor. And some drank from their glasses and looked

to the roof with redoubtable anticipation. Play
on Gabriel, play on. Then the fellow with the
fat fingers and the fellow in the checkered vest
joined in, the one pluck pluck pluck on the
strings of that bass, the other bang bang bang
on the keys of that piano. Then everything
and everyone began to shake. Or so it seemed.
The girl on top of the piano was the first. She
smiled down at the man name of Gabriel, him
blowing on his horn, smiling back, and then she
stood up on that piano and shook, she shook
her shoulders her hips her head, anything that
would move and a few things that wouldn't.
Then the girls all around stood up on tables, on
chairs, and shook shoulders, hips, heads, and
more. Some of the men shook just watching.
And every now and then the man name of
Gabriel looked up to the shaking girl on top of
that piano and smiled with his eyes, and every
time he did, she looked back and smiled with
her whole body. Then the older man, who was
not shaking, looked to the younger man, who
was, nodded again, and then spoke.

"This here's the second mistake."

Again a blank stare from the young man,
again the image of the coming train, again a nod
from the older man. And when the young man
turned to listen to the music of Gabriel and his
horn he found the music had stopped. Hours
had passed. Or so it seemed. The young man
looked from the tables the chairs to the floor to

the bar in back. Most of the dancing men and
women had left. Those who remained were
asleep, some in chairs, heads hung back, arms
stiff by their sides, some on the tables, hands
gripping empty glasses, empty bottles, and
some flat out on the floor, silk and satin soaked
with liquor. The man with the fat fingers slept
on the floor next to his bass, an arm draped
across, his fat fingers quivering some, but no
longer plucking. The man in the checkered
vest slept on the piano bench, his body bent
awkwardly towards the piano, his face uncere-
moniously plastered against the black and white
keys. The only two not asleep were the girl on
top of that piano and the man name of Gabriel.
She was resting easy now, her legs stretched out
behind her, her shoulders, her hips still shaking,
but ever so slightly, her head bent to one side,
and then she looked down at Gabriel and the
polished brass horn and smiled softly. Gabriel
smiled back.

"You wanna go somewheres else? Maybe
give this horn of mine a blow?"

"I sure do."

"Well come on, then."

And before Gabriel said another word, the
girl spun her legs around, slid down to the
floor, took the brass horn from the still smiling
Gabriel's hands and set it back on top of the
piano. Then she slid up into his arms, her whole
body smiling as before, and wrapped her legs

tightly around his waist. For a moment nothing
happened, as if time itself had stopped. Then the
man name of Gabriel carried the snake-hipped
girl out through the door of the honky-tonk. And
then time stopped again. The young man name
of Thaddeus looked to where Gabriel and the
girl had been, looked to the door, thought about
where they were going, thought to trade places
with Gabriel, have the girl blow on his horn a
while, and then he moved to follow the two, but
remembered the strength of the older man's grip
and stopped. The older man simply stared at
the brass horn on top of the piano, thoughtfully,
hopefully perhaps, and then he turned to the
young man yet again.

"This here's the third mistake."

The younger man looked from the older
man to the door and then to the older man
again, a look of impatience, a look of unwilling
complicity, a look of why-dont-we-get- off-the-
tracks-before-its-too-late. Then the older man
nodded a third time and the smoky, bright light
swirl of the honky-tonk was gone and the two
men stood inside the door of a tarblacked shack
at the bottom of the ridge on the other side of
the river. There was a stove in one corner, unlit,
a dresser shoved back against the wall, the
middle drawer missing, a dirty wash basin on
top, and a single bed in the center of the room,
a single cotton blanket, and no pillow. The
two stood silent near the door, the older man

waiting, stoic, unperturbed, the younger man wondering.

Then they heard voices.

"Aint much farther. Come on."

"I is coming."

"What the matter with you anyway?"

"I tire out from thinking on you. But don't you worry none. I is coming."

Then the girl from the top of the piano ran through the door, giggled, slipped off her dress, then lay down on the flat of the bed, nothing but her skin to keep her warm. Gabriel ran through next, stopped in the doorway, breath bursting from his lungs in short gasps, and then one long gasp and he stared down at the girl, forgot to breathe. Then the girl asked him where his horn was, giggled again, and before she said another word Gabriel had climbed out of his clothes and onto the bed and then onto the girl. Once again Thaddeus thought to trade places with Gabriel, once again remembered the strength of the older man's grip, and climbed out of his clothes anyway, a look of willing complicity now. Then the young man climbed on the bed. Or he almost did. For as soon as he stepped towards the girl he heard the rumble of a voice outside, a loud voice, a ways off still, but coming closer, and because the voice sounded angry, cornered, unpredictable, the young man stepped quickly back. And then Gabriel. He, too, had heard the voice, and so he slipped off the girl, off the bed, and into his clothes. But the girl sat up, a curl of legs and hips and smooth brown skin, and she asked him did he think he was through and where was he going, but Gabriel just shook his head and said it sounded like trouble coming and he wasn't one for trouble. So the girl became angry, hurt, or pretended to, said how all men were the same wasn't he ashamed of himself running out on her like this what was she going to do now, and on and on and on, her words blowing through the air like she wanted to blow on his horn even then. Then the older man turned to the nakedness of the younger man.

"This here's the end of it."

And before the young man could ask the older what it was he meant exactly, the door of the tarblacked shack shattered with the impact of a train, and the man in the checkered vest rumbled in, the forgotten horn of Gabriel in his hand, and he shook the horn in the air and shouted. "This here the last time I ever gone be made a fool," he said. "This the very last time. I gone take care of things my own way now."

Then he shook the horn again and looked to the bed, to the girl, and the girl leaned forward on her knees and said she wasn't his wife what was he thinking she was planning go off with sweet Gabriel here and who was it gonna stop them, and then the man in the checkered vest stepped towards Gabriel, towards the girl,

the horn raised and ready to come down on
top of the head of whoever was closer, the
man name of Gabriel Dupree looking to the
girl in disbelief, then knocking the man in the
checkered vest to the side and running out the
door. For a moment, the man in the checkered
vest didn't move. He looked at the girl now
crying on the bed, an angry but self-indulgent
look about his face, as if he had known all along
that he would catch her at it, and then another
look that said he'd be back to see she got what
was coming to her, and then he was out the
door after her understandably shy morning
pastime.

   Then the crying stopped, and the girl lay
back in the bed, still naked, and wiggled herself
into a comfortable position, but there was no
time for Thaddeus to even consider what to
do with her because the older man then raised
his arms, and the girl and the bed and the
backwater shack were gone, and the two men
found themselves in the black, black wood, the
older one walking slowly through the darkness,
chains rattling, the younger one following a step
or so behind, no longer naked.

-5-

   They were back in the black, black woods
now, in this myth of the young man⊚s making,

and at first the young man was thinking
about the snake-hipped girl and the regret
of a missed opportunity, but as they walked
deeper and deeper into the wood, with the
thickening, suffocating heaviness of the air
and the swarming mosquitoes and the midges
and Spanish moss flapping in his face and the
smell of a swamp somewhere up ahead and the
possibility of snakes or worse, the snake-hipped
girl was forgotten. All that was left was the
weariness that comes from walking too much.

"Where we going now?"

"We going the same way ol Gabriel done
went the day he done left that shack in a hurry."

"Why're we doing that?"

"Ol Gabriel he still out here somewheres.
Got his horn with him too. Folks round here
say they can hear him blowin that horn every
night from just after midnight till dawn. The
sound of that horn it rises up gentle through
the woods, through the swamp, then up the
river, the notes they is wavering in the air, and
then they's gone. Some say he trying to let folks
know he was done to death by that fellow in
the checkered hat. Some say he gonna keep on
blowin that horn till someone come along set
things right. Eye for an eye they say. I dont
know nothin bout all that. What I say is ol
Gabriel he just got hisself lost in these woods
and died before he could find his way out.
What I say is ol Gabriel he just want someone

come along and bury his bones in a proper way.
When someone do that ol Gabriel he'll stop
blowin his horn. Thats what I say."

Then the older man stopped speaking, his
words fading into the silence of the black wood.
The two men walked on, the older intent on
leading the way, the younger obliged to follow.
The trees were crowding closer together. The
black becoming blacker. Everywhere he looked
he saw the ghost of Gabriel Dupree. Or so it
seemed. He could almost hear the sound of that
horn.

Then the older man stopped, abruptly, eyes
peering into the blackness ahead. The young
man stopped also.

They stood on the edge of a swamp, the
prison-bar look of many cypress trees rising out
of the stagnant, dead water, and also many dead
ones at odd angles in the water and leaning on
each other and covered with moss. But they
did not go into the swamp. Then the older man
nodded in the direction of a great bald cypress
up along the bank, this one also dead, the
weight of the great tree sending its branches
into the water, the suddenly exposed roots
brittle and white from age and the lack of cover,
and there in the shadow of the roots the young
man saw the white almost phosphorescent
bones of a dead man, and beyond the bones the
tarnished brass of an old horn.

"Thems the bones of Gabriel Dupree."

The younger man nodded, staring at the whiteness of the bones, staring and wondering how the older man knew whose bones they were, how long he had kept the secret to himself, why he had chosen this particular moment to reveal what he knew. Perhaps he had heard old Gabriel blow on his horn one night. Perhaps he had spent his life searching for those bones. Then the young man shivered, and not from the cold. He knew how the older man had known about those bones.

"Aint nobody gonna hear that old horn blow around this swamp no more. Not after tonight."

The young man said nothing.

"Once we buries them bones old Gabriel he gonna rest them lips of his. He sure is. Till the good Lord come to call him up. And thats the truth."

The young man shivered again. He believed in the good Lord calling up the dead. Then he opened his mouth as if to speak, the words inaudible, almost.

"You sure about these bones?"

But the older man only grinned, a broad grin that seemed to fill in the black spaces between his teeth. He moved to the fallen tree and squatted beneath the mass of exposed roots, and then he looked into the ragged black hole where the tree had once stood and breathed in the smell of the earth and felt the earth with his hands and crumbled it with his fingers, and then he motioned to the young man and the young man joined him. For a moment they looked at each other, a moment only, each aware of the identity of the ghost reflected in the young man's eyes. Then they looked at the hole again.

"This here gonna be the place."

So the two worked to make the hole into a grave, hands digging deep into the moist, black earth, palms cupped, digging deeper and deeper. Then deep enough. Gathering up the bones, putting them into the grave, silently, carefully, even reverently, as if the fate of the older man's soul depended upon the proper and precise burial of his bones. Covering up the mistakes of this one-time trumpet player with the black, black earth. Then the startling whiteness of the bones was gone, and the young man felt that he had been given a glimpse of the future. Or maybe it was a warning of some kind? Was he going to end up like Gabriel? And what did that mean, exactly? Everybody ended up dead. But the young man could not untangle his thoughts. Then the older man set the tarnished brass horn on top of the earth to mark the grave and both men closed their eyes, as if in prayer, and then the younger man thinking, "It's no good, there aint no prayer in the book would do justice to what old Gabriel went through." And in that instant the younger man heard the sound of Gabriel's horn rising in the air, hesitant, wavering, the last gasp of a ghost, and then nothing, the younger man contemplating

the sound of nothingness, and then another
glimpse of the future in the guise of a dream,
but whether it was a future like Gabriel's, or
something as yet undetermined, he could not
tell,

   him running through the black mossdraped wood
mudstumbling over root and rock but not feeling the
straw of the branches sharp and sweeping against his
face just moving moving forward his hands thrusting
leaf and twig aside his shoulders slipping into the
shadows and then out again long shadows resonating
with the whistle of crickets the whine of cicadae and
then he came to the edge of the wood and there was
the slowmoving backwater warm water black like the
wood reflecting nothing not even the stars and he
stopped and looked at the water and wondered why
he could not see his face perhaps there was nothing
to see perhaps he was looking beyond his face
perhaps he was looking into the slowmoving water
of his own soul murky water that and though he was
not quite sure just what he was looking at he was
untroubled by his uncertainty for the blackness of
the water brought also a calmness of breath a sense
of tranquility as gentle and rhythmic as dying and
then he stopped wondering his eyes peering intently
into the dark dark air his eyes glowing bright blue
like two blue moons and he started walking along
the black wash each step measured precisely as if he
knew where he was going he walked until he came
to where the slowmoving backwater narrowed into
a grass-choked channel and there he found a hollow

*place up from the waters edge and in the shadows of
the grass there was an old rowboat scraped clean of
paint by wind and age cedar planks damp with the
smell of rot one oarlock missing the other heavy with
rust and he dragged the boat through the soft black
muck a gully where the keel had been and then down
to the waters edge and into the water and for a brief
moment he looked at the boat and he noticed how low
it lay in the water the curve of the bow how it barely
broke the surface but then he smiled anyway perhaps
the boat had lain in that hollow for years just so
he could find it and now all those years had come
together in a single moment perhaps the boat had
been made just so he could use it that spoke of some
kind of eternal purpose or so it seemed and then he
smiled again and climbed into the boat his hands on
the oars one in the rusted oarlock the other balanced
firmly on the rim and he began to row down the
grass-choked channel and then the grass giving way
and the channel widening slowly he rowed gauging
the depth of the water following the steady drift of
the current beyond the black shadows of oak and
cypress and pine beyond the lazy whisperings of the
long marsh grass beyond even the briny mire of the
naked coast and then out out into the cool salt air
of the open sea and the sea was strangely calm and
the sky was black and steadily he rowed his eye to
the horizon the chop chop chop of the oars echoing
in the blackness of sea and sky and the old rowboat
moving like a shadow among shadows chop chop
chop and after a time he wondered how long he must*

row how far before he could stop but at the center of
all that blackness such concepts as time and distance
seemed to have little meaning perhaps he had already
stopped rowing perhaps he had never begun perhaps
he had been sitting in that boat his entire life all
his experience neatly expressed in a single gasp for
air and when that gasp expired so too would his life
and his empty empty body would sink to the floor
of the boat and the boat would sink to the bottom
of the sea perhaps he said to himself but he kept on
rowing chop chop chop he kept on until he came to
an island rising white and suddenly from that black
black sea and then he heard a voice from inside his
head say stop rowing so he stopped the oars trailing
easy in the water the boat rocking slightly in the
shallows and then the voice said get out of the boat
and follow me and with that the voice from inside
his head leaped out through his eyes and there it was
dancing and laughing in the dunes follow me follow
me so he got out of the boat and waded through the
shallows and then dripping across the mooncooled
sand and into the long grass of the dunes follow me
follow me follow me the voice said and he thought it
was the voice of God which spoke and so he followed
it through the grass through the dunes shaking the
dust of sand and shells from his feet he followed the
voice along the edge of a marsh the smell of salt still
in the air and then up a grassy rise and three oaks at
the top but everywhere this grassy rise was covered
with crosses even up beneath the oaks white crosses
wooden crosses a thousand of them shining beneath

*the moon a thousand and a thousand more and he
wondered how there came to be so many crosses on
this particular slope who had put them up who lay
beneath them why had the voice led him here and
then the voice pealed with laughter a laughter that
seemed irreverent in the presence of so many crosses
and yet not irreverent and the laughter grew louder
and louder and then it was not the laughter of a
single voice but of a thousand voices a thousand and
a thousand more follow me follow me follow me and
in the din of so much laughter he became confused
which one should he listen to which one should he
follow and so he waded through this patchwork sea
of crosses the waves of laughter swelling swelling
and then the laughter was gone and he found himself
standing before a single cross a little smaller than
the rest and there was an old iron shovel leaning
up against this cross the handle broken the spade
a bit rusted an omen he thought at least as far as
omens go and then without another thought he took
up the shovel and began digging deeper and deeper
the smell of the black earth heavy with moisture
the smell of his sweat pungent just a trace of wine
perhaps the smells mingling surging upwards and
then he stopped digging and put the shovel down
and looked into the now open grave and there he saw
a tiny coffin made from pine a tiny coffin suspended
untouched by the blackness surrounding it or so it
seemed a childs coffin he thought and then suddenly
he felt that the child was not dead for the aura of
young life emanating from the coffin was too strong*

so he took up the shovel once again and set it to
the edge of the coffin and with three sharp thrusts
he pried loose the top and back and looked into the
coffin and there he saw a small child wearing a
white cloak a child with black hair cut close skin
smooth like porcelain the lips with a touch of color
the hands finely chiseled delicate a beautiful child he
thought and he wanted to wake the child for he was
sure it was merely asleep and so he reached out and
touched the child on the forehead but the moment he
did so the child vanished and now he was the one in
the coffin now he was the one in the grave and he
wondered how he came to fit in such a small coffin
and then he wondered where the child had gone and
then as if in answer to this second silent question he
heard the sound of a child singing and he looked up
from the grave and he saw the child from the coffin
looking down at him the child now singing in the
cold white light of the moon and he tried to speak
to the child but his words were frozen the child still
singing now taking hold of the shovel and he tried to
move to reach out to the child again but his muscles
were frozen as well then the child began shoveling
the heavy black earth falling upon his legs his arms
his face and all the while he heard the child singing a
happy song a song of innocence and then the last of
the earth fell upon him and he was surrounded by its
heavy warm blackness and then the singing stopped.

And when the dream had passed, Thaddeus
opened his eyes and saw that the older man was

gone. For a moment he could think of nothing.
The image of the ghost had fled, fading into
the grave of Gabriel Dupree, it seemed. He
looked to the grave, to the rusted brass horn,
then to the fallen cypress and beyond. The
night was fading also. He could see patches of
light filtering into the swamp. He wondered if
it was Gabriel had sent him that dream of the
future, and was it really his future he had seen.
But he could think of no answer. Once more he
looked to the grave. Then he moved down the
steep of the bank, past the dead, graying wood
of the cypress and the shadows there, then the
shadows flickering away in the steamy sunlight,
and then he was past that and into the morning
blue of the swamp and beyond, a voice now
beckoning, now urging, now laughing, the voice
from the dream: *follow me follow me follow me.*

So he did.

. . . and then one day along come a big big man,
maybe seven foot tall, and his arms they was ripple
sharp like he was made from granite, and when he
done heard that alligator roar, he come looking,
and when he seen that alligator up on that log, he
smile wide, and then he was saying say he done
come to wrestle that alligator and when he was
done it wunt go be no alligator world no more, and
with that the animals up in them trees they was
blinking they eyes in the mossdark look first to the
granite-man and then to the alligator and then to
the granite-man again, and they was all hoping how
he was go tear that alligator head clean off, and then
the granite-man he was stepping to the log he was
go grab hold of that alligator head, and he did, and
then he was squeezing hard as he could, only it wunt
doing nothing stop that alligator thrash this way and
that, and the granite-man he was squeezing harder
and harder, and the alligator he was beating his tail
up against the log was going dthunk dthunk dthunk,
and the animals in them trees they was holding they
breath for watching what goes, and then the alligator
he was rolling up in the air and back like so, and the
granite-man he was rolling up in the air and back
the same, and then they was both in the blackgreen
water, only the granite-man he done lost his grip,
and that alligator he was diving down for gobble that
big big granite-man up, and then he done just that,

and then he was out of the water and back on his log, and he was roaring and roaring some more he was saying say just me and my world, he was roaring till the dark settle down, and the animals up in them trees all they was doing they was shaking they heads for disbelief and saying say what was they go do now, only they knowd wunt nothing to do but stay up in them trees till morning, so that's what they did . . .

The Festival

-1-

Me and Ty we been sitting down on the stoop out front about an hour now, we waiting on Mama and Tramsee, and Im is wondering just where they at and what taking so long. Ty he saying say that how womens is, most likely they standing up front that old brass mirror hang on the wall in my mama keeping room and they primping with they hair the way they do it up and color they faces like they is thinking they still eighteen year old, only they aint, and Im is listening to Ty, only I really aint cause I looking up at the sky, and it almost dark and we go miss the parade they aint hurry up. Mama she and Tramsee been talking on that parade the whole while they been dressing theyself, and they voices floating out and down the porch like a shadow come before the rain.

"I aint live a day I be the one miss this parade," Mama say. "Why, we aint have one in eight or nine year now. You wunt here the last time."

"Well, I here now," Tramsee say, and sound like she smacking her lips together.

"It the cost of things what done most of them parades to death."

"Long as there a marching band, I aint mind the cost."

"You aint listening. You know how much
it cost they hire out a marching band? Every
dollar it worth you paying five."

"I heard a band one time up in Charleston.
They was blowing they horns and dancing em
up in the air and then down, and then they
gone down the street, wunt nothing left but the
drums. I'd a paid five dollar then and there,
only I aint have to."

"Well, you aint paying for this one neither?"
"I aint mind."

"You know who is?"

"Who?"

"Willie, that who."

"Willie! Who twist off his arm?"

"No need. Mose Heywood he say he let
Willie ride up in back of that old rust-out
firetruck of his and smile and wave to the folks
ifn he pay the bill, and Willie he take him up,
only he having a couple sign hang down the
sides the same. He say he need the advertising."

"He do, huh. Who he advertising for? He
have the only store anyone go to."

"Well, all the same he want the signs, and
that how come we a costume parade and a
marching band, even it is just a high-school
band from over the coast."

"Ever we need a mayor, he the only one go
run." "He running for it now."

And with that the voice-shadow it gone
and Mama and Tramsee they laughing, and

then come another shadow, and then some
more laughing, and it been going on like that
so long they aint never go see or either hear
that marching band, only time they come to
that bridge they be looking on someone else to
blame. Ty he tire and thirst he waiting so long
and he go inside, and then he back on the stoop
with a warm Co-Cola in his hand from out the
pantry and he saying say he aint mind none
no sir he done heard plenty of marching bands
in his time he aint go hurry about this one,
only just then Mama and Tramsee they come
stepping out the porch, and they both done
heard what Ty just said.

Before I knows what what Tramsee she all
over Ty saying say what he mean about that
crack aint he know this here a regular brass
horn marching band come all the way from over
the coast and it aint go cost him a plug nickel to
see it neither, and then what he doing a Co-Cola
in his hand, aint he enough sense to know he
making people late sitting there drinking some
and talk some like it a regular Saturday evening,
and then Tramsee she shoving him off the
stoop, and he trying to catch up a last swallow
from out that bottle, only she shove him too
hard and that bottle spill out in the grass. Mama
she letting Tramsee do most of the talking and
the shoving, but she angry just the same, and
soon as Ty he up on his feet and walking down
the walk, she shoving me the same.

Mama she wearing a blue shirtwaist, and you can see the cross of Jesus Christ hang round her neck, and Tramsee in something white seem to move around her whole body like air, and they both chewing they lips some about slow, monkey-butt men, and ifn they done miss that marching band, well, they aint know just what, but they is reliable for doing something, and that a fact. We lucky we aint been walking long before Mama she say hear that girl, and she talking to Tramsee, and it the marching band blowing brass, only we aint see it, and then Mama she looking back she saying say you catch up you want to but you stay out of trouble, you hear, and now she talking to me, and then Mama and Tramsee they hard feelings they melt off like hot butter and they running after that marching band, only it aint exactly running say it more like a twitching, and they aint looking back neither. Ty he watching them go, but mostly he watching Tramsee white behind twitching this way and that, and then mama and Tramsee they gone, and that white behind it gone the same, and me and Ty we left to walking by ourself.

"They sure is crazy," Ty say.

I aint know what to say so I aint say a word, and Ty he shake his head and laugh to hisself, and then he give me a narrow look and he start up again.

"You ever been with a woman, boy?"

I still aint say nothing.

"I aint mean a little girl, now. I mean a full-growd woman. Tramsee she been a woman since she twelve year old. She what I mean."

"I been thinking on it."

"You is what? Boy you losing some valuable opportunity you spend all of you time thinking on it. I must of been with damn near forty women I old as you. Some of them girls too. I aint waste none of my time thinking on it." Ty he stop talking, like maybe he thinking on it all the same, and then he give me a eye full up with confoundment and exaggeration.

"Boy, you making me thirsty something more than a Coke."

Time we up to the square, the festival lights they already on. The parade it done with, and most the folks they done circle back to the tables. I aint see Mama or either Tramsee for too many folks, but there Willie in front of the barbecue, and he smoke-shouting for everybody step on up and get some, and some they doing just that, and some they knocking about in the street and talking, and some they sucking down oysters or they eating a piece a pecan pie, and there all kind of laughter coming from the center of the square, only what it about I dont know, and Ty he walking past the tables and the laughter and the smell of barbecue smoke, and then he stopping in front of the volunteer firehouse, and I is stopping the same.

Five or six volunteer they sitting back on
some rickety wooden chairs they done pull up
to the edge of the street, and they got they feet
prop up on some old wood crates and they
drinking and talking and some they smoking
and some they checking out the people go
by. Aint much else to the place. The firetruck
it back now from the parade been park up
alongside the house maybe ten minute, but
it still have them two sign hanging down the
sides saying *Buy From Willie*. It aint really a
firetruck, just a old Ford pickup they done load
up with a couple three ladder and some axes
and a rust-out water tank almost empty in the
back and about fifty foot of hose. The firehouse
itself it just a one- story white cement block
with a couple door been painted black and a
couple three window cut out and that it, except
there a small black bell hang on the wall out
front for ringing ever there is a fire.

"How do you do, Ty?"

"How do you do, Mose," Ty say. "Where
you been?"

"Aint been anywhere different, tell you that."

"You want some of this here bottle," and
Mose he pouring some rye straight down his
throat.

"You done read my mind."

Then Ty he sitting on one of them rickety
old chairs hisself and he drinking and smoking
same as all the rest, aint no one talking now,

and I sitting on the ground, my feet curl up
beneath my knees, and Im is looking up to
them volunteers and watching what goes. Aint
nothing happen for a while. Then Mose he pull
a deck of cards from out his back pocket and he
slap it down direct on top of one of them crates.

"Who in," he say. Then the rest of them
volunteers they all pulling they chairs up
around that crate they saying say they in they
go win them some hard cold cash before the
night over, and Ty he saying he in the same,
only he looking down he asking me how much
change I brung, he know I a pocketful of dimes,
but he aint say another word neither he just
holding out his hand, and before I knows what
what my pocket it empty, and Ty he playing
poker with seven eight week of my working Mr.
Fludds truck farm, and every now and then he
throw a dime into the pot.

I is wondering how long I go be there before
Ty give me my money back, but Ty he aint
even look at me he so busy raking in pot after
pot. Some of them volunteers they mumbling
say maybe he good with cards but what about
women, and then they giving Ty a sour mean
look, but Ty he in such a good mood all he do
is smile and rake in some more. Then Mose he
start passing round another bottle of rye, and Ty
he about to faint from waiting he want to feel
that rye go down his throat, and then he doing
just that, and that bottle going round and round

and around, and Im is hoping Ty go shovel me
some of my dimes before that bottle go round
again, cause there a good chance he go forget
about the game it do, but he aint pay me no
mind at all.

Aint long before Ty he talking while he
playing, he talking back to when he was in the
United States Marines up at Montford Point,
and them volunteers they just nodding they
heads and letting him talk on and on. Ty he
saying say the first day he come to boot camp,
the sergeant, his name was Whitlow, he come
on up to Ty and ask him did he like full grown
women or little girls or maybe both, and Ty he
was grinning with that, his teeth they was press
down around his tongue, and he was saying say
where was they at and how many and he like
em both kinds every inch they head to they feet
only he aint never make it all the way to they
feet, and then Ty he was laughing with that,
only Sergeant Whitlow he didnt see the joke,
he start barking up in Ty face about how there
wunt no women nearby, no little girls neither,
how there wunt go be no one talk about the
female half for the next eight week maybe more,
wunt no one even think about them neither less
he give out permission, and was about then Ty
he start getting weak in the knees, and he was
praying to the good Lord say dont let it be true
Lord not eight week Lord knows he aint never
been without a woman that long not since the

day he was born, only the praying it didnt do
no good.

The next seven week Ty and the rest of them
boys they was marching all over the sandy flats
and into the pine woods and up and down
hills, and then they was wading through all
kind of creeks and ponds, and then more woods
or maybe a bog, and tripping over vines and
pushing they way through briers and blood on
they hands, and it was bad enough living in a
tent city in them ten-man tents, never mind the
flies biting you up and down, or maybe you
walking in a black black creek and you falling
into a trout hole you aint know how to swim
somebody has to pull you out, and the next
thing you know you sitting up under some
birch pine and you shivering from cold and
eating supper out a K-ration tin, and then the
tin it empty and you back at it.

Seem like all they was ever go do in the
marines was march, even it raining, and when
it wunt raining the sun it was laying on hot
and thick like barbecue smoke, and the boys
was all dragging, and then dragging some
more, and they arms they was dropping to they
sides, and then Sergeant Whitlow he was telling
them all say they aint raise they arms keep
them rifle butts over they monkey-butt heads
they go be marching the whole night through,
and then those arms they was coming up, look
like everybody want to surrender, but they

didnt know to who. It wunt at all like Ty done
bargain for, the rest neither, but they all kept to
it, only there wunt a day gone by Ty he wunt
thinking about a woman, and he say the rest of
them leather-heads they must of been thinking
on women the same the way they was talking
into they bedrolls every night. Wunt hardly no
one getting no sleep at all.

Well by and by them boys they was fed up
to here, it didnt matter there was only three day
left of them sorry eight week, and there they
was sitting on they cots or stretch out and they
was all of them tired from marching sixteen
hour. Some was saying how they wouldnt mind
it none if them yellow Japs come all the way to
North Carolina, if they wouldnt make em do
all this marching, the Germans neither, they
got there first. Some was saying there wunt
no such thing as the Japs or the Germans, that
was something made up to keep them out in
the field, no, the only enemy they had to worry
about was the United States Marines.

Then a couple was saying say it was
Sergeant Whitlow to blame, he didnt have no
idea what he was doing, hell he was a private
hisself ten week before, then a couple more they
was saying hell it could a been worse, but the
first two didnt think so, and then just like that
the four of them was going at it on the ground.
Then this big brown boy call Icebox Pete he
break it up, and them four was back on they

cots, and then Icebox he was saying say he just
hope he get a hold of the sergeant just one time
take his head clean off, and if he didnt swallow
it up in one bite it sure as hell wouldnt take
more than two.

Ty he wunt so full of outright pugnation
like Icebox, but all the same he was tire of
the marching and thinking he go on over the
fence that very night maybe head on down to
Charleston, just for the weekend, he knowd
a couple of pretty girl there, only he aint
seen them in a while. He aint never had the
chance. Soon as he think that Sergeant Whitlow
come into the tent, and this time it a surprise
inspection and the sergeant he was looking at a
couple footlocker, only they didnt measure up
so he turn them over dump everything out he
was saying say maybe they do a better job they
start from scratch, and then he was walking up
and down some more and smacking the palm of
his hand with a swagger stick and all the while
his tongue was running up around his mouth
like he a mad dog licking foam, and then he
was telling them boys say they wunt never go
measure up, none of them they keep on disre-
garding regulations, no, he was go teach them
once and for all, they had fifteen minute, then
they better be outside with full-packs and rifles,
they was going on a little march, maybe take
part in some maneuvers, the whole damn camp
was turning out.

Whitlow he march them boys down across
some river and into the black of some river
marsh, and they must of been out in that black
black muck the better part of the night, and
they hadnt seen or either heard of nothing
but some gray hoot-owls talking death, and
the sloshing of they feet, and maybe some
moaning, and some they done figure they was
marching straight into South Carolina, maybe
they was heading for Charleston anyway, and
some, the ones worry about them owls, they
was for turning back right then, and some they
just figure to find a good place to stop, have
something to eat or just lie down, and then they
come up from the water to a sandy, grassy flat
stretch cover up with mostly pine, and them
boys why they stop right there, but Whitlow he
keep on going.

After a time, dont know how long, Whitlow
he come on back for a look see what what, look
like he want to kick everybody head in too, only
he knew he was too small, so he was telling
them all he say you all better pick up you rifles
and you packs and get a move on you hear aint
no time to wait any of you monkey-butt boys
thinking the other way I go bounce you out
of this outfit so fast you think you back in the
jungle. Then Whitlow he was shouting loud as
he was able, only them boys they wunt none
of them listening, they was lean theyself back
against them pines and some they was falling

asleep, and Whitlow he was about to pull a gun, only just then Icebox Pete he was standing up look down at the little man.

"Aint none of them boys gonna foot it no more till they had some rest. They dead like dogs." And then Icebox Pete he done ruffle up his shoulders so he was big as he could be, which was more than enough empty out Whitlow courage, and then he was saying, "You aint like it none, you going through me."

Whitlow he was looking up to Icebox Pete, only he wunt smiling with what Pete done said, but he wunt saying nothing neither cause he didnt relish the idea of going through that big brown boy, so he stood there underneath them pines and he was sputtering to hisself the while, and then Icebox he decide he done spend enough time in the woods he want a real bed under his back, even it only a cot in a tent, and with that he say come on, and then him and the boys they was heading back. Whitlow he wunt so much a fool as he a little man, but all the same he was following those boys through them pines, and all the while he was planning what to do about Icebox Pete and the rest, and telling them so too, how maybe theyⓞd be breaking up rock the rest of they natural lives, but only if they was lucky, but every now and then he was telling them say he didnt mean what he said he forget the whole thing they just turn theyselves around and follow him some more, only wunt

none of them listening, and Whitlow he was
about to pull his gun again, maybe use it on
hisself, only just then the sky was rip open with
light and smoke, and a couple three shell come
crashing down through the trees.

Icebox he was the first to hit the ground,
and the rest of them boys they done the same,
only then the air it was raining with hundreds
of them shells, look like the sky was bleeding
to death, and then there was some more shells
and some more blood, and with that them boys
they was running like hogs every which way
look around for someplace to hide, wunt no one
particular, and after a while wunt nothing to see
but smoke. Ty he was the only one wunt cover
up, and he was wiping the smoke from his eyes
and wondering what he was go do, and then he
done seen a oak tree been rip up from the roots
and it look like a good enough place crawl to
and hide, only was just then a shell burst over
his head, and that was that, cause the next thing
happen he was waking up in a hospital room.

Ty he thought he was in heaven, cause
everywhere he look he seen white, and he
wouldnt of been surprise to see Peter hisself
coming through the door and he was thinking
what to say what all done happen how he wunt
look as bad as all that, maybe Peter just hold
him up to the light see his good side, but the
next thing he seen wunt no angel at all, was a
crop-hair nurse standing up by his bed with a

basin in one hand and two towel in the other.
She was waiting on Ty to open his mouth, only
Ty he couldnt get a word out he looking at
that nurse, and she seen he was having trouble
so she was telling him say he must of had one
sweet angel watch over him cause by rights
he should of been dead, and Ty he was asking
the nurse what she was talking about, only she
didnt answer except to say how she wunt the
doctor she wunt go talk about what happen it a
too too delicate matter he just have to wait, and
with that she done set the basin on the bed table
and then she took up a towel and full it up with
soapy water, and then she was washing Ty all
over.

Ty he was a bit confuse and tire, but he
sure didnt mind what that crop-hair nurse was
doing, and by and by he was feeling pretty
good. He didnt remember the last time a
woman been touch him like that, it didnt matter
how old she was, but all the same it seem to
Ty there was something missing, and with that
he was sitting up on his elbows and smiling at
the nurse try and catch her eye, but she wunt
interested, and even she was laughing some to
herself, and then Ty seen why. He could see
where she was washing, and there wunt nothing
there except her hands and the towel and the
soap and his own two skinny leg. There wunt
even a char-black stub grab hold of for luck, and
when Ty seen that, well he wunt sitting up no

more. He let his head fall straight back to the
pillow, and then a black-ice look come full up
his eyes.

The nurses at that hospital they was as
nice as they could be, and bringing him soups
and sometimes a piece of peach pie, and every
morning they'd be washing him down but good,
and sometimes they'd just come for relax and
some talk, but by and by, Ty he was done with
the hospital and them free-talking nurses, and
then he was standing up along side the rest of
his squad in a oak-panel room. They was all
line up, and Ty he figure they was all about to
get theyself a court martial, running out like
they did with Icebox Pete, and he was waiting
on Sergeant Whitlow come in and then they
go hear the worst for sure, only it was this
square-jaw captain instead, and he was talking
how sad he was they walk into them shells,
there wunt suppose to be no artillery for two or
three more hour, someone got the times mixed
up, but they done showed they was first rate the
way they handled theyself been wounded like
that, he was proud of them all, like they was
his own, and Ty he was looking around some
more for Whitlow and hoping he didnt show
up just yet, cause he knowd the sergeant have
something more to say, but then the captain
he was talking how sad he was about Sergeant
Whitlow, it was a damn dirty shame he been
kill dead by them shells, and the only one too,

he'd have been proud like the captain, wunt too many sergeants have a whole squad getting they purple hearts, didnt matter it wunt exactly the enemy, the captain he'd seen to that, and then he was talking how he was go find out who give the order on that artillery, even it the last thing he ever do, cause men like the good Sergeant Whitlow they was hard to come by. Then the captain was done with his talk and pinning on medals, and then he give them boys a white-glove salute, and then they was all out the door.

Ty he done talking now, and the volunteers they all nodding they heads like they done got purple hearts pin to they shirts the same, and then Mose he say for everyone to ante up a dime, and with that Ty he looking down at his pile of change, only there aint no pile, cause all the while Ty been talking he been losing, and then he looking down at me again and he asking me say you any more change, and I say I dont, and then Mose he say again for everyone to ante up a dime. Ty he give Mose a hard look with that, and look like Mose he turning blue too, only he dont say another word, and then Ty he the one look discomfort and disbelief in that blueface silence, dont know what he go do, and then he reach into his pocket and pull out his purple heart and he lay it on the crate. Well right off some of them volunteers they asking Ty what he do that for, that his only medal, whyunt he take it up, forget about this

here poker game and sleep it off, he only lost
a pocketful of dimes and they wunt even his
to begin with, but Ty he full of determination
now so much so he almost shake, and then
that blueface Mose he asking what it worth
he always wanted one hisself but he never got
the chance they bounced him out of boot camp
the very first week, and Ty he nod his head
and then he saying say it worth more than the
crown jewels of the state of South Carolina.
Aint no one know what he mean by that so aint
no one say a word, and then that blueface Mose
he nod his head and deal up the cards, there
aint no more betting this time on account of Ty,
and then everybody spreading they cards out
face up on the crate have a look see whats what,
only Ty he more hesitate and expectation than
the rest, and just like that Mose he break into
a blueface smile and then he raking in the pot,
and the last thing he do he fix that medal to his
shirt.

Poor old Ty. He just staring at them cards,
he aint move or either say a word, and when
Mose see that he reach over give Ty a bottle
all to hisself, even it almost half full, and with
that Ty he up from that rickety old chair, he
a little rickety hisself, and he look around a
moment like he see or either hear someone he
know come across the square, only aint no one
there, and then he sidle up to where that old
Ford firetruck it hunker down and he climbing

in with all them ladders and axes and that fifty
foot hose, and then he tip his head back and
start pouring that sweet rye liquor down his
sorry sorry throat.

The next thing that happen Im is walking
from the firehouse to the square wish on
something to eat, and I know I aint never go see
my dimes again so I just put it out of my mind,
and I just up to the barbecue grill when this
voice it come and full up my ears with a rustle
feel like smoke. It Jonas Lee, and he standing up
under a string of white light he swaying back
and forth and back and forth, cause he up on
some crutches, and he laughing all the while
like he go beat the tar out the devil his hide on
account of he has hisself another idea.

I know the best thing to do is keep on
walking cause Jonas he trouble and Mama
she tell me say keep away from trouble before
she done run off after that marching band,
but Mama she aint here, and Jonas he is, and
before I thinking what what we both walking
down along the square to Front Street, and
then we standing up front of Willies. I knows
what Jonas he wanting now, cause we been
here before, he wanting to get inside. Willies it
a whitewash dry- goods turn liquor store out
front, and a two-story weather- beat warehouse
been add on out back, only aint nothing up on
the second floor but some old newspaper, some

empty cans, and some empty bottle Willie been
collect the last ten year. Me and Jonas we been
try to get inside a couple three time, but Willie
he always come up behind. Jonas he saying
this here maybe our best chance cause Willie
he eating barbecue, and before he say another
word we both around back in the alley have
a look. There a small flatbed wagon shove up
against a double black door and a couple black-
out window up the second floor, and Jonas he
saying say all we do we pull that wagon up
under there, and he pointing to one of them
window, and then we climb up and in, and
Jonas he so impress with hisself he almost fall
over his crutches. I has to say he a pretty good
plan, but Im is wishing it was more better cause
I knows Jonas he aint go be pulling or climbing
cause he on them crutches, and besides, he too
small to reach up to them windows even he
standing on two three wagon piggyback.

Aint nothing come easy. I has my hands
wrap around the hitch of that wagon, and I
pulling and pulling, only the wagon it aint
move to breathe, and Jonas he saying say what
the matter what I doing now why dont I quit
my fooling and do like he say, and I like to
knock Jonas his mouth shut right there, only
I too busy pulling, and what keeping it I aint
know cause the wagon it empty but feel like a
team of mule dug in at the other end, maybe
worse, maybe it the devil hisself dug in, and

Im is thinking say maybe I better give up while
I can cause aint nobody win against the devil,
and that what I about to do, only just then
the wagon it pull loose with a lurch, and I is
landing in the alleydirt. Jonas he laughing now
and over to the wagon he bend on down, and
then he holding up a piece of chain link iron
and he saying say this here what you been pull
against it chain up to the side only it broke now,
and then he laughing some more, and I feels
like maybe I should knock him around double,
only I dont. Then I pulling that wagon to one of
them black-out windows and Jonas he pointing
the one he want, and then Im is climbing up.
Willie he done put in a brand new pane of glass,
but he left it up, so I grab a hold of the sill and
then I poking my head inside, and Jonas all he
can do he saying say what you see anybody
there what it is, but aint nothing to see cause
it too dark. Then Jonas he saying he gone go
around front and wait on me to open the door,
and with that he hobble off, and I hears the
scratch scratch scratch of his crutch on the
gravel as he go, and then I aint hear it no more,
and then I climbs on in.

It too dark to see much of anything, so I
hugging close to the wall with every step. Im is
walking through some newspaper scatter on the
floor, and I kick a couple three empty can smell
like coffee grounds, and then Im is coming to a
gray box shadow, which turn out it the stairs,

and the next thing I sees is Jonas Lee and he
at the front door and grinning like some poor
Joe strutting around the marsh found hisself
something to eat, and he saying say come on
come on, so I lets him in, and then we looking
up at the shelves see what what. It aint hard
to see now cause the light from the festival it
pouring through the plate glass windows out
front like soft yellow smoke. There everything
from glycerol cream to red bricks to beans to
hand soap and potatoes, but we aint after none
of that, and then Jonas Lee he stop he pointing
to some shelves in the back, and there twenty
maybe twenty-five carton of fireworks line up in
a row.

Jonas he saying say them fireworks they
time has come, and with that then Im is
grabbing hold of them cartons and stack em
up by the door, and Jonas he saying hurry on
up hurry on up aint no telling about Willie
he might be footing it over maybe get hisself
something to drink, and I trying not to listen to
Jonas Lee cause sometime he a aggravating way
about him, but all the same Im is thinking how
what we doing go cost something, and what I
go do if Willie come through that door, and I
almost drop a couple carton with that only I
dont, and then them cartons they all stack up by
the door. The next thing Jonas Lee saying say
where that flatbed we better move along while
we can, only by we he mean just me on account

of his leg, so I around to the back go pull that
wagon to the front, and then I loading up. It
one thing break into the back of a store come
night maybe see Willie ghost hover up in the
dark, it another load up with twenty twenty-five
carton been stole up under the festival eye,
and look like Jonas he thinking the same thing
cause he keeping a lookout for Willie or either
anyone else come along from the square. Every
now and then he waving his crutch in the air,
which mean stop, so I does, and when he satisfy
aint nobody seen us he wave for me to start
up again, which I does that too, and then the
cartons they all up on the wagon, and Jonas Lee
he hop up into the front and then he sitting, his
broken leg prop up against the hitch, and his
crutches laying up by his side.

Jonas Lee he say the best place to shoot off
them fireworks is on the other side of the square
by them live oaks lean out over the Governors
Wall, so thats where we heading. Then he say
what he would and wouldnt give see Willie face
time we fire his rockets, and then he laughing
some, and then he saying say it a swampblack
sky we about to full up with some jolly-roger
smoke outdo even Willie his barbecue, and
then he laughing some more, and the more and
more Jonas he talk to hisself, the more better
he impress hisself the same. We a long way to
go, but by and by we come to the other side of
the wall, and that wagon it pull up under a big

old live oak with moss hang down. I is already
tired. It have the feeling like my arms still
rolling with that wagon, and I is thinking maybe
I should stretch out and sleep, but Jonas Lee he
have other ideas. He hobbling through the grass
now and he saying say what you doing now
aint go be no show we dont set it up, and with
that I is lining up them rockets, and it don't take
too long, but long enough, and then Jonas he
say it sure go be something, and then he shove
a couple box of matches into my hands and slip
behind one of them oaks and aint nothing but
his two eyes blinking out through the moss, and
Im is looking at Jonas a moment, and it come
to me again what we doing go cost something,
but I shake it off. Then Im is looking to the
flatbed wagon and the shadow of the wall and
them fireworks line up and that box of matches,
and I aint know if I angry or either scare, but
something inside of me about to bust out, and
with that then Im is striking them matches,
maybe one for every five or six rocket, and them
rocket tail tips they glowing red and hissing
and spitting, sound like snakes, only I aint
bother none cause I moving down the line, and
then I done with them matches and I double
up behind the wall go watch a couple three
hundred snake hissing and twisting they way
through a swampblack sky.

   I aint never seen nothing like it. Like God
hisself laughing at the world. Some of the

rockets they aint go up high enough and they clipping folks up one side and down the other, and some they angle too high and they is heading for the low side of the square down along the Front Street stores, and there all kinds of dogs yapping they heads, and some of the folks they yapping they heads the same, and some look like they bleeding with the light from them rockets and then down on they knees and they praying the Lord go take them up cause seem like maybe it judgement day at last, and the ones from that marching band they aint marching now they all running to the dock, and aint but a couple three hang on to they instruments cause there all kind of horns and drums and pipes and even a brass tuba been left in the grass, they gone, but most of the peoples they running back and forth across the square, and back and forth again, and tripping over horns and such and cursing, they all in a panic like pigs, aint nobody have no idea what they doing or either where they is, and then Im is thinking say there aint no reason be standing by a couple empty box say fireworks on the side, and Jonas Lee he must of come to the same conclude cause he already gone.

The smoke it just starting to lift, and I see a shadow- crowd of people gather down along Front Street, and then I hear a couple shadow-voice come floating through the air, and they talking hush and disbelief.

"It a damn shame it go up like this."

"Poor ol Willie. He wunt but eating his barbecue twenty minute ago, now look what happening."

"Who you think done it?"

"Aint no one burn Willie down on purpose."

"Then how it happen?"

"It just happen. Thats all. It the hand of God."

"What God want to burn Willie down for?"

"He have something in mind."

Then Im is pushing my way up to the front of the crowd see what what, and everybody looking at Willies, which it on fire now, and they all watching the fire grow higher, higher, and then a couple more voice they mumbling by my ear.

"It aint them fireworks thats the cause of all this infernal combustion."

"It sure aint."

"It the fellow set them off."

"We oughta be out there right now looking see who done it. He cant be too far."

"He aint have no sense, tell you that much. Didnt he know the wind catch that fire, spread it around some of them stores, they all be melting like butter."

"You got that right."

"Someone oughta be looking."

"Oughta be is right. But what you go do?"

"Aint that the truth."

I aint hardly move the while they talking,
I aint want to give myself away, and then they
done and we all watching Willie his warehouse
burn. Seem like the fire done eat out the black
of that swampblack sky with a couple three
hundred red and yellow tongue licking up and
out, but aint nobody move cause they watching
the same as me till the bell from the firehouse it
clang clang clang clang, and with that then the
peoples they move a couple three step back and
that old Ford pickup come rolling by, and then
it stop, and it still has them two sign hanging
down say *Buy From Willies.*

Mose Heywood he the first volunteer off
the truck, he still wearing that medal, and he
telling folks say stand back stand back, and then
the rest of them volunteers they jumping off
the same, and some they out with they ladders
and they axes, though what good ladders and
axes go do aint no one know cause that fire it
burning so hot aint nothing to see pretty soon
but ash, and Mose he trying to hook up the hose
to the water pump, only every time he pull on
that hose it pulling him back the same. What it
is there a body curl up in the back of that Ford,
and that body it Ty, and he tangle up in that
fifty foot hose, he hugging a empty bottle too,
and look like he aint about to wake up even he
been on fire hisself. Every time Mose he give
a pull, he rolling Ty forward, and then Ty his
dead weight pull his ownself back, so Mose he

aint getting nowhere. All the same it take him
five or six pull make him convince, and then he
looking in back and see Ty tangle up, and then
he call the rest of them volunteers and then they
all tugging and tugging at poor old Ty, seem
like nothing go make him budge, and then all
of a sudden, Ty he come flying through the air,
it lucky a couple of them volunteer they catch
him, and that fifty foot hose come rolling off the
truck.

Them volunteers they done lay Ty down
in the dust of the square with that and then
they working get a hold of that hose, and some
from that shadow-crowd they looking at Ty
and shaking they heads with disengagement
and they saying say what he doing the back of
that truck he cover up with so much liquor he
reliable catch on fire hisself well that what come
of folk like him yes sir he and that Tramsee
girl they should of been a law against folk like
that coming here dirty up our town, and look
like a couple three they about to kick Ty in the
head, only is just then Willie his whole place
seem to heave up a shudder like it go explode,
and then it does, and then everybody down on
they knees they cover up they heads cause here
come a flock of bust up wood and bottle glass
and window glass and some broken plates,
and even some wicker baskets, and all of that
come sweeping over the street and then down,
and then maybe five six hundred potato sweep

down the same, only it aint sweep exactly cause
them potatoes aint small, and they coming
pretty hard, and knock some people out too,
and then someone saying say the fire must of
got to all that liquor aint nothing feed a fire like
whiskey and rye, and some they looking to the
fire with that, like they wouldnt mind being fed
some whiskey and rye they ownself, but aint
nobody move from they knees, not even them
volunteers.

The next thing happen Mose Heywood he
standing in front of that old Ford pickup and he
calling for help, and then some of them volunteers they climbing up on top pump out some
water, and some they holding on to that fifty
foot hose, and Mose he pointing the way, only
nothing come out but a snake-squirt of water,
which the fire it just swallow up, and they give
a couple three more squirt, only each time they
do the fire open it mouth and swallow some
more.

Everybody they back to they feet now, aint
nothing to do but watch Willie warehouse burn
to the ground, and some they saying it a awful
thing, they glad they aint him, but it sure do
look pretty, dont it, and some they saying say
it a shame some of them other buildings dont
catch, aint nothing in em, and they nothing but
eyesores anyhow, and then all of a sudden aint
no one talking, except maybe to theyself, and
they taking a couple step back, some one way,

some the other, and from out the shadow of
they faces come Willie hisself, and he stop in
back of them volunteers, they still feeding they
snake-water to that fire, and he breathing heavy,
and look like his eyes go fall out of his head.

Willie he furious and uncontrol at first,
he looking up at the fire and the smoke, and
pressing his hands up to his rumple-up bald
head like he trying to squeeze a orange, but
by and by he feel the folks they eyes prick up
against his back, and he know he have a crowd
waiting on him to talk the talk, and with that
then he climbing into the back of that old Ford
pickup he face up the crowd. Then he open his
mouth and the words they come rolling out,
they black like the smoke billow up from his
warehouse, and Willie he saying say the devil
he the one done all of this here the work of the
devil it always been mark by fire ever since the
Jews they done left the Pharaoh look at this here
fire look it you aint never seen a fire so bright
as that so red it red like blood you aint never
seen the sky bleed like this no you aint but it
bleeding now and that the sign of the devil
sure as you and me standing here only what we
go do about it the devil he go swallow up this
whole island with fire we let him so what we go
do we aint do nothing.

Everybody know what come next cause
Willie he aint never talk about the devil he
dont get around to old man Thaddeus, and

when he do it hard not to believe he talking
truth the way he get everybody work up. He
talking anger and revenge now, and everybody
listening they all full up with angry and
revengement, even they aint know they feel it.
Then Willie he open his mouth again nail them
folks eyes and ears back to the bone, and with
every word come rolling out of his mouth he
bigger, bigger, bigger, and pretty soon he big as
the fire itself, and with that I aint sure maybe I
dead or either dream cause

*Willie his bald rumple head it curl up under
the black-burn thatch of the sky, and his words they
sounding like the voice of God sit in judgement, and
Willie his eyes they burning brighter, brighter with
the snake- dance flick of that fire, and everywhere he
look folks they all falling dead to the ground, they
all burn up aint nothing left but a pile of ash and
some bone, and Willie he saying say we done burn
the devil burn him right out of them folks, and I aint
move to breathe cause I waiting he turn his snake-
dance eyes on me and thinking say what it feel like
be burn to ash and bone, only Willie he aint look my
way cause he happy enough for burning the rest of
them gather-up folk, and some they done try to run,
they fighting the urge of them fire-happy words, but
they burn up all the same, and then they all burn
except me, and Willie he open up a cat-shriek mouth
and laugh with that, and he laughing say he done
burn the devil from out of his tree aint no where the
old man devil he climb to now, only then Willie he*

*aint laughing no more, look like he cover up with
fire, and then all I see is a shadow use to been Willie
and a piece of that fire it break off and I sees it the
devil, and then the devil and Willie they both have at
it, they wrestling harder, harder, harder, and Willie
he cat- shriek some more he the devil in his hands
now and he aint about to let go, and then the devil
he throwing Willie to the black wood-ash what left
of the warehouse floor, and then old Willie he back
on his feet and it his turn throw the devil, and the
fire burning brighter and brighter, and Willie and
the devil they rolling this way and that through the
flames and back to they feet only aint no one turn
the advantage yet, and then it look like the devil he
a grip around Willie neck but then Willie he has the
same grip,*

and then Willie and the devil they gone,
like they been swallow up, and all what left is
a devil-eating fire burn my eyes, and maybe I
know better, and maybe I dont, but all the same
Im is stretching myself up to that fire to look at
it, to know it, talk it, breathe it, taste it, only just
then a voice it grab me from behind, and then
the fire it gone the same.

"Say, boy. You sure as hell aint gonna find
what you looking for in there."

And with that it like I been wake from the
dead, and I looking up, and there the pasty
white face of old man Thaddeus hisself, only
aint no expression to his eyes, and he done
caught me up around my collar with two hand

and he dragging me back from the smoking
black wood and the glass and the brick, and
then we back to the grass edge of the square like
we waiting on something to happen.

"This a better place," he say. "You see what
you want from here, and then we moving on."

Most the peoples they done give up
watching now and they walking back across
the square in twos and threes look like clouds
of smoke drifting up through the haze of them
festival lights, and then they gone, but some
they still shaking they heads they saying they
glad they aint Willie it a god damn shame a fire
swallow up everything a man own what God
he have in mind let something like that happen
must of had something in mind but wunt it a
good show all the same it sure was that, and
then they looking around maybe grab some
half-cook potatoes before they head off, and
then there the volunteers they all cover up with
black wood-ash hard to see who who, but they
too sleep-hungry mind about that and packing
up that Ford with they ladders and they axes
and they fifty foot tangle hose, and the last
thing they lifting into the back is Ty hisself, look
like nothing go wake him up a fire dont, and
they cover him up with one of those signs say
Buy From Willies, and then they all rolling on
back to the firehouse.

The only thing left still burning is Willie,
only he walking hush and intent through the

hot hot ash and the black wood chips and the soft smell of burn whiskey linger on, and all the while he mumbling to hisself about he aint done yet take more than a little fire to finish him off thats what it was a little fire no he the one go finish off that old man and it dont matter he the devil not one little bit, and then Willie he see me and the old man standing back in the grass, aint nobody move or either say a word we watching each other a while, and then Willie he squatting down into the thick of the wood and whiskey ash, he watching the smoke float straight up into the sky, and over and over and over he saying the devil, the devil, the devil.

-2-

The devil he come for eat my bones,
See he coming up a railroad track.
Been so long I coming home,
Slept last night in a brakemans shack.

Lay my head in a roaring fire,
I aint know I been so tire.
Devil he fixing some barbecue,
Aint nothing left for me to do.

Watch my bones they burn and crack
Devil he eating in a brakemans shack.

Watch the devil he wiping his maw.
Watch me stick in that old mans craw.

The next thing I knows the old man he
dragging me from the square, and he moving
a pretty good clip so I doing all I can to keep
from dragging down in the warm, moist
street-dirt behind him, and pretty soon we done
left the streets of that fire-stain town behind.
The old man dont say what he want, and Im is
thinking say maybe he go finish what start with
them crabs, and I aint want to bother about that
even he aint the devil, but look like I aint got a
choice. We coming to the dock now, and then
we up to the edge we looking out on the black
black water of the channel and watching the
grass sway back and forth, back and forth with
the wind, and then the old man he pointing
down to a old rowboat tie up in the water.

"Get in there, boy," he say.

I aint know what else to do so I climbing
down the ladder and into the boat, and the old
man he doing the same, and then he pick up
the oars and we moving through the water. A
couple time Im is looking down at the heavy
black water and thinking maybe I go dive in
swim for the bank, but I aint ever learn me to
swim, so I dont even try, and pretty soon it too
late even think about learning to swim cause
we moving through the deep wood now, past
the black shadows of water-root sycamores, and

oaks, and pine, brushing past moss hang down
from they branches, and every now and then
some hoot-owls come rustle-wing through the
air and crying they death-talk.

The old man he talking to me the while he
rowing.

"You sure is a quiet boy. What's the matter
with you? You afraid of something?"

The old man it like he read my mind, but I
aint let on.

"No, sir. No, I aint afraid of nothing."

"Thats good, boy." The old man give me
a hard look with that but he keep on talking.
"This here wood cant hurt you less'n you
afraid."

Then the old man he quiet up, look like he
trying to think of something more to say, and
while he thinking Im is looking to the black
of the wood and worry how the wood maybe
go hurt me, and then I sees a bluegray steam
rising up from the water for drift on through
the trees, only look like ghosts been talk about
by them hoot-owls, and every time a owl he
open his mouth, them ghosts they scatter back
to the black of the oaks and sycamores and
cypress and pine wait for them owls fly away,
and then the ghosts they drifting some more.
It almost more than a body can stand the owls
and the ghosts and the black of the wood, and I
just about to dive into the water anyway, I dont
care what happen, when the old man he talking

some more, and this time he talking how he
know about the wood, which it help keep me in
the boat.

The old man he use to been hunting alligator
a couple night a week time he first come to
the island, and every time he done it he been
camp out of this shack in the middle of the
backwater wood, only he aint been maybe
thirty year on account of Long Jim. It happen
like this. Thaddeus he done hooked up with
five maybe six boys been with him regular
hunting alligators and they done left town
about four o'clock in the afternoon. They was
taking the short way up across the island, save
time, was walking through the long grass with
they gear strap tight across they backs and
then skirting up through a couple grave-hump
hill, and all they all talking about was how
many alligators they was go get maybe sell
they skins up Charleston maybe go all the way
to Market Street, and then they was coming
through the trees heading down to the black
of the backwater channel, nothing to lead the
way but the sun dance through the leaves of
oak and redbay and maybe some pine, there
was sun-print all over the ground, and they
was climbing over stumps and down past some
water oak and some more pine, and was a
couple still talking, but the rest was chewing
on they words, and then they was down to the
shack.

Wunt much to see. The shack it leaning
back on the flat of the bank, had some holes
look up from the roof and some cracks running
to the moss-leaf ground, and it wunt but one
room with a old pine table and no chairs and a
small red lantern missing its glass, but the boys
didnt mind none, and Thaddeus he didnt mind
neither, and so they was dragging they gear
inside and lay it out on the floor. Was then this
long legged boy call Long Jim he put some fire
in the belly of that lantern and he start talking
about who the noosemens was go be and who
the gig and someone be carrying the knives and
a couple of lantern, and Long Jim was saying
say how he was go be walking the lookout,
and then maybe he the gig too, and them boys
they was all anticipate for jump the devil and
pressing they teeth together like they was all
grinning alligators theyself, and Thaddeus he
was grinning the same, and then they was all
out into the heavy wet green of the wood.

They was following close to the water, some
was in, and every step they was moving slow
even it early yet, but all the same they was
looking for alligators rest in the grass or maybe
up under the hammock or maybe slide through
the green black muck, and they was keeping
they feet ready to run they have to, only wunt
nothing to see or either hear but blueflies and
gnats skimming the surface, at least at first,
and then Long Jim he done give a owl-whistle

what meant there a alligator up ahead. Well
them boys they done freezed up with that for
looking to the blackgreen of the trees up ahead
of Long Jim, and Thaddeus he the same, like
they was all a flock of blue herons aint know
enough to fly off or not, and then there was all
kind of shouting and hollering and raking at
the water with hands, and then them boys was
knee-stepping up along the bank they want to
have a hand in the kill, and Long Jim his eyes
was iron and he was telling his noosemens to
keep they nooses pull tight cause that alligator
he was halfway down the bank a twisting and
turning try to get to his hole, watch out now he
maybe knock someone in the water on the way,
but he wunt fast enough for them boys even he
was swinging his head around try and take a
bite out of someone, no sir, no matter what he
try Long Jim noosemens they was holding on
tight, and wunt long before that alligator he was
out of breath, wunt hardly even give his tail a
twitch, and with that Long Jim he took up the
gig and come down, and then he done smile
cause he seen he done split that alligator head
in two on the first strike.

That was all she wrote for that there
alligator, and them boys they done whoop it
up and was waving they arms in the air like
they hadnt been dance since the juba days,
and some they was laughing about how small
that alligator was, wunt more than twelve foot

long, only didnt it put up a fight like they was fighting the devil hisself, and then they was spreading out in the grass to catch they breath. Long Jim he was resting the same up against this big black sycamore and scratching up at his head, like maybe he was thinking some more how he come down a top of that alligator head, he impress hisself with that, and then Thaddeus he was out with his skinning knife go cut that alligator down to the bone, and then a couple more they was cutting the same, and then they all done pack up the meat. With that then Long Jim he was up and saying say it time they move they feet go find theyself some more they full up they sacks, and then they was all slogging they way through the black backwater like they was before, only this time they wunt moving so slow cause they eyes was all fixed with the blood of that first alligator. Now by this time the sun had gone down and the backwater it was turning blacker with every step, and the trees they was like one black shadow been stretch out all the way to the edge of the bank, so the boys they fire up they lanterns and was swinging em back and forth, back and forth, but most of the light been swallow up by the waiting dark. Even the air it was heavy with some blood-wet predictiment, like the whole world waiting take a breath. And every step them boys was taking they was come on some alligator hiding in a hole or lay out in the

shallow, only it all in they homeless heads, and
then all of a sudden there come a bellowing
from somewheres out of the dark, only wunt no
one sure just exactly where, it sound like it was
everywhere, and them boys they was straining
they eyes they was looking to the trees and the
moss and the water and the hammock, they was
straining so hard the blood in they eyes come
pouring out, and the next thing what happen
this big blackblue alligator come a rumbling
through the blackblue shadow of the trees, must
of been thirty foot long too, and the branches
they was breaking off been kick up in the air.

That alligator his eyes was redmeat hungry,
and his mouth was hungry the same, and the
closest one to him was Long Jim, and before
anyone know'd what what, the both of them
they was twisting and turning up under the
brush and Long Jim he was hollering and some
of them boys they was hollering back, and then
three or four boys they done pull out some guns
with that, only where them guns come from
didnt nobody know cause they hadnt brought
any with them, and Thaddeus he had a rifle
in his hand hisself even he didnt own one his
whole life, but all the same they had them guns
in they hands, only wunt nobody know just
when to shoot cause didnt nobody have a clear
shot, and then Long Jim he was screaming for
his knife, only there wunt no way he could get
it cause it was strap down to his leg, and then

they was both rolling down the sides of the
bank, him and that blackblue alligator, all the
way down to the black, black water cause that
alligator he was dragging Long Jim to a hole.
Didnt nobody wait no more after that they was
all running for Long Jim and that blackblue
alligator, and a couple they drop they guns for
knives and was waving them in the air so Long
Jim could see, they was saying say hold on
Long Jim hold on, and Long Jim he was trying
to grab at roots, only look like it wunt no use,
and then them boys they done jump to the back
of that alligator, and the two they was hacking
at its backside with they knives, left them bury
up to the hilt in that blackblue hide, and the
others they done empty out they guns, one
upside that blackblue belly, the other upside the
head, but that alligator he wunt about to let go
of Long Jim even there a hundred knife stuck
out of his hide, and he wunt bother by the guns
neither except to make him chew some harder,
and there was all kind of steam rising up from
his mouth and he was lashing back with his
tail knock one of them boys to the ground, but
the rest they was hacking at that blackblue
hide some more, and empty out a couple three
more guns into that alligator head, and then
Thaddeus he step up with that babynew rifle
of his stretch out like a arm, and he empty it
out the same, and then wunt nothing heard
but a click click click they was all squeezing

they triggers dry, and with that the clock it
done stop, and that blackblue alligator he was
laying down the side of the bank, just laying,
half-in, half-out of the bloodblack water, and
was twenty or twenty-five knife bury deep in
his hide, and maybe eighty ninety bullet been
shot through his head and his belly, and wunt
much left even butcher it up for meat, but wunt
nobody thinking on that just yet cause that
alligator mouth it was still wrap around Long
Jim leg couldnt even see it, and when them boys
they done pry that mouth open and slide Long
Jim up, they done seen wunt much left of his
leg neither.

Long Jim he didnt do nothing but moan,
and every now and then he roll his head have a
look at what left of his leg and then moan some
more. A couple three they ease that leg up and
wrap it with a croaker sack been cut into strips,
and wunt easy cause some of the parts they
kept sliding to the ground, and the rest of them
boys they was butcher up all they could of that
alligator meat, which was more than it looked
at first on account of a thirty foot alligator it a
lot of meat, aint no sense let it go to waste, and
then they was all done with the wrapping and
cutting and they pack up the gear and the meat
and Long Jim and his leg, and they was heading
back to the shack. The whole bunch was worry
theyself with talk, and some was saying they
aint never seen a alligator big as that it wunt

no alligator must of been the devil hisself, and
then they was praying some on account they
wunt even close being inside maybe the devil
he come back finish them off, and then a couple
of lanterns swing through that black maybe
see the devil coming only wunt nothing to see
so they was praying some more, and then one
them boys, was a bald, rumple-head man, he
was saying say didnt nobody see the devil he
didnt want to be seen what we has to do we has
to fool the devil just set them two lantern up
along the bank somewhere on a stump when the
devil he come he see the light and that where he
go only we long gone by then, and the rest of
the boys they was nodding with that, and then
they was all running like a pack of ghosts from
the glow of them two yellow lantern wash down
across the blackblue water and then they was up
through the dark and over roots and dead logs
and brush through the moss, and they didnt
stop for nothing even they was lugging five
hundred pound of alligator meat and Long Jim
and his leg till they was up to the shack.

The first thing they done they was inside
they fire up that small red lantern cause it been
out a while, and then they was all flop to the
floor for laughing relief, only they was still scare
and tense from thinking on the devil, so it was a
thin, stringy kind of laugh barely stretch across
the floor. The only one wunt laughing was Long
Jim, but every now and then he give another

moan, which maybe sound a little like laughing you was just listening to it the way the air kept breaking up in his throat, but it wunt anywhere near to laughing you was looking at what was left of his leg. Then the laughing it stop, and they was all looking to Long Jim and his leg, look like something out of somebody dream the way that red lantern running its thin strings of soft-yellow light down across the shadow black floor, wunt hardly enough light see they own hands let alone who next to them, and then they was talking what to do, they voices stretch out thin in the dark of that shack like the light.

"What we do now," said the first.

"We do what we can," said the second.

"We doing that now," said the third. "Aint nothing to do. We aint none of we going outside. Aint nothing but trouble we go back out we all end up like him. Look at him, man. There death in them eyes."

"You all cant let a man die like that," say the first. "Leg chew up and spit out like tobacco. Could be you lying there on the floor instead of him."

"Could be."

"That what I said."

"Could be any one of we here, but it aint. It Long Jim no matter what we saying."

And it was just about then Long Jim he was clutching up at the air like he was thinking he back in the water with that alligator chewing

his leg, and he done pull hisself up to almost
sitting, he was prop against the leg of the
pine-wood table, and then he was calling out for
his knife again. Thaddeus he was the closest one
so he take up a knife put it into Long Jim hand,
and with that Long Jim he lay hisself down
to the floor again and he fell asleep, a couple
string of soft-yellow light stretch across his face.

"That man he need a doctor," said
Thaddeus.

The rest of them boys they was looking to
Thaddeus when he say that, most of they faces
all wrinkle up with amusement, but some they
was stiff with silent rebuke, and then they was
all talking with theyself some more.

"What kind of doctor he talking about?"

"Aint no doctor on this here island."

"Have to head up the coast. Even then aint
find many take colored folk, lessn they colored
theyself."

"Long Jim he aint have to worry about that.
He be dead before he cross the water."

"Man, he lucky we dont talk him to death
here and now."

"Aint that the truth."

Then that rumple-head man, he'd been
listening all the while from the dark of the
corner, he give a jerk with his arms and roll
hisself up to his knees, and with that he done
corner the rest with his black-arrow eyes dart
back and forth, and then he open his mouth.

"Aint no doctor ever cure a devil-bit leg," he said. "And that a fact. Only thing cure that is a conjure man, and that what Long Jim need."

And with that the rumple-head man he fold hisself back into his corner, he was waiting on what happen, cause he wunt the one go for a conjure man and everybody knowd that, but before he fade into the dark complete, one of the rest he was up from the floor and he was saying say he'd be back with the conjure man even he have to kill dead a hundred alligator to do it, only it didnt sound like he mean a hundred, didnt sound like he mean even one, but then he was through the door all the same and moving through the blueblack of the night. The rest they was left sitting in the middle of the floor, and they was satisfy they was doing all they could for Long Jim so they was busy now scrounge about for something to eat, maybe a cup of cold beans or rice go along with some ham, they didnt even think about some of that deaded alligator meat, and they was talking some more too, but it was about conjure men how most was good with colds and maybe fever and some could call the rain but only a few could bring back the dead they didnt want to come. Long Jim he done roll hisself up under that pine-wood table, maybe he was thinking he get away from that alligator in his head, and he done left a stringy blood- stain on the floor where his leg it been drag. He didnt hear

a word was said about conjure men calling rain
or how maybe one was coming, but it look like
he was needing one soon by the way he was still
calling out for his knife even he had one in his
hand.

No telling how long they was waiting, but
by and by them boys they was done with they
food and they talking done drop to a slow,
heavy roll around the room, like they eyelids,
and they'd a been asleep another minute only
was then the conjure man he come busting into
the shack, and the other one what went for him
he done slip in behind.

The conjure man he was a big bone man
the color of dark plum, and he was wearing
a red skullcap and holding a small black bag
in his hand, but he wunt looking too happy
on account of he'd been woke up out of bed
and rowed five maybe six mile through the
backwater wood, but soon as he seen Long Jim
laying there a smile come busting up on to his
face. First thing he was over to the table he was
sending Thaddeus sit by the door, and then
he was hunch over Long Jim leg and he was
mumbling to hisself and shaking his head, and
didnt nobody have no idea what he was saying,
but the meaning come through clear enough,
and then the conjure man he was dragging Long
Jim out from under the table scatter the rest of
them boys up against the walls, and then he set
Long Jim up in the middle of the shack. Long

Jim he was moaning still, but wunt as bad as
before, which was saying something about the
touch of this here conjure man, and he even
drag Long Jim by his chew- up leg too. Then he
took out his chalk and make a circle up around
Long Jim, and he done it smart, and then he
done fire up some candles, one for the head,
one for each arm, each leg, even the chew-up
one, and then he was dancing around that circle
and calling out to the spirits, and every now
and then he'd reach into his black bag and pull
out some chicken bones or some feathers and
he scatter them down across Long Jim and his
chew-up leg, but some was landing on the floor.

The conjure man he was dancing in
everybody eye, except Long Jim eyes they was
shut, and the soft yellow from the small red
lantern it mix up with the yellow from the
candles it was all dancing the same, but look
like the conjure man he wunt having much luck
with Long Jim and that leg no matter how long
he dance, like maybe the devil he done eat up
too much of that leg, but just then there come
a dancing wind it seem to answer the conjure
man call, and it come dancing in through one
side blow out the candle light and the lantern
light, and them chicken bones and them feathers
they was swirl up, and then the wind it was
dancing out the door take the door and the
bones and the feathers with it, and then the rest
of them boys they wunt watching the conjure

man dance cause the wind it was coming back
for dance some more, they was all hanging on
to arms and legs keep from following after the
bones and the feathers, and the conjure man he
was watching the wind the same and hanging
on to Long Jim, and then all of a sudden a smile
come wind-dance across his face, and with that
he was shouting out to them boys how this here
storm was the spirits doing wunt nothing for
them to do but wait it out. It was almost like
being outside.   With the wind come a couple
crack of lightning so sharp was like a whip
beat across the back of the sky, and then come
the blood- warm rain through the holes in the
roof, and it didnt let up. And every time that
whip done crack, them boys they flinch up like
it was they own backs been whip, and some it
looked like they was bleeding real blood in that
flashing light and then the light it was gone,
and didnt none of them boys move at first cause
they was too scare, but after six or seven stroke
they was all moving for huddle up under that
pine-wood table, all except the rumple-head
man fold-up in the corner and Thaddeus by
the door and Long Jim and his leg stretch out
in the chalk circle. The conjure man he was the
first one under, and he kept shoving the rest
of them back into the rain saying they wunt
enough room they wunt enough room, but just
as he clear them out a fifth time the wind it
come again and dance some with the pine-wood

table, and that surprise even the conjure man, and then the table it was dancing out the door and down the bank to the water, only it have to go break-leg cause it was too big to fit through any other way, and with that the conjure man he was saying say now huddle round huddle round, which the rest they done it.

By and by the wind and the rain they blowd theyself out, and them boys they was shaking water out of they hair and wiping it from they eyes, and Thaddeus he was doing the same, and the conjure man he was looking to the still black sky from out the middle of that huddle of shaking hair, and his eyes they was full up with rejubilation, only then he wipe away his enthuse along with the water, and he was saying say he done his best he call the spirits down and they come wunt nobody say they wunt he been in this room see what we seen and wunt nothing more to do neither but wait on Long Jim see if he wake up come the morning sun or either gone off with the devil. With that the boys they was nodding they heads, even the rumple-head man in the corner, and some they was looking to Long Jim with respect or either scare, but wunt nobody saying a word just yet, and then the conjure man he was saying say he thought it looking pretty good for Long Jim, but he'd been wrong a couple time before only both time it been on account of a white man, and with that them boys they was all looking

to Thaddeus they eyes slicing him up like he
another alligator, and the conjure man he was
watching satisfy he done made a name for
hisself and then he fell asleep, and then one by
one them boys they was all falling asleep, but
they was mumbling to theyself the while, was
all the same thing, they was saying say they go
kill theyself one more alligator kill one for Long
Jim they have to it the last thing they ever do,
and maybe give Thaddeus another look, and
seem like everybody say it five or six time, and
then the mumbling it stop. The only ones wunt
sleeping was Long Jim and his leg, and they was
stretched out dead in the middle of the room,
and the other was white man Thaddeus, and he
was sitting up by the door and wondering what
he was go do next.

Turn out wunt nothing else to do. Thaddeus
he seen Long Jim wunt go be waking up
anytime soon, and he knowd exactly what them
boys would be thinking they wake up see Long
Jim nail-dead on the floor, so what he done he
took hold of Long Jim by his arms and he start
dragging him to the door and he was praying
some too maybe none of them boys wake up
before he make it. It wunt easy cause Long Jim
he was already stiffen up, and he have to almost
break his arms to get him through, but then he
was, and without thinking where he was going
next he was dragging Long Jim through the
thick green wet of the brush pile up from the

storm, he was heading for the water, and all
the way Long Jim his leg was bouncing side to
side. Was then Thaddeus he seen the conjure
man patch-up rowboat pull up to a tree, and
the next thing he done he heave up Long Jim
and roll him in, and then they was both in, and
then Thaddeus he pick up the oars and push
away from the bank and then he was rowing up
through the backwater wood.

Thaddeus he still didnt have a idea where
he was going, but he was going just the same,
and every now and then he'd ask Long Jim
what he want to do next, where he want to go,
but Long Jim he was just laying low in the boat
with his head flop up against one side, and his
arm trailing low for ripple in the black, black
water. Wunt too long Thaddeus he see the light
of them two lantern left to fool the devil, and
why they was still lit he couldnt say cause the
storm must of swept up this way the same, but
he wunt thinking too hard on coincidence he
was thinking say it pretty dark too dark to be
rowing aint some kind of light, and so he row
on over to the edge of the bank, and he grab
the two lantern off the stump set them down by
his knees, and even they didnt give off enough
light except for maybe light up Long Jim face,
well Thaddeus he didnt mind, he was saying
say light is light, and then he was rowing some
more. He must of been rowing a hour fore he
pull up his oar and toss the light of one of them

lantern around, and he still couldnt see much of
anything cause the warm wet dark it swallow
up the light before it reach down to the water,
but all the same he knowd it the right place,
could feel it more than see it, could smell it,
taste it maybe, taste like it almost a deep deep
swampwater lake, and then he shine the light on
Long Jim face give him one more look, and then
the lantern it was down in the bottom of the
boat again and Thaddeus he was shoving Long
Jim over the side.

Soon as Long Jim he hit the water there
come a rush of white water, and Thaddeus he
hold out the lantern some more and he seen
ten or twelve black shadows steaming for the
boat, and they red eyes they was steaming the
same, and Thaddeus he wunt about to wait for
them to come up under the boat cause they
was a swampwater pack of alligator and like
to knock him in the water they trying to get at
Long Jim, so he was pushing back quick with
his oars give them alligators room, and then the
alligators they was fighting theyself and bellow
in the water, and there was red eyes everywhere
dipping down and then back up again, and
everything was getting wet, even Thaddeus, and
he was fifty foot away by then, and then all of
a sudden the fighting and the bellowing and
the white water stop, and the shadows they was
dipping down some more, but only to cool off
they tempers, and there wunt nothing left to see

of where Long Jim went under except maybe
some steam rising up off the black, black water,
and with that Thaddeus he was thinking to
hisself say it wunt exactly what the conjure man
done said, but wunt no one else gonna know, it
was close enough.

By the time Thaddeus he coming back, the
sun was coming up, and the blackblue of the
backwater wood was drift up like a ghost. He
didnt waste no time tie up the boat he was
scramble up through the warm wet brush, and
he was bringing the two lantern along, they
was burn out by then, and he wunt thinking
a thing except get hisself through the door,
and then he was. Wunt nobody awake just yet
they was all huddle up on the floor smell like
wet mules been lock up a week or more, and
then Thaddeus he have hisself a idea, and he
set them two lantern where Long Jim he used
to been right in the middle of the conjure man
chalk circle, and he was dancing with a smile
hisself he do that cause he could hardly wait
and see everybody faces they wake up, and then
he was laying hisself up against the pine- wood
wall like he been there all the while, and he
close his eyes like he asleep.

Thaddeus he didnt have to wait long before
that huddle it shake itself awake, and didnt
none of them boys say a word right away, and
the conjure man he didnt say a word neither,
the truth was they was all staring at them two

lantern where Long Jim should of been. It hard
to say how long nobody said a word, but they
was looking more and more like mules too
stupid even to kick, they wunt even blinking
they eyes, and then one of them was saying say
thems the lanterns they done left for fool the
devil, and they was all nodding they head with
that but didnt none of them ask how they got
where they was, and then another he was saying
say anybody see where Long Jim done gone
to, and they was all looking around the room,
only Long Jim he wunt there, and the boys they
was looking impress and scare and hungry
and tense, and all at the same time too, but the
conjure man he wunt looking anything but scare
the way his eyes going round and round that
shack like part of him was wondering what it
was he done only most of him didnt really want
to know, and then another one of them he was
saying say maybe the devil he carry Long Jim
off just like the conjure man done said, and with
that then the conjure man he done had enough
he was up from the huddle and he was saying
say wunt no trusting the devil wunt a hundred
hundred men full up his appetite no sir we
better make tracks fore he change his mind
come back for more, and with that the huddle it
break up and everybody scrambling around that
shack, they was packing up the gear and the
five hundred pound of alligator meat and they
brand new but empty guns, they was packing

up everything except them two lantern in the middle of the floor, they was worry about that, and Thaddeus he was scrambling right there with them, only he was having a hard time keep hisself from laughing out loud, and then they was all through the door into the leaf-washed light of the morning sun, and the conjure man he was leading the way.

-3-

The old man he still aint say a word about where we going or what we go do, aint nothing but the swish swish swish of them oar, maybe some tree-groan, some owl- shriek, but by and by he slowing down, and I sees we coming to a moss-cover bank with one black sycamore lean over the water. The first thing we do we sliding that boat up from the edge and tie it to that tree, and then the old man he saying say look up through them trees, which I does, and there a small tarpaper shack bury up in some dark- needle pine, and a deep red glow coming through a red- curtain window make the black of the wood look blacker still.

"That's where we spending the rest of the night," he say, and then he nudge me up the bank and up we go.

It the same shack he been with Long Jim, only there a couple of chair lean against the wall

now, and someone been fix up the door and
that broken-leg pine-wood table the same as
new, and that deep red glow from the outside
it yellow now we is inside and it coming from
two lantern stand up on the floor and one small
red lantern missing its glass its up on the table.
There aint no blood-stain wood, no chalk circle,
it all scrub bare bare, even the holes in the roof
they been patch, only who done it and when
and where he gone there aint no telling. Then
the old man he look at me like he know what I
thinking. "Aint no one here, boy, except you and
me," he say. "Aint no one else been here must
be thirty year now."

How he know that make no sense cause I
can see the door and the table and them three
lantern, and who done lit them I aint know but
must of been somebody. But the old man he
aint bother about that, and then he pull out two
green shoulder-pack stack up under the table,
and he going through them see what there. In
the one there some brown bread and a couple
can of peaches and look like some cheese, and
in the other there a couple of rib-tooth knife and
some fold up croaker sacks and a couple three
roll of twine, and the rest I aint see for the old
man shadow, but seem he satisfy with what he
see cause the next thing he do he sitting in a
chair his hands a hold of his knees, and then he
leaning out into the wash of the yellow lantern
light and he talk some more.

"You gonna find yourself a mat over there in the corner. You get yourself some sleep as best you can. I aint never close my eye I been in this shack, and that almost thirty year, but that my problem. Tomorrow come we gonna pack up the boat and head out into the backwater hunt you up a alligator."

With that I moving to the corner and rolling out the mat, and then I laying down, I aint know what else to do, and the old man he aint move from his chair he watching me all the way, and when he see me looking at him he give me his waiting-smile. Then he turn down them lanterns, and with that aint nothing to see but three red fuzz ball floating in the black, and Im is staring at them fuzz ball and staring and then it like they all just one fuzz ball, and it look like the devil's eye for sure the way its hovering there and red like it is, and then just like that the shack and the old man in the chair and them lanterns, everything is gone,

and there I is standing at the bottom of some ghost-white stone steps rise almost straight up into the sky, and with that Im is thinking say maybe I dreaming, I has to be, but it seem too too real be a dream, and with that I aint know what to think I just standing there on them steps and must be four or five hundred folks standing there with me crab-stiff on them steps, they heads arch back and looking up cause it just starting to rain, and some they wearing black hats and black coats

*and some they wearing black dresses and holding
black fans out from they sides, and then they all
grumbling to theyself and checking they watches for
the time saying say how long before the doors they
open up aint they been standing long enough this
unbelievable keep folk waiting round like this have
to take this up with someone, and then the man a
step above me he turn he saying say we all be here as
long as it take but some folks aint happy lessn they
something to complain about, and then he look down
to me with his brown ball eyes and he take off a black
bowl hat and give a patient, waiting nod like so, and
then he saying say he only been waiting maybe five
year but they saying some, the ones at the top, they
been here over a hundred, and then he black bowl his
head again and turn his brown ball eyes to looking
up some more.*

*I aint even try to think what five year waiting
feel like, but then it happen I aint have to worry
none cause a sigh of repent and relief come roll
down through that crowd of black-hat folks, and
then we all is walking up. By the time we to the top
of the steps the rain it gone, except some dripping
down from the hats and the fans, and we standing
up front of a ghost-white clapboard church, aint a
whole lot bigger than Willies store and warehouse
before the fire. The folks they passing through two
polish oak doors and then they sitting down on some
polish oak benches, only everybody hunch over a bit
cause aint no backs, and then the doors they shut,
and everybody restless and waiting. Aint nothing*

*happen. And then a couple hanging lantern is fire
up down front, only aint no one I see done it, then
a couple more and a couple more all the way to the
back, and seem like the air it burn red with smoke,
so much so the peoples they mopping up they faces
just to see, and then the smoke it clear some, and the
red from those lantern come down to a glow, and a
preacher he step to the box.*

*The preacher he wearing a fire-bright suit like
he the devils own rooster, not even Willie has a suit
like that, and his eyes they is fire-bright the same,
and everywhere he look he burning something, three
hat catch fire, a young womans dress crumble up
to ash, a couple old grands they cant keep still they
shoes is smoking, but mostly he burning out eyes till
they nothing but empty white sockets staring back.
Is then the preacher he talking, only it aint exactly
talking, more like we is thinking what already been
said, and it only one thing, start out a whisper,
but it a growing thing too, over and over and over
again, the words they saying say aint nothing be
afraid of folks nothing at all, and then the folks
they take up chanting them words, louder, louder,
some they mopping they faces some more, some they
slipping out of they coats, hats falling to the floor, a
couple more dress ash-crumble, and all the while the
preacher he keep time with his fire bright eyes.*

*Aint long and the church it full up with the ash
from all that white-socket chanting, so the preacher
he wave his arm once and he bring that chanting
down, and then he wave again and the fire from*

*them hanging lanterns is bleeding up along the
ceiling and then down along the walls, and then he
out the box he wave a third time calling everyone
to come on down the aisle, and then they doing just
that, and the preacher he saying say what you afraid
of, and I aint exactly hear what anyone say back, but
it look like they all afraid of something cause they
nodding they heads, and some even reach out to grab
the preacher by the hand, and then they stepping
past, only where they going I cant say cause there
too much ash from the words and smoke from the
fire to see, and then it my turn, and the preacher he
saying say what you afraid of boy, and I know what
it is, only I cant say it, and then the preacher he
pointing to a big big kettle sitting up there past the
steps, and a big big fire underneath, and that where
all the people been going, only they aint people no
more, look like they crabs been boil for supper, and
soon as I see that the preacher he laughing, and the
fire from that kettle it laughing the same, and then
a hot hot flash, and just like that the church and the
preacher and that kettle full of people-turn-crabs is
gone, aint nothing left but some church-ash swirl up
around my face, and that laughter echo round in my
head.*

*Well, with that I sure hoping this a dream. Then
the ash it settle down, and the laughing too, and
Im is standing in front of a black iron gate open
up to a boneyard. There three black and scraggly
sycamore huddle up in the middle of a small-hump
hill, and four or five hundred cross pin-stuck in*

the soft black earth, and look to be some dirt-wash
headstone lean up against a black iron fence one side,
they am almost turn green for wait on the devil,
and the other side there a one window slate-gray
shed, only nobody home. Aint nothing more to do
so I climbing over the gate for a look, and past the
four or five hundred cross, and past the turn-green
stones, and this been a dying place a long time in
anyone rememory cause look like the names and the
dates all been wash away, and I is just stop up under
them sycamores time I hears a shallow scrape scrape
scrape and then a rustle sound like wings.

I aint move or even breathe in the dead-leaf
shadow of them three black sycamores, and it a lucky
thing too cause from out that slate-gray shed come
two singing men. They singing shovel songs, cause
they both a shovel slung over they shoulder, and
then they down the other side from them sycamores
and they singing death songs, cause that what they
shoveling, and one he doing most of the work, and by
and by he a pretty good load of dirt pile up behind
him, and the other one he doing most of the singing,
but every now and then he shovel up some black and
let go over his shoulder.

Then they both done stop with they shoveling
and they singing, and they leaning on they shovels
for catch up they breath, and the one done the most
shovel he mopping his sweat with a fade red rag
and he brush away some of them green-eye boneyard
snapflies, and the other one he aint so tire so he start
up talking.

*"Aint no need dig every man a grave," he say.
"After a while it pretty hard tell one from another."*

*The first one he aint catch his breath just yet so
all he do he just nod.*

*"The devil he aint mind who bury where. Come
judgement day he go open up every grave hisself
have a big old meal of bones. He aint look see he a
old man elbow in one hand and a young girl ankle
the other. He eat em all."*

*The first one he nod his head some more. The
second one keep talking.*

*"No sir, the devil he aint mind at all," he say.
"That why I saying say dont you bury me. Just
throw me to the fire till my bones they crack and
burn. Watch me stick in the devil craw then. Aint he
be surprise."*

*And with that the singing men they laughing
to theyself, and then the first one he say come on,
and he shoulder up his shovel, and the second one he
laugh and do the same, and then they both walking
down to that slate-gray shed, and they singing a
fool-the-devil song now.*

*Soon as they gone, I out from the sycamore
shadow and down for look at the grave they been
digging. There a bone-rot smell rise up from the
hole, even aint no one in it just yet, and then Im
is wondering who it for and how long he been died
and what from, and then I sees the stone up one end,
and soon as I see it I know there been a misunder-
statement somewhere down the line cause that stone
have my name burn into it, and then just like that I*

aint looking at the stone no more, Im is lying in the black rot of that hole looking up to ghost-white sky, and Im is trying to move my arms my legs climb out of that hole, only aint nothing work, and then I hears them singing men again, and sound like they coming back from the shed, sound like they singing some more shovel songs too, and then the singing it stop, and I sees the two of them standing on the edge of the grave, they shovels prop up on they shoulders, and they talking some more about fool the devil, only they aint look down and see me, and I aint know what all been happening or either why, all I know is I scare and confuse, and Im is trying to call out, only my mouth it aint work neither, and then the singing men they start up singing some more, and then down come a pile of soft, black dirt, and look like nothing go keep them two from singing and shoveling, singing and shoveling, and then everything goes black.

The next thing I know my eyes is open and I looking around the shack. The way the sky shine a deep blue through the cracks in the wall it look to be late evening, and I wondering where the old man is cause them two green shoulder pack they gone, and so is them two lantern for fool the devil. Aint a sign the old man ever been there. Then Im is thinking say its time I heading home, I sure as hell aint go spend another night in that shack, not with everything happen last night, even it was

only a dream, I aint go stay. But then Im is
thinking say if it was a dream, then who done
send it, and why, one thing for sure, I go be
on the lookout for a big big kettle. Then I aint
thinking on nothing no more and I get up and
head outside, and Im is standing up against
the shack in the shadow of a couple of pine
tree hang over the roof, and listening to the old
man sing. He down the bank by the water, he
stowing them shoulder packs in the boat and
a couple of croaker sacks and then he reach
over put something else in and then he looking
around see if he sprung a leak, and all the while
he singing about the devil and his daughter,
how she was a pretty young thing had a way
of putting men on they backs when they wunt
looking and every now and then she©d up and
marry one for spite only she wunt never able
to hide nothing from her daddy. The old man
he singing like he know the girl hisself, and I
thinking say that does say a awful damn lot,
only then the old man he stop singing and look
up to the shack. He see me standing in the
shadow of them two pine tree.

"It about time you get up, boy" he say.
And then he say, "What you waiting on? Come
on. Aint nothing left for you to do now. The
boat it already loaded up." And he sitting on
the side of the boat.

I aint feel like move, but I moving just the
same, and then it seem like I scrambling down

the side of the bank and clutching at roots maybe bust my neck, and the old man it all he can do not to bust out laughing. Then we both in the boat and the old man he push us away from the bank with his oar, and then we moving up through the blackblue water, and he singing some more about the devil his daughter, and all of a sudden it have a funny feeling, like all the time the old man singing Im is belly up inside a alligator, aint nothing to hear or either see except maybe the wind whistle down through some alligator teeth. Then the old man he aint singing no more. He just whisper some. He telling me to watch out now cause he can smell some kind of alligator lurk about in the water, or maybe up along the bank.

Well I looking with that. I looking so hard my eyeballs peel back raw like onions, only aint nothing but the deep blue shadow of pine and sycamore and cypress twist up on the black-green bank, and some they branch-nails digging into the water, and they all cover up with moss. But the old man he just tell me to reach back and pick up a gig, cause there no telling how many alligators go be swimming past the boat by and by. Then he dont say nothing, and I wondering just where it is we going there so many alligators, only then it come to me. The old man he taking me to where he dump Long Jim in the water. My whole self go numb with that, and it feel like I been there before, and then the old man he saying say ready with that gig boy say what you doing I said ready he go get away without even a scratch you dont hurry up.

The alligator he sunk low in the blackblue aint nothing but two red eyes bubble up above the water give him away, and then he rise up a bit in the water, look like he give a alligator smile, like he been waiting on us maybe his whole life long, and then aint nothing but a wind-ripple where he gone down and under. The old man he see that smile same as me and he shaking his head he saying say we in trouble now a alligator smile like that mean only one thing mean all you can do is watch and wait and the alligator he know that the same so he watching and waiting aint nothing go outlast a alligator and when you just about ready to give up then the alligator he come lash out of the water and before you know it you and he you both is fighting on the same terms. The old man then he looking to the water, he almost resting on his oar, and I looking the same, only it hard to rest with a gig in my hand, and I wondering if that alligator he as much trouble as the old man been saying, maybe he aint even coming back.

Im is just about settle myself he aint when the old man he up in the boat and shouting and the alligator he rising fast from the blackblue water, his two red eyes burning holes in the

air, and Im is coming down with the gig, but
everything moving too too slow, excepting the
alligator, and all I coming down on is water,
and the alligator now he twisting around in
the water he curl his tail up around the boat,
and the old man he shouting for me to watch
that tail, and so I does, and then the tail it
come smashing down on top of the boat, and
before I done raise that gig again, it out of my
hands and in the water, and is then I heading
in after it, and the old man he heading in the
same, and then we both sinking down in the
water we alligator bait, only that alligator he
aint bother none cause he too busy smashing up
the boat with his tail. Im is trying grab a hold
of something, even that alligator, only everything slip away, and the more and more Im is
trying, the faster I going down, and deeper too,
and then it seem like there aint no reason try
any more, cause aint no use, so I stop, and the
only thought what come to me it about Long
Jim how he was eat up by a alligator and look
like the same damn thing go happen to me. It
hard to say what all happen next. First it feel
like something grab a hold of me from behind,
up around my collar, and I aint know exactly
what to do with that so I start kicking at it, and
I thinking say as long as I has both of my legs I
be going down kicking, only it dont do no good,
and then I feels the black of the water rushing
up around my head, and then around my arms

and legs, and I dont know ifn I at the bottom of
that swampwater lake or either up in the belly
of that rowboat-smashing alligator, and then
the rushing it stops, and then it feel like I being
drag up from the water and up along the bank
through the wood, and then it feel like dry, stiff
grass, and I aint know how long I been drag like
that, or where to, but then the dragging it stop,
and with that then I hear the old mans voice
saying say come on boy come on boy come on,
and then he grabbing hold of my legs and he
pump them up and down and up and down,
and before I knows what what I coughing up
some swampwater, taste like I coughing up a
couple three barrel of axle grease, and then I
open my eyes.

The old man he leaning over me and
rubbing at my arms and my legs, only all I see
is a ghost-white shadow up against the deep
blackblue of the sky, and feel like I aint any
skin left he rubbing so hard, and all the while
he saying say that the biggest alligator he ever
seen and he seen a few we just lucky he wunt as
smart as he was big that all he wunt too smart
must of got hisself a belly full of wood by now,
and Im is wondering if all that wood feel worse
than a belly full of water, and Im is hoping it
does, and just then the old man he stop with
the rubbing and the words, and he give me a
pig-knuckle smile like he know all along what
Im is thinking about, and then he sit on back

in the long dry grass and he staring up at the
sky, and his face it looking like he done had
all he want to eat and then some, and then it
sound like someone saying say I told you boy
aint nothing be afraid of, and maybe it the old
man talking, and maybe it aint, I aint hear just
where the words they blowing from, maybe it
the wind.

. . . *now when the next morning done come,*
along with it come a second man, and he wunt big
big like the first, but he had hisself a long black knife
hang down from his belt, and when he done heard
that alligator roaring and roaring, he done come
looking just like the first, and when he seen that
alligator sitting on top of that log, he done smile
wide he was saying say he was go teach that alligator
what was what and then it wunt go be no alligator
world no more, and with that the second man he
was waving his knife around like he was trying to
cut the air in two, and the animals up in them trees
they was looking out through de moss same as before
they was asking theyself what go happen this time
hope this second man he do better than the first they
been treed too long, and then the second man he
done jump on that alligator back he was holding his
knife up against the hot yellow sun and riding that
alligator like he on the back of a horse, and he kept
trying to stick that knife somewhere in the alligator
head, only it wunt as easy as he thought on account
of that alligator was thrashing this way and that,
and snapping at the air every time that knife come
down, and after a while it look like that second man
go ride that alligator three hundred day if that what
it take, and the animals they was cheering him on
like the three hundred day almost up, but then the

alligator he was up in the air roll back like he done the first time, and then the second man and his knife and the alligator they was all tumbling into the water, and the second man he was twisting around look see where his knife was at, only all there was was the blackgreen water full up with a bluegreen alligator, and with that he didnt know what to do, so he start swimming for the bank, only he wunt much for swimming so the alligator he aint have no trouble come up from behind grab hold of a leg, and before the second man he even think to give a kick, that alligator he done gobble him up same as the first, and with that he was back on his log and he was roaring and roaring say just me and my world, and this time he done roar all the way through the night, and the animals they was shaking they heads some more they was saying say they wunt ever go get out of them trees, and it was looking like they might be right . . .

Songs

-1-

A great deal of time has passed, almost without his noticing, which is, perhaps, not so unusual for a man who has lived his life outside the normal bounds, outside of time, so to speak. So there he is now, sitting inside his cabin in the summer-hazy isolation of an old man. It is a too too hot evening, early evening, and also moist, and the sky is a heavy, sickly green color, which means that from somewhere a storm is coming. But Thaddeus does not bother about the storm. He seems almost oblivious to its coming. He is sitting there with the windows closed in spite of the heat, and he is shivering slightly even as he is perspiring in the closed-window   stuffiness of the cabin, and he wonders how it can be cold in August, but he does not really mind. He is sitting at the table eating crabs and the lamps are not lit and the sickly green light from outside does not seem to penetrate the hazy, enveloping dark of his eating, and he does not mind this either. Then he looks to the window and blinks at the dying green light which does not come in and he thinks that even the sky is dying and then he looks away from the window to the crab bones scattered carelessly about the table, finds one with a scrap of meat clinging to it, gnaws on it,

chews the meat, and while he chews he begins
reliving his life, though quite without meaning
to, from the time of that visiting Reverend's
daughter to the time of Kilby and the crabs, but
it's all mixed up in his head, fragments, parts
left out, the confusion of a dream, as if the life
that was is slowly merging with the life that
is, the inevitable mingling of the past with the
present. . .

> *O come and join our boisterous band,*
> *Our women and wine we'll share;*
> *We soon shall reach the promised land,*
> *And drink whatever's there.*
>
> *We'll grab a jug, it wont be long,*
> *We'll empty it by and by;*
> *Then arm in arm we'll sing this song,*
> *And laugh until we cry.*

The show had not yet begun, and a young
Thaddeus was thinking about the girl from
Charleston, he'd been looking at her a while
but he didn't know what to say it was like his
mouth didn't work and that troubled him and
then today she'd come up and they started
talking and then she said why didn't the two of
them get together after the meeting her daddy
had gone down to Jasper county for a couple
of days there wasn't nobody to bother them,

and Thaddeus he had said that he would. He
was part of a group of men standing outside
the tent, but not really a part, and the men sang
and laughed and whistled at the pretty women
who flashed by on their way into the tent, and
some not so pretty. They sang mostly taproom
ditties, although when the more prominent of
the town passed by they dropped the words
and it sounded a little like they were humming
hymns, and when they whistled at the women
they made suggestive gestures with their hands
and laughed when these were noticed and then
abruptly ignored.

One of the men, grizzled, whiskey on
his breath, an old brown coat in spite of the
warmth, nodded at Thaddeus and asked if he'd
heard this here preacher the last time he come
to town, they had themselves a real good time
then, why the sheriff himself he had to come all
the way out break things up, of course everyone
knew he would, the sheriff, he didnt hold too
much with tent preachers, especially those
that liked to sing and dance and maybe have a
drink, not since he was married he didnt, his
wife she believed in a dry state, at least ever
since they passed the Prohibition.

Then the grizzled man laughed.

"Them deputies gonna have a hell of a time
tonight if the sheriff sends „em over this way,"
and he pointed to a single car parked on the
other side of the road maybe a hundred yards

away, the car turning black in the late evening
light, a couple of deputies sitting on the hood.
Then he laughed some more.

Thaddeus looked to the deputies, two skinny
men, each a shadowy reflection of the other,
like twins, black hair, not so tall, unshaven,
guns stuffed loosely in their belts, looked to be
talking quietly, not paying much attention to
the men and women gathering beneath the large
white tent.

Then the others started talking, laughing.

"What you wanna bet that young Sheriff
Aikens come busting in by nine o'clock," said
a longnosed man in mudgray workpants and a
faded yellow shortsleeve. "And his Uncle Walter
in the crowd too."

"You mean the Judge," said a man with
bigred ears, bigred hands.

"That's the one."

"He'd be crazy bust in on the Judge."

"He would at that."

"But it'd be something to see now, wouldn't
it. Like two pigs in a poke. I'd pay five dollar
see something like that. Cash money too."

"I'll bet you five dollar the Sheriff dont
do nothing," said a man in corduroy pants
smoking a Pall Mall. "He probably home right
now busting into that pretty young wife of his?
You ever see the way she wiggle her hips when
she walk down the street? Man, I wouldn't let
nothing get in the way of me and them hips."

The men murmuring with enthusiastic agreement, laughing some more, the possibility of encountering the softwiggling hips of Mrs. Albert Aikens eclipsing all thoughts of a nighttime raid. At least for the moment. Then a puzzled voice coming from the man with the bigred ears, bigred hands.

"What he doing with a wife like that?"

"Not enough, that's for sure."

"You think he know that?"

"Hell, no. He too busy busting up revival meetings."

The men laughing some more, then the longnose and the Pall Mall man giving five dollars each to the bigred to hold, then shoving their dollarempty hands in their pockets, fat, wagerhappy smiles spreading across their faces.

"They gonna have a hell of a time," said the grizzled man, and then he turned to Thaddeus and asked if he wanted a snort, and when Thaddeus shook his head the grizzled man smiled, relieved perhaps, slipped his hand into his coat and pulled out a jug of whiskey, uncorked it, took a snort, corked it and then back into his coat. Just in case this show wasnt as good as the last one he said, and then he smiled again. Then the men sang some more.

Again Thaddeus looked to the deputies and wondered how long it was going to be before the sheriff arrived. He remembered the last time they played Barclayville. Someone put

a couple of shots into the Conover piano and
an old woman in the front row fainted from
the excitement. Thaddeus laughed to himself.
Then a blackbooted usher stepped from the tent
and announced that the meeting was about to
begin it being eight o'clock or close enough and
anybody who wanted a seat better grab one
now there wasnt gonna be no one putting out
more chairs, and with that Thaddeus and the
barbershop four of his waiting there lilted into
the tent and sat down in the back.

The crowd did not quiet down immediately, did not really ever quiet down. Some
were singing taproom ditties not unlike the
song which the grizzled man and his friends
had sung outside. Some were drinking on the
sly, look about to see who was watching, then a
snort or two, just in case. Some were laughing,
and every now and then a woman would cry
out stop that, and the laughter would swell.

Then the grizzled man poked Thaddeus in
the stomach.

"We're gonna have a hell of a time tonight,
deputies or no deputies" he said.

Thaddeus nodded politely, noncommittally,
but all the while he was thinking he sure as
hell hoped so, but he was thinking of later, then
the grizzled man took another snort from his
jug and Thaddeus looked away, waiting, then
looked to the platform. The Reverend Jacobs
was sitting there, an inscrutable calm about the

man, and beside him sat the other one, the one
not gone to Jasper county, his hands fluttering
about uselessly, from fear of crowds, perhaps.
Then the aging, genderless one behind the
piano struck a note, and the three pearl-throated
women and the four soft- singing young men
of the choir behind them began to sing a
Presbyterian hymn, though at first the song
was barely audible on account of the boisterous
almost savage nature of the crowd. But soon the
music began to swell and the crowd grew silent
with anticipation and the air grew still and it
seemed for a moment that everyone was holding
their breath.

Then the Reverend Jacobs was standing at
the podium and he motioned to the choir and
the singing stopped, and everyone exhaled,
slowly, but the Reverend did not speak. He
looked at this crowd of withering expectation
with the practiced eye of a dealer in horse flesh.
Then he pulled out his black leather bible, held
it high in the air as if it were a ringleaders whip,
and then he snap snapped it with a supple jerk
of his wrist, and the men and women in the
crowd jumped.

Then he spoke in a low, gravelly voice.

"Ladies and gentlemen, I have not seen, I
say I say I have not seen such wickedness in a
congregation as I am witnessing here tonight.
Not in forty years, ladies and gentlemen. You
ought to be ashamed of yourselves. But you are

not. You ought to bow down before the Lord
and ask his forgiveness. But you will not."

And he stepped into the crowd and shook
his black bible fist at the people.

"You will not, and do you know why you
will not?"

The people shifting uncomfortably in their
seats.

"Do you know why you will not bow down
before the Lord? Yes, you. And you. And you.
You will not bow down before the Lord because
you have made of your world a new Sodom and
Gomorrah. Yes you have, ladies and gentlemen.
You all are living a life of depraved and
repugnant excess."

And the Reverend held in his gaze the pale
faces of those he had pointed out with his bible,
and the others in the tent tried to look away, to
either side of those flashing, bible-black eyes, to
avoid, perhaps, being pointed out themselves.
But they could not look away.

"But you will not escape the vengeance of
the Lord."

Then the snap snap of the black bible whip
and the crowd jumped a second time and the
good Reverend was now roving back and forth
through the crowd, a contorted leer of satisfaction and contempt on his face.

"Yes, ladies and gentlemen. I say, I say
you will not escape. No one escapes from the
vengeance of the Lord. But you, you are like a

man I once knew, all of you are. He thought he
could escape. This man I once knew, and he was
a giant of a man, stood well over seven feet tall,
he thought he could escape. But he could not.
He lived a life of the wildest, most beguiling
depravity, and thought he was a world unto
himself. But he could not escape the vengeance
of the Lord."

And the men and women beneath the white
canvas bigtop began to sway back and forth,
back and forth, listening to the words of the
ringling Reverend Jacobs with the rare and even
unsettling attentiveness of those hypnotized by
the mystique of the center ring.

"But let me tell you, ladies and gentlemen, I
say I say let me tell you now all about this man
I once knew, so you may judge for yourselves
the truth of what I say. He belonged to a circus,
but not just any circus. No, indeed, ladies and
gentlemen. The show of shows, the sign said, a
panorama of the uncommon, the unusual, the
unheard of. It was a scene of the most profligate
extravagance to rival anything the ancients had
ever experienced. This was a show you did not
want to miss."

The image of the circus beginning to take
root, the men and women longing to witness the
show of shows.

"And this man I once knew, he was the
most uncommon of them all. Yes he was ,
ladies and gentlemen. He claimed to be the

world's strongest man, yes he did, and the
most beautiful as well, and so he was, a seven
foot colossus of the modern era to rival the
likes of Hercules or Apollo himself. And some
wondered why they were not as strong or as
beautiful, and they despaired, they looked
deep down into their immortal souls and they
thought the Lord had done them wrong."

A flurry of soulful, despairing looks.

"And the most beautiful women in the world
would throw themselves at his feet, and he
would devour them, as a savage beast devours
its prey."

A few in the crowd getting down on their
hands and knees, becoming savage beasts
themselves, looking for something to devour.

"But they paid their dollars. I say, I say
they paid their dollars to see this man who was
a beast. They paid their dollars to partake of
the savage and yet beguiling depravity of that
circus among circuses. Yes they did ladies and
gentlemen."

Snap, snap, snap.

"And afterwards some were invited to go
still further, for every night these people of the
high wire threw an after- midnight extrava-
ganza in honor of their seven foot savage, and
always on board their libertine circus train, a
train over one-thousand cars long, a train which
never went anywhere more than once, a train of
consummate excess."

Snap, snap, snap.

"And for a single dollar, ladies and gentlemen, I will show you what they saw. Yes I will. For a single dollar I will show you this man who was a beast and everything he was a part of. I will help you feel what they felt. And all for a single dollar."

"A single dollar single dollar single dollar dollar dollar."

And the crowd of men and women were overwhelmed by the words of the Reverend, or so it seemed, and they roared in uninhibited appreciation, the ringling Reverend smiling again, the satisfied, leering look still perched on his face, and then he cracked his blackbiblewhip and two ushers in black ties and black jackets got up from each end of the platform and made their way down the sides of the tent to the back, each with a large golden plate in hand, the genderless piano player playing an earthy, eager, almost unrestrained rendition of *Where Cross the Crowded Ways of Life*, the pearl-clad choir joining in, and the men and women of this circus-train congregation rummaging madly through their pockets and purses and wallets and then piling dollar after dollar upon the passing-by plates. Even the sour-smelling, grizzled acquaintance of Thaddeus added to the pile. And when the last of the money had been collected, the ushers hurried to the platform, the plates piled high with single dollars and their

hands on top, the ringleader Reverend now
smiling a broad smile at the dollarempty faces
of the men and women, at the two ushers, at the
plates, a carnival barker smile, a get-what-you-
can-while-the- gettings-good smile, smiling and
nodding and smiling,

    this is it ladies and gentlemen snap snap
snap

    i've seen you looking at me

    the moment you've all been you've what
waiting for

    i've seen you, but i don't mind

    now you will see for yourself

    you don't

    he's got them now, the young man thought
to himself, it's gonna to be one hell of a show

    snap snap

    unh-uh

    snap

    and he wanted to join in the fun, for there
was something compelling about what the
Reverend promised

    now my daddy would mind

    one hell of a show

    but i dont

    you don't?

    i've been looking at you too

    but he did not join in

    snap snap snap

    The ringling leader Reverend now whirling
his way through the crowd, up towards the

platform, towards the podium, and then back the other way again, and all the while cracking his blackbiblewhip, and the crowd ducking with every snap snap snap of his arm, and some howling, the rage of bestiality in their eyes.

"See the longest circus train in the history of circus trains pull out from the city of Charleston, over one-thousand cars of the most scintillating entertainment found anywhere in the civilized world. The greatest assortment of man and beast ever assembled."

From somewhere there was the sound of a train pulling out.

"Hear the howling of the monkeys, the growling of the lions caged in the rear, the rumblings of the elephants as they stumble against each other, the coarse shrieks of the majestic birds of prey. Yes, ladies and gentlemen, I said, I said hear all these strange and exotic sounds, and many more besides, direct from that darkest of continents. The faraway continent of Africa."

"The darkest of the darkest of the dark." More men and women becoming beasts. snap snap snap

"See the seven foot colossus, the wonder of the modern world, upon that very train. See him walk from car to car, the cloak of a sheik upon his back, a willing throng of men and women following his every move. And see him remove that cloak."

And it seemed to the men and women who were beasts that the good Reverend removed his own heavy black coat and hat as he spoke, and also the too too white shirt underneath, and then everything but his socks, and with that they fell upon each other, ripping shirts from backs and skirts from hips.

snap

"See the women of his harem dance rings around his nakedness, their hands upon his chest, his arms, his legs, his body rubbed with oils from arabia, his face smiling the smile of a sheik, then this majesty of the circus train taking the women one by one."

snap snap snap

And the men and women howled with glee, for they were all of them beasts now. The lust of the ringling Reverend's words danced within their newly naked souls. Or so it seemed.

"See the men of this traveling-by-rail sheikdom taking those that are left, one by one then none. See the unbridled lust of men and women become savages, the naked arms, the naked legs, the naked breasts, the naked hips."

snap snap snap

"Yes, ladies and gentlemen, yes."

(And the ringling Reverend snap snapped his whip to the rhythm of his words and the men and women who were beasts squirmed faster and faster)

snap snap snap

(their naked bodies squirming in the grass
beneath the white canvas bigtop)
    snap snap snap
(and then some up on all fours and howling
and barking as if they had treed the devil and
then back down in the squirming seething grass
of the Reverends conjuring)
    snap snap snap
(the whip of the ringling Reverend urging
them faster and faster and faster)
    so you
    snap
    so you doing anything tonight, i mean after the
show
    snap, snap
    no i, i wasn't doing a thing
    snap
    i was hoping you'd say that
    snap
(then the naked bodies of the men and
women who were beasts lay panting on
the grass under the large white tent their
backs bared to the good Reverends stinging
blackbiblewhip)
    ladies and gentlemen
(the ringling Reverend back at the podium
now and he snapped his whip and the men
and women who were beasts became men and
women again)
    i said i said ladies and gentlemen
    snap snap snap

(and then the men and women sat down on
the benches still naked still panting and they
saw that the Reverend was fully clothed)

ladies and gentlemen just look at yourselves
you ought to be ashamed

snap snap snap

you are just like that man i once knew the
man on that irredeemable circus train well let
me tell you what the good Lord had in store for
that one let me tell you about the vengeance of
the Lord for when he looked down upon that
train he saw the very wickedness of sodom and
gomorrah come to life a second time and he
could not believe his eyes so he called a council
of angels and they looked down from heaven
and they all agreed that such a phenomenon
was most unquestionably unnatural was in fact
a natural impossibility and should therefore be
destroyed immediately and the Lord agreed and
commanded that the train be struck from the
tracks

(the men and women moaning with despair
at the thought a protracted ohhhhhhhhhhhhhhhhhhhhhhhhhh whirling around the tent or
maybe they were just shivering in the nakedness
of their no longer being beasts)

and when the Lord had spoken a single
angel departed from the host and came down
from heaven an angel of the most prodigious
muscular capabilities why his right arm alone
was thicker than the mightiest of the great

cedars of ancient Lebanon and the angel held
aloft a mighty sword a sword forged in the
fires of a time before man a time before time a
time of volcanoes and molten rock this sword a
sword of fire itself and when the angel neared
the train he heard the sounds of that most
primordial passion and down came the mighty
sword and the sound of steel on steel echoed
throughout the land

(and the moan again for the nakedburning
men and women could hear that coming down
sword)

some thought those terrible giant lizards of
a thousand millennia past had reawakened from
their paleozoic slumber deep within the darkest
catacombs of the earth and walked again across
the continents of the modern world

ohhhhhhhhhhhhhhhhhhhhhhhhhh

(the Reverend thinking of an even larger
second collection)

and some thought the incandescent immor-
tality of the sun had collided with the earth that
the end had most assuredly come

ohhhhhhhhhhhhhhhhhhhhhhhhhh

and some thought they heard the raging
voice of God as if God himself had descended
in judgment upon all mankind yes indeed ladies
and gentlemen the sound of that sword upon
that train was unlike any sound heard within
the memory of man

snap snap snap

but what of us what of us what of us us us

(and the ringling Reverend heard their
words the leering satisfied look expanding and
he spoke again)

i see a most sombrous sight awaiting you a
most sombrous sight of carnage and destruction
yes i do ladies and gentlemen for like that man
i once knew you are also riding that circus train
yes you are you are all riding into the railway
darkness of sodom and gomorrah see the naked
corpses of men and women scattered across the
side of a mountain their bodies twisted beyond
recognition amid the wreckage of wheels and
twisted iron

snap snap snap

(the men and women saw the wreckage)

see the stunned survivors looking from body
to body in a naked disbelief most profound

(the men and women looking at each other
in the nakedness of disbelief)

see the savage beasts of those darkest of
jungles acquire a most immediate taste for
human blood

snap snap snap

(the men and women shuddering)

see the majestic lions of africa run down the
shrieking sheiks

(and some heard the roar of the lions
prowling outside and ran from their chairs and
hid beneath the platform and some did not
know where to hide and some just fainted)

see the hordes of howling monkeys feast
upon the flesh and bones of the dead and dying
     (and some heard the howls of monkeys
echoing in the air above and fell to their knees)
     yes indeed ladies and gentlemen see a sea
of cataclysmic upheaval a scourge of dynamic
dimensions yes indeed a veritable rain of fire
and death fallen upon the immoral heads of the
wicked each and every one
     snap snap snap
     (and with that the men and women who
were no longer beasts cried out in earclutching
prayer)
     save us Lord save us from the fire of the
howling sword of the monkeys prowling in the
fire of the fire of the save us from the lions of
the Lord
     (then the ringleader Reverend snap snapped
his whip a final time and those who were not
kneeling joined those who were and they all
bowed down their heads before the imagined
incendiary might of the Lord all of them naked
still even the grizzled man who had offered
Thaddeus a snort went to his knees though
he seemed more concerned with the where-
abouts of his somehow missing jug than with
the possibility of death by fire but the young
man name of Thaddeus was not kneeling not
praying he was thinking again about the girl
from Charleston so he stood up and walked out
through the flap a pause then one more look

and then he turned from the nakedglow of the
men and women at prayer the dollarglow of
the two reverends on the platform then looked
out into the darkness of the night and he saw
the black shapes of wagons maybe some trucks
moving in from the road towards the tent they
were moving and he walked to meet these
wagons these trucks a step or so he walked
and then he stopped watched waited then the
wagons and the trucks slowed and then stopped
a dozen or so in all each with a dozen or so men
and then the men climbed out down a joggle of
arms and legs assembling in the grassy heavy
heaving dark then the joggle marching towards
the nakedburningorangeglow of the tent
bubbling up against the dark dark sky the joggle
marching with the rigid yet nervous dignity of
men who carried guns but had never had the
opportunity to use them)

    snap snap snap

    (and as they neared the tent a thin wiry
shadow separated itself from the group and
then a thin wiry voice)

    load em up boys goddamn jaybird naked
evangelists load up as many as you can get a
hold of

    (and with that the dozen dozen men ran past
the watching Thaddeus and into the bubbleglow
of the tent some waving their guns in the air
and shouting and some not and then came the
thin wiry shadow and Thaddeus saw it was the

sheriff though not so tall not so old not the kind
of sheriff one expected in a small South Carolina
town the sheriff watching his men and then
smiling at Thaddeus giving him an elbowpoking
angled up)

thems good boys to have at your back

(then the sheriff laughing a thin and wiry
laugh also then running into the nakedbub-
bleglow of the tent himself)

load em up boys load em up

(and the men and women saw the dozen
dozen running wild through the flap the sheriff
running also the men and women no longer
praying no longer contemplating the incendiary might of the Lord or so it seemed and the
Reverend saw them also him kneeling by the
plates and stuffing his pockets with dollar bills
and then looking out again and the other one
the one not gone to Jasper county still sitting in
his chair not sure just what a reverend should
do during a raid his hands still fluttering about
uselessly and the men and women now scrambling over chairs and under them the men
and women naked still some hiding beneath
the platform some of them sifting through the
mostly abandoned clothes on the ground then
grabbing whatever they could the grizzled man
sitting on the ground between two chairs at the
back of the tent sitting on the folds of his coat
the missing jug in his hand and all the while the
piano player was playing though the choir had

fled and the sheriff and his boys riding herd
through the crowd their guns waving wildly
in the air a couple of shots then a couple more
then a shout and then grabbing at this arm at
that some of the men and women struggling
and some not and some not knowing what to
do)
    load em up boys loademup
    snap
    (and then some of the men and women were
edging under the sides of the tent then running
into the night the tent stakes popping loose
behind them the tent collapsing the white of the
canvas settling down upon the ground like a
shroud down upon the naked men and women
and the still-playing piano player and upon
the dollarhappy reverend and the other one his
hands fluttering still and upon the sheriff and
his boys and their guns and the young man
name of Thaddeus scrambling away from the
settling shroud back through the dark moist
grass of the field then stopping looking to the
ghostly white of the canvas spreading out upon
the ground the sound of the piano drifting
above it all like the very soul of those beneath
the sound escaping up into the next world or so
it seemed then the voices of those underneath
the men and women shouting)
    this way no this way no this way no this
(then the sheriffs thin wiry voice)
    we got em now boys we got em now

(then some laughter then a shout then a
gunshot then a gruff and gravelly voice)
   you best tell your boys to let go of my arm
Albert (then silence)
   (then the sheriffs voice a bit thinner now)
that you Uncle Walter
   you heard me
   yes sir Uncle Walter sir you heard him boys
say let go of his arm that Uncle Walter
   and while they at it you tell em to let go of
the rest of them folks then head on home
   you heard him boys we done enough for
tonight
   (then the ringleader Reverends voice
billowing up and out)
   bow down your heads i said i said bow
down your heads
   this way no this way no this way no this way
   (then one by one the voices slipping out
from underneath the edge of the tent some
becoming naked men and women some
clutching clothes in their hands some not then
off into the dark then some becoming the
deputies no longer waving their guns in the
air no longer in pursuit then to the black of the
wagons the trucks one becoming the sheriff
another becoming the sheriffs uncle a large
pink man pink ears a pink belly a white but
bootstreaked shirt the sheriff hanging on to the
uncles elbow the uncle buttoning up his shirt
tucking it in his pants)

i sure is sorry about all this Uncle Walter i
mean i mean i sure is sorry

come eight o'clock tomorrow morning you
best be at the courthouse you hear me Albert

yes sir Uncle Walter i will i mean i do i mean
yes sir yes sir

(then the uncle rolling his pink ears his pink
belly

buttoned now into the black of a carriage
then hip switching then off into the black of the
field the sheriff watching him go then into an
old ford the sheriff nodding firmly to his boys
a time-we-went-home kind of nod then the rest
of wagons the trucks rolling off into the black of
the field also)

-2-

He had felt the island before he had actually
seen it. And then it loomed before him, a gray
lump spreading out against the heavy, black
horizon. He rowed towards the shore, and then
he felt the rowboat scudding over the sandy
bottom and he got out and pulled it up onto
the narrow stretch of beach. The moonlight
glinted off the sand, and Thaddeus thought
to himself, it is more like I am dreaming now
than when I first saw myself coming here. Yes,
this is the place. And he was certain of himself
this time, for he had been to several islands the

past month, many islands, or so it had seemed,
each one rising up out of the seagrassy sea of
that beckoning voice and then he would be
standing on a beach and watching the seagulls
and the fish that had washed up or he would
see the hazy, early morning silhouettes of
people in the distance but when he got closer
the people would be gone or maybe he would
stumble across the twisted remains of a dock
half-buried in the sand and that's all there
was, but none of these islands had measured
up to the image from his dream, none had felt
right, there had been a vagueness about them,
an emptiness, an incompleteness, and then the
voice would start up again and he would get
back into the boat and try another island. But
he felt a completeness here. He felt like he had
come home. The voice from his dream would
bother him no more. Then he left the boat and
went dripping across the mooncooled sand and
up into the long grass of the dunes, but not
far. Stretching out in the sandy, grassy earth,
his heels digging in, he fell asleep. But he did
not sleep long, and when he woke he heard the
sound of men talking, and the spit and hiss of a
small fire. The men and the fire were very close.

"What you mean about de devil?"

"He dont mean nothing. Willie here been
talking bout de devil since before you was
born."

"What you mean?"

"I mean I seen him dat's what I mean. I was out here one night was after midnight, must of been dis very spot too, and I wunt doing nothing jes sitting thinking maybe looking to de dark blue waves come rolling in and den from out de dark I done heard de slap slap slap of a oar and den in come a old patchup rowboat look like it was about to sink.   It was den I done seen a man standing up in de bow of dat boat, only he wunt no ordinary man, no sir, looked like de devil hisself come to life."

"How'd you know he was de devil?"

"I jes know'd, dat's all. He was wearing a black coat, a black hat, had hisself a gold chain hang round his neck, a couple of gold ring, and he was holding on to looked like de staff of Moses only it had de head of a snake on it, and all de while he was riding in dat boat he was staring across de waves his eyes looking straight at de island, and red too, like he was trying to burn everything down. De next thing I know'd he was out of dat boat and we was standing face to face down de beach a ways, and de devil he give out a crooked kind of laugh seem to be coming from everywhere, and den he done said it was about time he made my acquaintance, and den he done stuck his Moses staff in de sand like dat and den everything bust loose. De snake head it open its eyes and start twisting and turning and flicking its tongue and den it give a hissssssssy sound like it dying, only it

wunt, and den a red fire come out of its mouth
burn a circle in de sand, dere was fire all de way
around, and me and de devil we was standing
in de middle of it, and den de devil he grab
hold of my shoulders toss me to de sand and
we was wrestling like we both born to it. Some
of de time de devil he was up on top and some
of de time was me, legs and arms and shoulders
and hips churning up de sand, de sand flying
dis way and dat, de hot of dem flames burning
red across my face across de devils face almost
looked like we was wrestling wid fire, and
den de fire it was gone, and de devil he was
standing by his boat been pull up on de sand,
only he was looking too spit and polish to been
wrestling like he was, wunt even a button pop
off his coat, and den he done look me over and
he said de night was almost over but he'd come
back some other night and we'd wrestle some
more, and den he give me his crooked smile
again and step into his boat, and den he was
gone. And dat de truth."

"What kind of truth you talking about?"

"Truth is truth."

"He was gone cause he wunt never dere, and
dat de real truth."

"Truth is truth."

"Say Willie, when you think de devil he go
come back and wrestle wid you some more?"

"Dont know for sure. De devil he didnt say,
and no way of knowing neither. I expects I jes

has to keep my wits about me. De devil he show up any time he feel like it."

Thaddeus was sitting up now on the grassy slope of the dune, but the three men had not seen him in the uneasy glare of their talking and the glow of their fire against the night. They had been there only a short while, but already there were scads of empty beer bottles scattered about. But they didn't bother about these. They laughed and talked and drank and tossed a few more empties to the sand and then they talked some more. The one doing most of the talking sat furthest from the fire, almost in the shadows, the bald arc of his head glistening with only the faintest flicker of light, the posture of a prophet, or so he seemed to think. And the one doing most of the listening did so with almost ritual misgivings, a little round face leaning forward, slowly, looking into the fire, then to the other two, then leaning back and looking to the jagged darkness beyond with pleading, perspiring, round-faced eyes and the unexpressed but religious hope that dawn would come suddenly and brightly. And then there was the one doing most of the drinking, a heavy-set man in a faded, grease-soaked baseball cap, a lazy dignity in the way he leaned slightly to one side, mostly drinking, but every now and then looking up at the other two and then a word of advice.

"You suppose he go come tonight?"

The voice belonged to the little round-faced man, and he hunched up closer to the fire. The bald-headed prophet smiled. The man in the baseball cap looked up from his almost empty bottle and shook his head.

"Man, I told you Willie here he jes talkin. Aint no devil comin back. Tonight nor any other night."

"But jes supposin he do?"

The bald-headed prophet smiled again.

"Ifn he do he do. I aint seen de devil but once in my life but I done held my own. I expect I can do de same again. Ifn he do."

And with that Thaddeus slipped from the grassy dune of his concealment to the sandshadows of the beach and into the light of the small orange fire. The three men stopped laughing, stopped talking, stopped drinking, their eyes fixed on this figure of their superstition come to life, their eyes brittle like church glass, the unanimity of their silence like church glass also. Thaddeus cocked his jaw as if to speak, but he didn't, and then he sat down. For maybe five minutes he stared at the silent, waiting, firesinged men, and they stared back, but they were looking through him more than at him, as if the reality of what they saw was still sitting back among the shadows of the dunes. He smiled at these three unmoving almost shadows of men, but still they did not respond. His face was beginning to sweat in the orange

glow of the fire, and he wiped the sweat from
his brow and his hand on his pants. Then he
thought perhaps he would become the devil for
these firewaiting silencesinged men, a thought
so random and absurd he almost burst out
laughing, and yet it was also intriguing. Then he
smiled a second time.

"What are you boys all doing out here?" The
three men said nothing.

"You dont mind if I join you, do you?"

The three men still said nothing, their eyes
filled with the image of a squatting, sandspitting
devil, their eyes about to burst into a thousand
pieces, a single image becoming a thousand then
a thousand more. Then Thaddeus looked into
the kaleidoscope of their eyes.

"I come over in that rowboat over there?"

Thaddeus nodded towards the gray,
shadowy heap of the rowboat several yards
from where they sat, the boat turned over and
pulled up from the water, but not all the way.

"I've been going up and down the coast in
that goddamn boat for how long only the devil
knows. Seems like I aint been on dry land in
a month of Sundays. You all have any more of
that beer? I could sure use a swallow."

But with that the eyes like church glass
broke into a thousand thousand pieces. The
little round-faced, round- eyed man was the
first. He looked from Thaddeus to the gray,
heaping shadow of the rowboat and the waves

lapping there to the one named Willie, the little
man's round face getting rounder, and then
he scrambled to his feet, kicking sand into the
fire, and then he was gone down the beach. The
one in the baseball cap was next. He looked
first to the not-yet-empty bottle of beer in his
hand, then to Thaddeus, to Willie, and then he
dropped his bottle and scrambled after the first
one. Willie was the last. He looked from the
orange-glowing fire to the seemingly smoky
silhouette of Thaddeus squatting in the sand
to the heap of the rowboat and the swelling
memory of his story and the devil he had fought
and finally to the shallow craters where the
other two had been, a look of fat desperation
dripping down the sides of his face, unwilling
to believe, it seemed, in the efficacy of his own
bald-headed prophecy. Then Thaddeus moved
closer to the prodding warmth of the fire and
looked up and grinned, but before he could say
another word, the prophet named Willie was
running after the other two.

Within weeks of Thaddeus coming to the
island he had seemingly forgotten about the
Reverend and the girl and even Gabriel and
the grave beneath the fallen cedar and how
Gabriel's life had been a warning to his own.
The delirium of his sudden banishment and the
time spent with the chain-bound trumpet player,
all of that seemed now like some fragment

from a childhood nightmare, and so he had
put it aside. Even the dream that had brought
him to the island he had forgotten. Instead, he
abandoned himself utterly to the unthinking
festivity of Pappa Toms, and so it was that
ten years quickly passed. Grab a beer and sit
down. Talk to the girls and watch them bounce
up the stairs and the men following and then
fuck like the devil and then bounce back down.
And sometimes he'd pay a dollar himself and
go up the stairs and some of the ones he paid
for would ask if the stories were true and he'd
say what stories and they'd say the ones about
him turning into the devil soon as he got home
they'd always heard about the devil and how
big he was but they didnt know maybe it was
all talk, and he'd say there was only one way
to find out and then off they'd go for a couple
of nights, maybe even a week. And when ever
there was a new girl, Pappa Tom would point
her out and Thaddeus would think up some
excuse to go talk to her, though these conversa-
tions never lasted more than a couple of beers.
Of course Thaddeus had no single criteria for
the women he selected, though being young and
new was certain to rouse his interest, and he did
have a thing for blue blue eyes, or at least eyes
that could be mistaken for blue, but he never
became emotionally involved with any of them,
he was against that. Women were something to
be enjoyed, he thought, like the beer. But he'd

be damned if he'd let them sneak in and take
over his life. His life was not to be like other
lives. It hadn't been. It wasn't. The ramshackle
cabin of his indifference and the black squirrels
nesting in the eaves above or the raccoons in
the crawlspace below, and every afternoon catch
some crabs, and make a few dollars that way,
and then head on down to Pappa Toms and
buy a girl. Or maybe she didn't even need to be
bought. He hadn't bought half of them, they'd
just come up on their own and opened up their
legs. He didn't mind. But none of them had
ever said a word about the primitive, earthy,
dissolute squalor of his existence, not the ones
he'd paid for, nor the ones he hadn't, and god
damn anybody that did. His strength lay in the
doing of things his way.   And that was that.

Then he met Kiri Girl. For almost ten years
nothing had happened to challenge the dissolute
squalor his life had become. And now there she
was sitting there in the orange- gleaming light
of Pappa Toms, the two of them sitting at a
small table shoved up against the stairwell and
the shriek and smash of laughter all around,
like the sound of bottles breaking. Her sitting
directly across from him but looking away,
and him not remembering when she sat down
but wanting to ask. But he said nothing to Kiri
Girl. Not at first. Which was goddamn odd, he
thought. But it seemed that his mouth didn't
work, and he vaguely remembered the same

thing happening one time before, one time
before a woman had troubled him, or perhaps it
was a girl, but he couldn't place the other one,
and so he just sat there, staring at this woman,
this girl with blue blue eyes. And there she sat
with an air of noble almost scolding indifference
and those blue blue eyes staring off into space,
and it wasn't just Thaddeus she ignored, but
the sounds of the piano and the laughter and
the dancing and drinking, all of this whirling
around her and she did not respond. And then
it came to Thaddeus that maybe this girl was
not a girl, maybe she was a work of art, even
her face had the finely cut precision of a marble
statue, and with this in mind he leaned up over
the table and peered closely at the finely worked
skin of this unmoved and unmoving beauty,
so close he could almost taste it, feel it, yes, he
thought, she's one hell of a statue, his hands
moving up to confirm his suspicions, and then
quite without his expecting it, she did move,
sharply and suddenly, and he blinked some and
sat back a lump in his chair. Yes, once before he
had been troubled by a girl, but in the nearness
of this sculpted work of art, he had forgotten.
Then Kiri Girl spoke to Thaddeus, though even
he did not see her lips move.

"What you want from me."

He coughed some and blurted out a
response.

"You want to dance some?" he said.

"That what you want?"
"Yes."
"That all you want?"
Again the coughing.
"Yes."
And then his throat was clear.
"All right by me."

So they stood up in the smoky light of their watering eyes, the white and yellow string of bulbs flickering from the rafters, on then off then on then off again, an unending barrage of shadows flickering across his face and hers, or perhaps they were smiling at each other, but who could say. But they did not move from the table, and all the while they stood there they were looking at each other, eyes hooked into eyes, as if the piano and the music and the others dancing and laughing and drinking did not exist, as if all that they did not see were but a dream, and all that they did see were the only reality. They stood and stared at each other and then each became an image in the others eye, an image of a time that once was, like each was a mirror of the past, or at least she was, an image of youth, of beauty, an image of the sacred, and then the images were gone, and all that remained were the mirrors, empty mirrors waiting for some new image to fill their frames. Or so it seemed.

"You sure."
"Yes."

The music of the piano slowed, no longer a racing staccato now, it was something smoother, like the gentle roll of the black tidewater, and the dancing shadows of the others also slowed, even the walls were now rolling with the tide, a lazy black tide it seemed, hips curling around hips, arms curling around arms, and Thaddeus and this girl who was taken for a work of art waded into that black and rolling tide, arms curling around arms, hips curling around hips, then they were lost in the sweaty, heaving, swelling blackness, hallelujah. Later they had gone up to his cabin, though who had suggested it Thaddeus could not remember. But there they were, sitting at the table shoved up against the half-open window and the heavy, warm dark from outside coming in. The faint, faintly warm, yellow glow of an oil lamp showing itself in streaks on the table, and also faintly on the face of the girl.

But Thaddeus was turned away from the lamp.

"You know about me?"

"I know what they been saying."

"And what's that?"

"They been saying you is the devil."

"What do you think?"

"If you wants to be the devil that all right by me. Maybe I like the devil."

What she saw in this man who might have been the devil she never said. And he never

asked. But there was something there. It was
in the way she spoke, the coppery insistence of
her voice, and also the way she moved about
the room, a haughty indifference in every step,
and yet also a measured willingness. Then they
both moved from the table and the lamp to the
darkness of the back room and the sagging,
gray shadow of the bed and the lamp light not
reaching there, but they did not mind. Then
they were in the bed.

"So how bout I show you what the devil can
do?"

Kiri Girl smiled.

"What ever you want to do you just do it."

And then he was finished he rolled off the
girl name of Kiri Girl lay back in the sagging
bed of his exhaustion his head to one side to her
side propped up on his elbow he looked into
the blue blue of her eyes brightly shining blue
even in the dark and saw himself his nakedness
shining wet in the darkness of the pinetimbered
room a languid lover now the girl name of
Kiri Girl looked up and smiled her nakedness
shining in the darkness also she smiled again
and for a moment the darkness was gone as if
her whole body had smiled with the light of the
moon or of the sun her whole body the pliant
curve of her neck to her shoulders and arms
the slippingaway arc of her breasts slipping up
then down with every breath the gentle slope
of thigh to knee to calf her whole body smiling

with the light of the moon or of the sun and
yet he did not return her smile to do so would
have been to risk eternal damnation he felt
certain of that in this moment of his conquest
to do so would have been to tear off a little
piece of his soul and give it to the devil yes
that was it soon he would have nothing left and
the devil would have it all yes of course there
was nothing wrong with taking a woman to
bed especially one as willing as this one it was
perfectly natural an urge but nothing more and
there was nothing wrong with giving in to those
primitive urges nothing wrong with worshiping
the sun or the moon yet a man could only go
so far yes there was no use getting emotional
over such a thing as a woman and for a moment
the memory of the other one took root in his
brain and it was sharp and piercing and he
winced and then the memory was gone and it
was Kiri Girl once more yes, there was no use
getting emotional no it was better to curtail
the emotional part get rid of it entirely or if
that was not possible then give his emotions
to something else yes that was the trick let her
stay as long as she liked but not give in to the
emotions of it yes yes but all the same he better
watch out with this girl if he didnt well God
only knew what might happen if he didnt then
the man name of Thaddeus watched the girl
name of Kiri Girl and he fell completely into
those blue blue eyes and he knew that every-

thing he had ever thought or felt or hoped for
up till that moment had been a lie she was the
light of the moon or the sun and if she wanted
his soul it was hers for the taking and so he
watched her lying there next to him until he was
no longer sure why he was watching then the
girl smiled once more curled her hip around his
and closed her eyes and with that the light of
the sun was gone or perhaps it was the light of
the moon . . .

Ten months have passed in an instant. Or so
it seems. Ten months which he thinks he's just
forgotten. Like the ten years before Kiri Girl
and before that the dream of his banishment
and before that and before that and before that.
The years gone by in a shimmering, weaving
blur like rain. Or maybe the past never was.
Yes, that's it. He has always been here, the
living of his life and the salt-sweet smell of
the ocean and the breeze coming in and the
nights with Kiri Girl, and the mornings too.
This is all he has ever wanted. He does not
remember anything else. Him standing there at
one end of the porch. At the other end a clump
of blacks huddled together, a lantern hanging
above them, the lantern lit, swinging gently in
the night air, the yellow light mixing with the
shadows.
N o i t h u r t s n o i t h u r t s n o i t h u r t
s noithurtsnoithurtsnoithurts.

The voice of a woman screams through the
cracks of the pine-timbered walls and claws
at the ears of Thaddeus and the blacks. Then
Thaddeus moving to the window, and the heavy
silence that comes after such a scream, but still
it is there, the scrape and wretch of it, in the
pit of his stomach. But he does not show it. His
body does not even flinch, though this could
be just a trick of the light, the lantern flashing
across his face, and then shadows. He puts his
face to the window and it sticks there. He sees
Kiri Girl lying in bed, the brown bubble of her
stomach half-hidden by the white of the sheets
spread across her knees, her skin glowing with
the heat of perspiration. A covey of black-
womenfaces hovering around the bed, the girl,
folding and unfolding sheets, the women boiling
water on the top of the black stove, stroking her
arms her legs her brow with a cool, damp cloth,
singing softly, slowly, almost moaning, a song
about the birthing of a babies. Thaddeus listens
to the words a moment, the song lingering.
Then he turns from the window, absently,
helplessly, and waits for the next scream.

Then the blacks at the other end of the
porch, talking softly.

"She sure can carry a tune."

"She sure can."

"Aint like any music I ever heard."

"What music you talking about, you damn
near deaf, why if you done cover up you ears

with you bigknuckle hands wouldnt make no bit of difference."

Then the one who had spoken presses the flat of his hands against his ears and opens his mouth in silent song. The others laugh, a knowing laugh, some looking to the open-mouthed jester in their midst, some looking to the door, the windows of the cabin, and some looking to Thaddeus, a solitary figure leaning against the unfinished cut of a corner post, and then the laughter lessening, lessening, then lost in the darkness beyond the porch. Thaddeus puts his pipe to his mouth, strikes a match against the post, then brings the match to the pipe and inhales, the flame catching, the smoke rising, a cloud of white above his head. Then the woman screams again. And the blacks turn from the scream, some rubbing their ears, and talk some more.

"Sure hopes she has dat chile of hers soon enough," says one.

The others nod, some still rubbing their ears.

"It aint hers," says another, the voice almost inaudible.

"Dont care whose it is. I cant be listening to dat singing of hers much more."

"I said it aint hers."

"What aint. What you talking about?"

"If she keep singing like dat much more my ears they go fall off land on the floor."

"Mine too."

"I said de chile it aint hers."

The voice speaking with the determined febrile assurance of a prophet,speaking to willing ears, the absurdity of the statement obscured by the faintest possibility of its being true. Or so it seems.

"What you mean by dat?"

The others nod, no longer rubbing their ears, puzzled, intrigued.

"She giving birth to it right now."

"She givin birth but dat chile aint hers. Aint hers. Dat chile de chile of de devil hisself. You mark my words. De devil he jes using dat girl bring his chile into dis here world. You mark my words."

The clump of blacks huddle closer together beneath the light of the lantern, the blacks marking words perhaps, the voice of the prophet drawing them in. The prophet stands motionless in the middle of the clump, his bald head shining in the swirl of light and dark. Then the voices of the others break from the huddle, a swirl of light and dark, also.

"How you know dat Willie?"

"Yeah, how you know dat?"

But the prophet name of Willie simply raises his hand and the swirling voices stop. Then the prophet speaks again.

"De devil he done come among us. So says de Lord. De devil he done come to take our women for hisself. Jes like de serpent done in de

garden of Eden. You all know what Im is talking
about. He been doing dat ever since he done
come to dis here isle and we been let him too. Is
time we done put we heel to his snakeuglyhead
and give we heel a turn. Dat de only way deal
wid de devil I know of."

And with that the prophet name of Willie
retreats into the comfortable shadows of the
porch, the trace of a smile spreading across his
face. The clump of blacks huddle closer still, no
longer needing to mark words it seems, some
looking to the man name of Thaddeus who
has now become the devil, some looking to the
cabin again, to the girl inside giving birth to
his demon child, some hiding their faces in the
shadow of Willies smile, all of them aware of
the presence of the serpent at the other end of
the porch, the serpent coiled around the corner
post, all of them grgrgrinding the cups of their
heels into the soft wet pine- wood of the porch,
the grinding unconscious, perhaps, instinctive,
the heels turning faster and faster and faster.
The man name of Thaddeus turns at the sound,
looks to the clump of heelgrinding blacks
beneath the lantern, but says nothing, smokes
on his pipe some more, and then the tobacco
is used up. Then the blacks become frightened
and turn to the bald head of their prophet once
again.

"What you mean by we heels?"
"What we supposed to do?"

And the prophet hears the words of their fear and for a moment he does not answer. There is no answer, it seems. And the blacks wait for the prophet to confirm their suspicions. They wait a moment longer. And then the woman inside screams a third time and the silence of the prophet is forgotten.

"There she go some more."

"Aint she done?"

"Sound like she done hit the highest note on de scale."

"Sounds like it."

"Sounds like she done, you mean."

So Thaddeus turns from the darkness beyond the porch when the woman inside the cabin screams, turns once more to face the window, the door, the smoked-out pipe in his hand. Then the scream fades and he opens the door and steps inside and makes his way over to the woman and the bed and the child. The clump of blacks clump in behind him, silently, as if they are a reluctant shadow, and then they spread out against the wall. There is a heavy, warm, stifling stillness about the cabin. And also an emptiness. Kiri Girl lies in the bed, the sheets pulled up to her shoulders, she is sleeping now, the rhythmic rise and fall of her applehard breasts barely noticeable, a testament to the pain of giving birth perhaps. And the women who eased her pain stand stiffly behind the bed, almost bitterly, the hollow of their eyes looking

through him, he thinks, as if he were a doorway
to some other world. And then the door closes
and he sees the child, a small blueblack raisin
of a child in the arms of one of the women. The
child does not move. And then Thaddeus is
holding the child, he looks at its wrinkled face,
its wrinkled hands, and does not move either.
The child of the devil, the voice says. A whisper
from the shadows on the wall but Thaddeus
does not hear the words. The face of the devil.
The hands of the devil. Then the voice stops
for a moment and Thaddeus steps with the
child to the door and then they are outside. The
shadows on the wall become blacks again and
clump through the door and stop beneath the
light and dark of the lantern.

   Then the voice begins again.

   From that moment on Thaddeus did not
speak to the girl named Kiri Girl, or even really
think of her until after she abandoned him to
his misery of solitude some five years later,
and then when he did think of her in later
years it was with bitter, halting recollection,
not because she had left, but because he could
not separate the memory of her being there
from the unbreathing quiet of his still-born son,
and he did not speak to any one else either,
except for maybe a few words to get his crabs
sold, and that went on until after the end of
the second great war. But it was those first few

years that were the worst. He expected biscuits
for breakfast, and coffee, though how they came
to be on the table he never bothered to ask,
and then he would spend the day up along the
ocean side of the island and maybe catch some
crabs, at least that's what she thought he was
doing, but he rarely came home with anything
but an empty basket. At night he would
grumble over the beans, but never a word
directly her way, and then he would grab the
small red lantern and light it and off he would
go down the hill and vanish into the black black
wood. She used to stand there sometimes on
the porch and watch that red bead of light as
it bounced along, smaller, smaller, and then it
would be gone. And sometimes she was still
there in the morning when the light broke up
from the beach and settled in a soft, hazy blue
about the cabin, and there he was coming back
up the hill, and the light in the small red lantern
was out. But most of the time she was asleep.
And then this was always true. Of course she
often wondered where he went during the
night, and sometimes she would wake long
after midnight and feel the stifling emptiness of
the cabin closing in and she would imagine her
Thaddeus had gone to the devil, but most of the
time she figured what he did was his business
and let it be.

The only thing she never forgave him for
was taking the child without her say-so. Even

if it was dead it had been her child as much as
his. More so, she told herself, it was my stomach
it done come out of. He didn't do nothing but
stand on the porch and wait it out. But he never
told her what he had done with it. And she
never asked him. And then one day Kiri Girl
decided to leave. Why she had stayed so long
in the silence of his misery even she did not
know. Perhaps she had no where else to go. But
she left all the same. She watched Thaddeus go
off with his basket and his net and his pail of
rotting chicken heads, and then she packed up
her suitcase and headed into town. And when
this old man of her last day came back later that
afternoon, and he was an old man by then, or
at least he looked it with his suddenly white,
stringy, tangled hair and his black, black eyes of
hunch-backed bewilderment, he hardly noticed
she had gone.

-3-

"What you think he doing"
(dreaming)
"What you think"
(or not dreaming)
"Maybe he dead"
(his eyes closed)
"Maybe he aint"
(or half-closed)

But Thaddeus did not move. Perhaps he
could not move. He had not moved in almost
twenty years, or so he sometimes thought. The
birth of the stillborn child had robbed him
of his strength. But even though he did not
move, he watched with growing interest these
two adolescent boys of his half-dreaming as
they ran up along the sunwarmed beach and
then stopped to have a look at this old man
sleeping in the sand. They looked carefully,
suspiciously at the sunwarmed but strangely
white white face. As boys will when meeting a
would-be devil for the first time, a mixture of
awe and fear shaping their features. And then
they were the ones not moving. They looked
from the devilmaybeface of the old man to the
basket of crabs by his side to the pattern of
sticks and strings inching across the sand to the
murky yellow-green of the tidewater channel.
They saw fishheads drifting in the shallows.
Or maybe chickenheads. They saw a basket of
big blue crabs, the crabs fighting for a place in
the sunwarmed basket, the click click of their
claws sounding harsh, discordant, alarming
in the warm, sunny air. Then the smaller boy
seemed about to run off with the basket of click
click clicking, and the bigger boy was about to
follow, but then they stopped. The smaller boy
now with a smile stretched across his face. And
all the while the watcher watched.

click click

you see em, yousee
click

For a moment time stopped. The ripple of
the murky, yellow-green waves became like
glass, a glass of possibilities, perhaps. And
the two adolescent boys looked into this glass
and saw themselves, but were unaware of the
possibilities, or so it seemed. Then they looked
beyond themselves and they saw four giant
crabs crowding around the remains of a chickenhead, blue crabs, each as big in the eyes of
the boys as the sun or the moon or some other
celestial body, a phenomenon caused, no doubt,
by the refraction of light in water. Then the
glass became a ripple of yellow-green waves
again, the tidewater rolling in over the crabs,
the chickenhead, up the sandy bank, and then
back out, the crabs eating undisturbed, and
now the bigger boy down in the sand, taking
hold of the string, winding the string around
his wrist, winding slowly, slowly, the chickenhead moving through the sandsifted water,
and also moving slowly were the four crabs,
still undisturbed, following the half-eaten head,
the smaller boy so excited now he could fly
to the moon, or to the sun, then the smaller
boy shouting to the bigger boy, the bigger boy
blinking in the sudden glare of shouted words,
and then shouting himself

wheres the wheres the
click click

net

im is looking im is looking

wheres the

click

the smaller boy wondering where he was
going to find a net, wondering if the old man
had one, was sure he must, and the old man
no longer sleeping, suddenly rising from the
hardpacked sand, his eyes burning with the
white of the sun, or the moon, then shouting
about his crabs, his basket, the bigger boy
not moving, not saying a word, as if time had
stopped once again, the smaller boy turning,
heels sandkicking, the smaller boy then moving
through time, or so it seemed

cmon

not a word

you click click boys think you can rob a man
of his click click crabs and click click like that

what you

not a word

what you waiting for

you boys got a thing or two coming ifn thats
what you click click think

not a word cmon

then the smaller boy was running down the
beach as a smaller boy will run when being
chased by something larger older the devil
perhaps and the bigger boy eager to follow
tearing string from wrist then up and after but
catching his foot on the old mans basket the

bigger boy down in the sand a second time the
basket sandtwisting the once imprisoned crabs
now rolling towards the sea clickety clickety
clickety click the bigger boy wondering what
the devilmaybefaced old man had in store for
him the boy watching the blue crabs vanish
into the waves him wishing he could set free
the crab part of himself locked inside and then
vanish in the waves also as if his true soul were
that of a giant blue crab a kindred spirit to those
vanishing in the haze of the tidewater refuge
then the black of the old mans shadow looked
down on the boywannabecrab then down came
the net on the bigger boys head bigger but not
so big and whoosh his eyes went wide with the
fear that comes from being netted . . .

   Several hours later, after the boy had left
his cabin for home, Thaddeus stepped out onto
the porch.   There was still the smell of beans in
the air, and he breathed that in, and then there
was the night and it had come in heavy and
dark and there was the promise of a summer
storm and he breathed that in too, but no storm
came. Then Thaddeus went back inside and
fumbled a bit with a kerosene lantern and lit it
and then came back out, but the lantern only
made the darkness seem darker. So he stood
there a moment on the porch in the gently
swinging glow of the lantern light and watched
the orange sparks of the fireflies blurring and
weaving their way through the tree shadows

along the bottom of the hill and then fading
in the deepening gloom, and ever so faintly
he heard the sound of the sea. He started off
down the hill and moved through the black of
the trees and the moss slapping him in the face
and the low- waiting branches whipping back
and stumbling over roots or almost and also
the gnats. He moved through all of this, though
just where he was going even he did not seem
to know, away from the faint sea-sound and the
porch and the smell of twice-cooked beans, and
then the air was still and hot and had the feel of
being dead.

It was good, he thought, that thing he
had said about fear. He hadn't known just
what to say to the boy, all the way he'd been
dragging him up through the marsh grass
he'd been wondering what'd he say and how
he'd say it, give him a thing or two to think
about, that's what he had told himself back
at the beach, which caught the general drift
of his mood concerning the boy but it didn't
help much with the particulars, and then he'd
been sitting on that Co-Cola crate and getting
worried by then but he figured he might as well
give the boy a couple of good whacks for the
crabs and get something to eat, and if he
didn't think of anything by then he'd maybe
give him a couple more. But then there was
the way that boy looked when he ate up those
beans, like they were the last beans he was ever

gonna eat, him spooning them in as fast as he
could but his eyes weren't watching the beans,
that's when it had come to Thaddeus, him now
remembering the words, *most folks is so afraid
of living they cant wait to go to war and they is so
afraid of dying they cant pass up a church without
going inside.* But the boy didn't show the same
kind of fear most people had, hell no, not the
way he kept to himself and his eyes always
watching, why he didn't even cry out from the
hickory, he just stood there waiting for more,
not insolent or defiant, just detached, and for
a moment Thaddeus had felt he was looking
into his own eyes. This is what Thaddeus was
thinking when he looked at the boy. He could
still see him eating there and those eyes above
that spoon. Goddamn it, and he was laughing
to himself now, I bet that boy would've been
shitting beans if I'd of taken up that stick again.
Then Thaddeus laughed out loud, but then just
as suddenly became quiet again, thoughtful, for
it seemed to him a profound wisdom he had
spoken to the boy.

Then the thinking was done, but Thaddeus
was still walking through the black black
woods. He walked in stiff, unthinking silence,
and then he came to a small tar-papered shack
overlooking the black black channel water
several yards below, and he went inside. The
very same shack where more than thirty years
earlier Long Jim had bemoaned the loss of his

leg and the two lanterns had been left. But it was dark now, for those lanterns had long since expired, and Thaddeus set his own on a chair by the door and then took a stick and lit the two still there on the floor, and also a small red lantern in the middle of the table, and then he sat down in another chair. The last time he had been there was eight or nine years after the child and he had made a new door out of a piece of pine and dragged the broken table up the slope and fixed that too, but he hadn't done anything about the chalk circle. It had seemed almost burned into the wood slats of the floor. And so he had left it as a reminder, a marker of sorts, though of just what he had only vaguely articulated to himself. But in time even this circle had disappeared from the floor, and everything was as it had been before Long Jim and his leg, except for the two lanterns.

It's been a too, too long time, he thought, and then with unhurried movements he reached underneath the table and pulled out a canvas backpack and opened it and pulled out a can of peaches, or maybe it was pears, and a can opener and then opened the can and sniffed at it and it seemed tolerable in spite of the years so he slurped down the fruit and then the sweet, sticky juice. Then he left the empty tin on the table and put away the can opener and the backpack, and then he picked up the small, red, now red- glowing lantern and was

out the door, glancing but briefly at the dark
gash of the backwater channel below and then
making his way around to the rear of the shack,
and there he stood a while contemplating the
dark, sloping grade of a small rise, and then
beyond that it dipped away. Then he started
up, the dim yellow glow of the tar-paper shack
unfelt against his back, but he was walking
more cautiously now than when he had come
up through the wood, more slowly, almost not
moving at all, as if in nearing his purpose in
coming to this place he had suddenly changed
his mind, or forgotten what it was, or was by
some invisible, oppressive hand being forced to
a stuttering, halting, but inevitable abnegation
of things. Of himself, perhaps. Of the way
things had been the past twenty years and him
not giving a goddamn. From somewhere a
wisp of wind fluttered against his face and for
a moment he thought he could smell the sea,
and then the wind and the sea-smell were gone
and he was standing at the top of this small rise
and looking down into the spreading darkness
below him. He knew near enough where it was,
but he couldn't see it in the dark. Thinking,
*damn, I should of been back long before this, what
if something dug it up, what then, or maybe there
was water got in and floated it away, this goddamn
swamp you cant keep it in one place before its
bubbling up somewhere else, goddamn it, what the
hell I been doing.*

Uncautiously now, he trundled through
the darkness, the small red lantern bobbing its
light this way and that in enthusiastic but silent
accompaniment. But the dark did not give way,
and seemed even to suck up the light as he
reached the bottom, so he ranged back and forth
through a dark, thickening clutch of willow oak
and some bay, and there was also a tangled,
viny mass of muscadine and wisteria, all the
while punching at the darkness with the lantern,
his free hand pushing through the branches and
the vines, and then dragging himself through.
He was no longer merely a watcher of things,
or so it seemed, but was once again a doer.
And then suddenly he found it, a small clear
patch among a few pine, and he set the lantern
down and knelt and pulled at the vines that had
crept over the mound and the three flagstones
he had put there to mark the grave, and the
vines came loose and he brushed them away
and also the loose dirt and then re-stacked the
flagstones neatly one on top of two, and then
he was satisfied and sat back some. Still he kept
his eyes on the grave, an intent, silent, aching,
but also bewildered look about his face, as if he
had suddenly and unexpectedly seen his own
newly-dug grave in the now soft, humming
dark. Thinking, *I should of been back long before
this, but I've been here some and that's more than
she can say, hell, she didn't come even once, she
didn't even ask, and it was hers as much as mine.*

And from a distance there was only the small lantern glowing like a red bead against the night, for the old man had seemingly vanished into the moist, enveloping shadows. But still sitting there. Thinking, *but maybe she didn't want it, that would explain it, maybe she even wanted it born dead and that way she wouldn't have to bother.* And then *hell, it wasn't hers at all, not ever, it was always mine, only and always.* And then even the light from the lantern was gone.

-4-

And then he had come to the end of it. The end of a life and the death that was to be. And he was not afraid. In the brutal solitude of his old age he had come to appreciate the directness of death, the unblinking honesty of dying. He thought of death and dying as he might think of a quiet conversation with an old friend, no eye of God watching over your every step, no hand of the devil trying to trip you up, just two old friends talking for eternity, an endless stream of words, *what you doin here i been riding in this here car for more years than i care to count on account of these chains on my feet i been riding around hope to come across someone help me break free is that what you doin here is you the one . . .*

He tossed the overgnawed crab bone to the pile of white at the center of the table the

bone clattering among the many bones. Then
he stood up from the table and walked to the
door the walk of a man having eaten too much
each step somewhat rounded him moving to
the openness of the porch he stopped a moment
the sickly green sky having become a deep
heavy purple the storm beginning now the first
few drops of rain pelting the ground and him
listening to the rain, and the mingling of past
and present was complete, or so it seemed, him
looking over to the boy *whyunt you just pull
up them pants and sit yourself down i aint gonna
eat these goddam beans all by myself* and then he
saw that the boy had finished with an endless
stream of big blue crabs had finished the last
of the words his words and then the boy was
gone and instead he saw himself in the deep
of the backwater wood the black shadows of
the water oak and the pine and the redbay
becoming a single shadow the wink- on-wink-
off-wink-on-again light of the fireflies patches
of bright yellow flitting from branch to branch
wink on wink off like the souls of the dead
flitting from the here to the hereafter lost souls
perhaps wink on wink off and the man name of
Thaddeus followed the winking dead through
the trees *follow me follow me follow me* a thousand
voices winking a thousand and a thousand
more the voices winking with laughter in the
dark dark *follow me follow me follow me* and he
followed the patchwork of beckoning laughter

then the bright yellow dimming the laughter
growing softer and softer with every step and
the laughter was gone and he saw the wrinkled
face the wrinkled hands of a small child a
small blueblack body in his arms the child not
breathing the fingers curled toes curled and
there he was in a small clearing him now laying
the child of his devilmaybesorrow by his side
him then remembering the voices on the porch
and her pain and then the silence then him
digging in the earth the warm soil moist in his
hands digging deeper and deeper the weight of
the earth the weight the click click click of crab
toed feet then the black boy almost a man inside
the cabin his face pressed up against the glass
of the window and then he Thaddeus kneeling
before a small black hole him breathing hard
his lungs filling with the quiet dirtdamp air
then him laying the child in the hole and he had
wanted to give this child something of himself
a sense of life and some words to live by but
there were no words now not for this blueblack
child and him feeling wordless voiceless but
only for a moment the grief the inadequacy the
fear then pouring out up and then the body of
the blueblack child changing then changed the
blueblack white the white white of the moon
it seemed the wrinkled face not wrinkled the
fingers the toes not curled and him sprinkling
the black earth upon the body sprinkling slowly
the whiteness of the child rising up to fill the

hollow places in the sky then the whiteness
gone him kneeling before the mound of a newly
filled grave him kneeling now in prayer the
voice of his grief and the whiteness of his words
rising up to the sky also, *you there and then im*
here and then i do not understand and then you
were not meant to understand and then why did
this child have to die and then what child and then
the child buried in this grave my child my flesh
my blood my bone and then i do not know children
are born children die i do not know why there is
no why only living and dying and then but why
this child i do not understand and then you were
not meant to understand there is no understanding
you must root out the memory of the living child
from the hollow black of your brain and bury that
memory alongside the body and then it is more than
memory and then then you must become the child
and take your place in the grave and the child will
be of no more consequence that all you want yes all
right by me, and for a moment the past became
the past once again and the old man name of
Thaddeus found himself standing on the edge
of the porch still standing there still looking to
the stormy blackness of the sky but he did not
seem to notice it the harsh pelting of the rain
now against his face but he did not seem to
feel it him moving now to the cabinside of the
porch a lantern hanging from a hook above the
door him lifting the glass of the lantern taking a
match from his pocket then striking a flame the

light sputtering a moment in the breezy stormy
dark then catching then filtering through the
yellow yellow glass and mixing with the dark
him stepping from the lantern and the swirling
light and dark and sitting down in a cane-back
chair the rain sweeping across the edges of the
porch now but not where he was sitting him
sitting there listening to the voice of a child the
child singing then the last of the earth would
fall upon him and he would be surrounded by
its blackness its warmth and the singing would
the singing would him taking his pipe from his
pocket putting pipe to mouth the pipe unlit him
listening to the words of the song, what was
now is what is now was, an endless stream of
words . . .

. . . but the very next morning, along come a
third man, only he didnt look like much, he wunt
big big like the first, and he wunt wearing a knife
like the second, and the animals they thought they
done seen enough they was just shaking they heads
some more they was saying say it wunt go be long
fore this one in the alligator belly just like the rest,
but the third man he didnt pay them tree-sitting
animals no mind, maybe he done heard that alligator
roaring and roaring and come looking the same as
the first and the second, but he wunt coming too fast
or either bold, and he wunt talking neither, cause he
knowd a alligator wunt nothing fool with, all he did
he just stop along the edge of the swamp and he was
looking to that alligator sunning hisself on that log,
and next he pull out a piece of rope he make hisself a
noose and that was it, and all the while that alligator
he was waiting on the third man same as the rest,
and he was waiting and waiting and waiting but
wunt nothing happening, and by and by the alligator
he done look to see what was what, and all he seen
was a man with a rope aint make no move, and the
alligator he wunt sure what to think with that, and
the animals up in dem trees they wunt sure neither,
and then it seem like the end was coming cause the
alligator he wunt go wait no more, he was sliding
from that log into the water he was go show that
man whose world it was, only before that alligator

make it halfway up the bank, the third man he done
slip a thick thick noose around them alligator jaws
and pull it tight, and with that the alligator he
wunt able to open his mouth, and he was shaking
his head this way and that try to shake hisself loose,
only wunt nothing he could do, and the more he was
shaking, the more tire he was, and pretty soon all he
wanted was to slip way into the cool of the swamp
maybe hide in a hole, but the third man he didnt let
go, and when the alligator he done tire hisself out,
the third man he done pull on that rope some more,
and then he tied it off, and before that alligator he
knowd what was what, the third man he done grab
him by the tail and he was swinging him round and
around and around, and when the third man he done
let go of that rope, that alligator he went rising up
through them trees, and then the alligator he was
gone . . .

The Storm

-1-

It been three week since I seen the old man, not since he pull me out from that alligator, which it just go to show how Willie and the rest of them they all been wrong. He aint no devil. The truth is most people just dont know him, and he dont care. Then Im is thinking say just why it is I aint seen him and what it is he been doing, and soon as I thinking that it have the feeling like the old man he waiting on me this very minute, and then it aint the old man at all it like I is supposed to go do something or something go happen, and then it the old man again. It sure is strange thinking like that the way it shift back and forth. Then Jonas Lee he come hobble along on his crutches and I aint thinking on nothing no more and Jonas Lee he look like he some kind of crab the way he moving through the dust of the street, and then he go through the gate and bang it shut, and before I can say a word he sitting next to me out the front stoop.

The first thing Jonas do he smile he saying he another idea, and that the last thing I want to hear, but aint nothing I can do cause Jonas he already talking. Jonas he saying say he wanna head on up to Pappa Toms maybe slip inside and he aint wanna go all the way by hisself

maybe I come along, didnt I always want to
stick my head on the inside, of course I did,
didnt I know the same stories, I'd heard them
too, anyways what was I doing round here
the middle of the afternoon, wunt nothing for
excitement like Pappa Toms, so what I say. Is
just then my mama she call out from the back
of the cabin she saying say I best get inside help
her tie down the windows aint I look to the
sky there a big big blow coming look to be here
a couple of hour maybe three, and mama she
right about the sky it a pale graygreen stretch
out to the south, but there aint much wind
yet, and there aint no rain far as I can see, and
before she open her mouth call out again, Im is
walking up the street with Jonas Lee.

The whole way we walking Jonas Lee he
telling me about his brother B. J. how he done
walk in all by hisself the first time he ever
been to Pappa Toms, how the lights they was
burning low from the walls, and was all kind
of grease-heads and chaw-talkers from over
the coast sitting at some darkwood tables and
drinking rye or whiskey and laughing and
humming and talk about the girls, and some of
the girls they already found theyself a partner
they was dancing out front or maybe up the
stairs they already had enough to drink, and
there was a whole lot more waiting to wet they
throats, but B. J. he couldnt move even to lick
his lips. Was then a couple of them girl they

done come up to him, and they was giggling
say what was he doing there didnt he want to
come upstairs or was he nail to the floor, and
B. J. his eyes they was smiling up and down
them girls he looking to catch some skin, and
then they was moving up the stairs, the two
girl in front they was wiggling they hips side to
side, and B. J. his eyes they was wiggling side
to side the same, and then they was up in some
room and the door shut, and every now and
then they voices was drifting down, first was
B. J. saying say he ready he waiting, and them
two girl they was giggling, and then B. J. he
was saying say what they do like that for there
room enough on this bed for three, and then
them two girl they was giggling some more, and
the next thing what happen them two girl they
was running down the stairs and out the front
and then they was gone, and B. J. he was at the
top of the stairs and shout about them two girl
he was saying say they done rob him stole his
pants off the chair, and sure enough, he wunt
wearing nothing but his shoes, and the dancers
and the drinkers down the first floor they was
all laughing, and some what knowd B. J. was
saying how you like you first taste you must of
liked it a whole lot cause look like you hungry
for more, and then everybody was laughing so
much was hard to think, and B. J. he was down
the steps, he took them three at a time, and then
he was out the front the same as them two girl.

Pappa Toms it shining with a couple
hundred orangewhite light strung along a black
shingle roof, they winking on and then off and
then on and then off again, look like fireflies
floating up in the black of the wood, and there
a heavy crowd of peoples going up some blue
blue steps and across this low hang porch, and
there a fat head he be nodding evening from top
of a blackwood stool and he saying say hope
you all have you some kind of ruckus tonight
storm or no storm for blow, and the peoples
they all nodding they heads, only some they
turning they eyes have a look at that graygreen
storm-coming sky, but only a moment, and they
all going through a couple of blue blue door,
and then they gone.

Me and Jonas Lee we watching from back
in the hammock, and Jonas Lee he saying say
the only way we moving past that nodding fat
head is through the back door, and with that
we moving down a narrow blackwood walkway
stretch around to the backside of Pappa Toms.
We moving up along from the water, past a
couple three rowboat tie down in the water
and something else look like a barge, past some
old wood boxes and some empty bottle toss
down in the grass, and then we sliding inside
of a black screen door almost fall off its hinges,
and the next thing I knows we is sitting at a
two-chair table shove up in the corner, and aint
nobody seen us come in.

For a while we just watching what goes.
There a couple three talking heads sitting next
to us, they saying say there be some storm
coming tonight and that the truth, and then they
laugh, and then they drinking they beer. Most
the mens they drinking bottle beer and some
they drinking whiskey or rye, and some they
sitting hunch over they tables slap anything
on the behind it come for wiggle by, and some
they just tapping they feet to the music, and
some they wearing white string ties and stub
toe shoes and they out there on the dancing
floor they saying say come on wind come on
rain aint nothing look bad you riding a train,
and a whole lot of other things aint make no
sense, but them girls they giggling no matter
what they say and moving up close, and then
the mens they all shouting some more. All this
happening to the sound of a brown- bear piano
man sitting up front at a tin pan piano and bang
away at the keys, and he smiling like he a whole
other piano stuck up in his mouth, and his
head it bobbing back and forth with every note,
and the music it swell up in the smoke-yellow
glow of the lights, bigger, bigger, and bigger,
and them dancing people they moving faster
and faster and faster, pretty soon aint nothing
to see but arms reaching up and legs kicking
out, how nobody been kick I aint know, and me
and Jonas Lee we watching everything like we
watching a movie.

Is then a long-legged woman come walking
into the roadhouse up front she move across
the floor, she wearing some kind of gold wrap
around her body and she has two yellow-
brown eye match her yellow-brown skin, and
a long thick braid of hair hang down her back,
and everybody they staring at her the way she
moving through Pappa Toms, they aint dancing
or either drinking, they aint doing nothing no
more, and she swishing this way and that like
she some kind of river, and then some they start
up when she pass by, they saying say look at
that Jordan she the only woman in this place,
she the land of milk and honey come to us,
aint no river you need to cross you on top of
her, but the woman she just smile and dont say
nothing, and all the while me and Jonas Lee
we just four blinking eyes, and wouldnt it be
something talk to a woman like that, only what
you go say, and then wouldnt need nothing to
say, just looking at her all I want to do, and all
of a sudden it look like she coming to me and
Jonas Lee, only what she go do that for I dont
know, and then she standing right there, she
looking me up and down and smiling, and I
wondering what Jonas Lee go think only just
then Jordan she leaning down real close, and
the way she smell, like apricots or something,
it knock Jonas Lee out of my head, all I care
about is breath that Jordan in, and all the while
I breathing, that gold wrap it going swish swish

swish, and then Jordan she running her fingers
through my hair and whispering in my ear, she
saying say come with me sweetie you follow
me aint nothing you need to worry about I only
go show you a thing or two maybe you like it,
and the next thing I knows she kissing me on
my neck and then around to my mouth, and
the way she smell like apricots and her tongue
curling up around mine, it almost knock me
out, and then she pull away and she pulling
me away with her, and she saying say, come on
sweetie if the rest of you move like that we go
have us some sweet time.

First thing Im is thinking is I aint never been
on a dance floor before, and all that twisting
and grinding and kicking and shouting, well I
just dont know, but just then that brown-bear
piano man he slowing things down, he playing
a grief-song now about some girl been left by
a railroad man but then she marry his brother,
and maybe I can do that, only Jordan she must
have some other idea cause we moving past the
dancing and the heat of that sad sad song, and
Jordan she saying say come on sweetie aint too
long now, only she aint say where we going,
and the next thing I knows we heading upstairs,
up these rickety old steps been cover by an old
blue rug, and Im is looking back at the dancing
and the piano man and Jonas Lee he still sitting
at that two-table chair in the corner only look
like he have his own trouble cause a couple girl

they got a hold of his crutch, aint nobody let go,
and then Jordan she saying we almost there it
wont be long, and we moving down a lamp- lit
hall.

I aint never seen a hall like that. The lamps
they aint giving off much light, it like walking
through a blueblack cloud, and there doors all
over the place, and Jordan she trying every door
she see, but they all lock, and Im is trying a
couple myself, and one door it do come open,
only out come a bony arm man, and he waving
a bottle of rye in the air and he saying when
the fire too hot the wick most likely go soft,
and then he rattling with a bony-arm laugh,
look like he about to head downstairs, and
then a voice come calling out say I aint mean
it Horace you come back now, and Horace he
wink at me he saying happen every time, then
he back inside and shutting the door. Is then
Jordan she calling me from the end of the hall
and she saying she found one aint too big she
hope I like it, and with that Im is following her
through the shadow and into the room. There
only one window, so it pretty dark, and look
to be getting darker too cause the graygreen
sky outside it almost black now, and the rain it
running up against the window, and every now
and then the wind it blow like a freight train
coming through. Then Jordan she turn on a floor
lamp bring a little light, and then she slipping
out of her clothes, and I aint know just what to

do she do that, maybe look around find a towel
to give her but there aint even that, and Jordan
she laughing all the while she saying say she
aint mind that storm even it blow the roof away,
and then she spread herself out on a rumple
sheet iron-post bed, and the soft yellow light
from the lamp it running up along the inside
of her legs and then down again, it all I can do
keep from staring with my mouth.

Well, I aint know just what I doing after
that, and then Jordan she saying say come on
sweetie she only go bite a little bit, and then
she laugh, and before Jordan she say another
word I climbing up beside her on the bed, and
where my pants and shirt they at I cant say
for sure, I aint remember taking them off, but
somehow Im is still wearing my shoes, and that
some comfort, only Jordan she see that and
she laughing some more she saying she aint
heard of nobody keep his shoes on his feet, only
what she have against shoes she aint say, and
then she reach up pull me on top, and her legs
climbing up around mine, and Im is thinking
to myself aint nobody downstairs dancing this
close when just then that freight train storm
come slamming itself into the side of Pappa
Toms. With that then the window in Jordan
room it bust into a couple hundred piece slice
through the air, and then the stormwater rolling
in come roll across the floor knock the floor
lamp out then on to the bed, and me and Jordan

we aint wait around see what happen next, we
scrambling through the door and out into the
blueblack of the hall.

Looks like there water everywhere, but me
and Jordan we the first ones running down
the hall, and some they peeking out from they
blueblack doors see what what they saying say
Lordy they aint never seen so much water full
up a house before where it all coming from
sure hope them people downstairs they all
know how to swim, and then everybody out
in the hall and everybody naked too, and we
all running for the stairs, only we run smack
into them downstairs people they running
up, and someone say aint nothing down there
except you a fish, and then everybody stop,
aint nobody know just what to do, and all the
while the water in that hall keep rising, it up
to our knees now, and then another voice call
out he say there some stairs the other end of
the hall go all the way up to the roof, and then
everybody they off running again, aint nobody
even mind some is naked and some aint, and
a couple three more they even taking off they
clothes as they go just to be polite, and then
everybody up on the roof come face to face
with that freight-train storm, and there so much
water now Pappa Toms look like a raft, and
some of them peoples they aint wait for the
water get any higher, they diving off the roof
maybe swim to a tree, but the rest they just

huddle up hold on to anything they can, and me
and Jordan we doing the same, and then all of a
sudden there a stormwater wave come roll over
that roof wash everything clean.

-2-

The next thing I know, the storm and the
water and Jordan and the trees and Pappa
Toms itself they all gone, aint nothing but a
black, black haze cover everything up, and I
cant move about see anything different. If that
aint dead I dont know what. But maybe it aint
so bad being dead, it aint like people been say,
seem like it go be a comfort just lie there all day
all night aint nothing more you has to think
about, not the old man and everything he been
saying and doing and is he waiting on me and
what I suppose to do, and not Willie and all his
devil talk and how he aint never go stop till he
meet up with the old man face to face like two
railroad trains run smack into each other, not
worry about what you go do next and is you
afraid or aint you, all of that you done with
when you is dead, and all the while I is thinking
like that, the black black haze it lifting, slow,
slow, and then all of a sudden there a nighttide
sky with a bright blue moon, and I is walking
through the thick of the wood, brushing past
moss and branches, and climbing over the wet

of dead logs and up around the ghostdark of
palmetto stands, only where exactly I is and
where I going I cant say, and by and by I sees
a small blue fire burn in the distance, and then
from out the blueblack of the wood I hears some
voices and they talking about all the crabs they
done caught and how they done shell a couple
three thousand they done boil them and eat
them up and my oh my how soft and sweet that
crab meat is it aint never taste so fine before
what they go do they run out, and then they
cackling like they knows they aint never go
run out of crabmeat, and the cackling it getting
louder and louder, and it must be coming from
some witches cause who else sit around under
a blue moon munch on a couple three thousand
crab, and the next thing Im is standing on the
edge of a small clearing, and there am three
witches sitting up around a smoky blueblack
kettle with a small blue fire up under, and the
witches they all wearing black tatter skirts,
black tatter shawls, but they eyes bright as
smoke, and all they all doing they eating and
talking and grabbing for crabs out of that kettle,
and they look to been eating crabmeat maybe
two three year the way there crab bones pile
up all over the ground, and look to be some
stony chip crows poking they beaks through
them piles turn over the bones, they scrounge
abouts theyselves looking to eat some scrap of
crabmeat and clawing at each other they find

some, and then they looking to them witches
they blue bead eyes full up with hungry and
crow-squawking sound like throw down some
more throw down some more throw down some
more, and them witches they acting like they
aint heard they just keep adding to the pile, but
every now and then they squinting some then
fling some crabmeat to the crows, and with that
the crows they flapping they wings some more
and snapping at the meat in the air, and it gone
before it ever get to the ground, and with that
Im is stepping back slow and easy, the last thing
Im is wanting is them witches see me hiding in
the trees, and I just about to turn and run off
into the dark when them witches they stop they
cackling and turn they smoke bright eyes to the
wood, and the crows they turning they eyes the
same.

"Aint nothing you need to worry about,
honey," say the first. "We been expecting you."

The other two they be echoing the first one
words, and then they all cackling to theyself,
but it aint seem like they know exactly where
I is the way they looking out through all them
pile of bones and into the blue black of the
night, which all right by me, but why I aint
even think to run I dont know why, and then
the witches they all calling out they saying say
now honey come on now honey come on, and
it all I can do be resist with that, and then they
aint saying now honey no more, and the first

one she raise a bony white hand and she snap
her bony white fingers in the air crack crack like
she cracking the bones of one of them crabs, and
with that then them crows they up from they
piles they flapping they wings and squawking
some more, only this time it sound like break
all his bones break all his bones, and then they
swooping up through the heavy black shadows
of the trees, and the witches they cackling some
more, only they more appetite in they voices
now, and Im is wanting to run, only them crows
they closing in they smoke eyes burning aint no
where to go, and then the witches they saying
say here he come he coming now, and the next
thing I knows Im is floating in that smoke black
kettle, only how that happen I aint know, and
the crows they sitting down around the edge
of the fire they in a stony chip ring looking up
to them witches they all expectation like maybe
there some crabmeat coming to them by and
by, and I looking to the crows, and then to the
witches and them piles of crab bone, and what
I go do now I aint even know where to begin,
and the witches they cackling say wunt too
many boys running round the wood in nothing
but they shoes, and then they laughing for feel
the pluck of my arms and legs with they bony
white hands, and then they cackling some more
they saying say what a fine figure of a boy,
fine figure, he almost a man, you feel that juice,
we having we some kind of feast tonight, we

is, more better than all that crabmeat, even the
bones, they aint go be hardly nothing left for
the crows eat up, nothing, but that the way it go
sometimes, and then they asking me say they
hoping the water it hot enough, and I saying
say it is, feel like the meat of my bones been
boil away for soup, and I knows I dont find me
some way out of this pot I aint go be fit keeping
company with even them crows, only seem like
Im is all lock jaw cause I cant move for even
pray, and then the witches they dancing around
that kettle they cackling some more and singing
and chanting,

> *The devil he dance for eat them bones,*
> *See he dancing in a brakemans shack,*
> *Then the devil he done and going home,*
> *Pick his teeth with a wooden jack.*

> *Up and up and up the smoke,*
> *See the kettle boy start to choke,*
> *Time he done it time for eat,*
> *Aint that kettle boy tasting sweet.*

> *The devil he say he coming back,*
> *All he find is a empty shack.*
> *Been twenty year that kettle boy gone,*
> *Been twenty year we sing this song.*

And the words of that song they rising up
with the steam from that kettle, sound like

someone ringing a bell, and then the steam it
burning white and whiter, and pretty soon that
all there is, and from out of that white come a
voice, sound like it me talking to myself, and
the voice it saying say them witches they done
spend they time getting fat off the bones of dead
folk only I aint dead so what I doing I want to
end up a twenty year kettle boy course not then
what I afraid of aint I enough sense know what
to do aint I the sense God give a bean there aint
nothing be afraid of just do what you have to,
and with that then the voice it gone, and Im
is climbing up over the side of that kettle, and
then Im is running from the smoke smell rising
and them stone-chip crows waiting around to
eat and them piles of crab bones scatter in the
grass and them song-singing witches the same,
and I knows I been that close to dead, only
I aint, and then just like that I is running up
along the beach, feel like I been running three
whole day too, and look like it close to supper
time the way the sun hang low in the sky, and
the next thing I know I aint running no more,
Im is looking to the dark blue water, and aint
nothing run through my mind now, it gone
numb, and then Im is sitting stretch out on the
cool cool hardpack sand and feel the waves
wash around my feet.

It take me a while know just what I go do
next, feel almost like I done crawl out the blue

blue water instead of sitting there looking at it,
and then I is thinking on what done happen to
me, only I have no idea, but I too too happy I
aint dead to worry now, I go figure it out soon
enough, and then I is asking myself say when
the last time I been eat, been too long aint it,
wouldnt some of Tramsee peach pie hit the spot,
maybe she cook up some of her fried chickens
go with it, and with that then Im is heading for
Ty and Tramsee shack, almost taste that sweet
peach pie, and then I there. Look like no one
been out since the storm to put it back together,
look worse than the last time too there boards
bust up all over sticking out of the sand, a iron
post bed turn over its side, a couple pillow and
the mattress fold down a top of some sea oats,
some pots and plates and spoons and soup cans
and empty bottles and magazines and shoes and
a old tire too, they all scatter up one dune and
down the next, and then off to one side, look
almost like a photograph, there Ty he sitting
in a cane bottom chair sea weed all up around
his feet, he wearing the pants from a blue serge
suit, and a cotton shirt, but he done forgot about
his socks and shoes, and all he doing he looking
to the sea and working on a bottle of rye.

Ty he aint see me yet, so I walking up to the
chair and come up behind, and then I saying
say what you waiting on Ty, only loud enough
in his ear give him a jump, only he dont move,
he just sit there mumbling to hisself, he going

on and on, how there must have been a couple
hundred peoples moving through the backwater
wood and all the way down to town they
looking for somebody, only who it is he aint
say, and some they was busy dragging chains
through the blackgreen water and the heavy
heavy hammock and every now and then they
was calling out to stop and have a look and
then they was shaking they heads and dragging
some more, and some they was flipping through
what left of Pappa Toms, which Ty he was
saying there wunt enough Pappa Toms left sell
for kindling, and then Ty he going on about
how it was too too hot so hot feel like the air
itself melting and most everybody was too too
tired go on with them chains, and then Ty he
talking how Willie come up the road just then
and Willie was saying wunt nobody go find
nobody that boy he must a been eat up by the
devil that wunt no natural storm that was a
devil-come-take-me storm and that just what
the devil he done too he done take that boy for
eat him up wunt nothing left to do now but go
to church Sunday give that boy up to God that
the only thing help him now, and then Willie
he was heading back to town and everybody
else was going with him, and with that then
Ty he start whispering now, he saying say get
ready, it almost time, it almost time they done
move it up, it aint go be Sunday, it be this here
night, Friday night, then we all go see God

face to face, and then Ty he just stop like that,
he looking straight into my face like he just
seen me then, only he dont say a word, he just
clutching that bottle of rye, and the next thing
happen he up from the chair and he stumbling
across the sand.

I aint know what to say the way Ty he run
off. Im is standing next to that cane bottom
chair and thinking say it something what a
bottle of rye can do, but that aint right, cause
Ty he aint never act that way before even he
drink a hundred bottle, but it sure hard to say
just what he talking about, and then it come
to me say I aint wearing nothing but shoes,
what else a drunk man say and do a naked
boy come at him from behind, and with that
I kicking the sand and laughing, and then I is
looking through what left of Ty and Tramsee
shack maybe find me something to wear, only
aint nothing but more shoes, aint even a hat,
and the next thing Im is edging down along
the beach make my way to town, aint no telling
how many peoples eating they supper or either
done and sitting on they porches talking some
or maybe just watch the red of the sky fade a
deep blackblue, and what they go say they see
me jaybird naked I aint want to know so I best
find me a place hide out till they all go to bed,
and then something inside me say hide out in
the church, which it make the most sense, cause
aint nobody go to church on a Friday night

no matter what that crazy old Ty was talking
about.

I aint been long inside when the church bell
it start ringing out, and what that mean I aint
know, and I trying to think, only nothing come,
but the church is the last place I want to be that
bell keep ringing, so I back to the welcome room
and open the door, only it too too late cause the
whole town they walking up the street, look like
they all mules been tied to a plow they walking
so slow, but they coming all the same. Nothing
to do but crouch down back of some old sofa
been left inside for waiting, pray nobody think
to look my way, which I does just that, and
then the door open and in come the town, and
the mens they in they Sunday black suits and
Sunday black hats even it only Friday, and some
they wiping they faces with handkerchiefs and
talking grim and low, and some they kicking
the dust off they shoes and straighten up
they ties and they aint saying a word, and the
womens they in they Sunday black dresses and
hats the same, and some they reading out from
they black bible books and they walking with
they words, and some they singing, sound like
grief songs, and some they just talking to hear
theyself talk.

"What a boy like him doing a place like that
I like to know," say one.

"Hell, he a boy like any boy," say a second.

"One thing for sure," say a third. "There

plenty of worse ways to spend your last day on
this here earth."

"Aint that the truth," say the second, and
then they all laughing low and looking to sit
theyself down maybe somewhere in the back,
and the next thing I know everybody inside and
they sitting down the same, but just who they
come to see off I dont know, and then it come
to me maybe it Jonas Lee Porter, cause I aint
seen him come in, only what he get hisself kill
for, he know more better than that, but then I
is thinking maybe Jonas Lee he aint dead like
everybody think, maybe he playing the devil
go fool everybody else, and if that the case then
the peoples eyes they go jump soon as he walk
through the door and this I has to see, and with
that then Im is up from that old sofa and edge
up along the welcome room wall go take me a
look inside.

It sure is something to see. The church it
lit up with oil lamps burn from one side and
the other, but they aint give off a whole lot of
light, mostly shadow. There aint been so many
peoples stuff up in there since Mister Baxter his
funeral, and was so many then must of been
thirty or forty pass out on the floor. The only
thing different there aint no coffin, which it only
make sense cause Jonas Lee he aint dead, but
all the same the peoples they aint know. Some
they bending they heads most down to they
knees they moaning and rubbing they eyes, and

some they singing more of them grief songs,
and some they looking to they black bible books
they saying say sweet Jesus sweet Jesus over
and over. Even Mama and Tramsee they sitting
up front they holding each other hands and
they aint saying a word. Seem like nobody see
it coming but me, except maybe Ty, he know
something up cause he sitting back of Tramsee
whisper something in her ear and then she push
him back and he look around like he waiting on
a ghost.

Is then the Preacher Barnes he stepping
down from the reading desk, he look like a
shadow float through the gold flake lamplight,
and he walking back and forth across the front a
while, like he thinking on what to say, and then
he turn face out to the peoples, and he open
his mouth.   It have the look like he about to
swallow everybody there.

"We all know grief, brothers and sisters," he
say. "Aint none of we strangers."

And a couple womens they calling out they
know honey they know.

"We all go miss that boy, been missing him
already, but he in a better place, I knows that
been told by the Lord."

And some more they praising the Lord sweet
Jesus thank you thank you. Then the Preacher
Barnes he start talking a narrow, harsh voice.

"Aint all of us go be so lucky though," he
say.

And them praising voices they saying no sir we aint no sir.

"I knowd of a railroad man he been work the boiler of a engine up and down the South Carolina rail line must of been thirty-five year and he wunt so lucky. Every time the Lord call him he turn the other way face the devil."

And then them voices again.

"Sweet Lord Jesus no."

And the preacher he stepping down the aisle now, and he a black bible in his hand, and his voice it like a knife-thin whisper cut to the bone.

"That right brothers. That right sisters. He turn to face the devil instead of the Lord."

"Sweet Lord Jesus."

"Then one night the devil he give him his due. Railroad man he was having some trouble with a pop valve talking so much steam it was slowing things down, and hot too, but it wunt no ordinary trouble, brothers and sisters. No it wunt. A railroad man he know how to deal with ordinary trouble. No brothers and sisters, the trouble he face was the devil working his devilment."

And a couple women they fainting with that, and a couple more calling on Jesus save em save em now, and the Preacher Barnes he keep talking, only now his voice it rising with the steam from that boiler.

"The engineer he kept on calling back for more steam, and the railroad man he was trying,

he done about everything he think of, only it
wunt no use. That pop valve kept on hissing,
that hot kept on burning, and wunt long before
the railroad man he done lost his head and pick
up a shovel and he knock that pop valve hard
as he could, only time he do that the steam
from that boiler it done bust loose and burn him
dead."

And there voices come from all over the
church with that they saying say Lord a mercy
Lord aint nothing help him now sweet Jesus
dont let that happen here sweet Jesus Lord, and
then the Preacher Barnes he pull his voice back
a bit for everyone to hear.

"That railroad man he just like we all right
here we done turn face the devil instead of the
Lord and the devil he go give us our due we
dont turn back."

And some of the peoples they nodding they
heads like they know they been facing the devil
but they ready to turn the other way, and some
they saying, "No sir, no sir, we aint been face
the devil, no sir" and then the Preacher Barnes
he waving that black bible book of his in the air.

"You want to turn from the devil?"

And a whole lot of voices saying yes they
do.

"You ready turn from the devil face the
Lord?"

And them same voices saying they ready,
they ready now.

"Then this here the ticket take you where you wanna go, this here the fire of Jesus words, the fire of his name come burn away everybody sin, you wanna turn from the devil face the Lord you gotta have this ticket, then you be riding a train all the way to the promised land."

And the Preacher Barnes he walking back up the aisle now and he saying say aaaaaam-meennnnn brother, aaaaaammeennnnn sister, and the peoples they saying aaaaaammeennnnn back and swaying with the hum of them preacher words, sound like he the train he talking about, and it coming closer and closer,

and then all of a sudden Im is standing on a platform my face up against a crossstitch iron gate for wait, and there am all kind of people they waiting with me we all naked as the devils daughter, and we all waiting on a train, can hear it coming, only aint no one know just who go get on board, and then this wrinkle old man dress down in black bib- overalls and a black cap he stepping across the black of the rails, he a blue ball lantern swing loose by his side, and then he up on the platform the same, only he on the other side of the gate, and then he fixing that blue ball lantern on a hook and he waving his cap in the air, and with that a blackblue train move up along the platform, its wheels they whining angry with the slowdown, and then there a cloud of steam come hissing up from under, it curl up hot and heavy and roll up through that gate, but the people dont seem to mind cause maybe it go be more heat

where they going they miss this train, and then
everybody looking everybody else they thinking now
who got a ticket, and some they rifling through they
pockets they almost cat-crying say where they done
put it where it at and then my oh my oh my, and
then down on they knees and cat-cry some more, and
some they looking to buy, but aint nobody want to
sell, and some they shaking they fists in the air they
saying they go ride that train even they aint got a
ticket, and some they just staring into the white of
all that steam . . .

And then the Preacher Barnes he back at his
desk and he waving his bible some more. "But
dont you miss that train. You miss that train you
go be left to the devils own, that right brothers
and sisters, and then the devil he go feast on
your black barbecue bones hisself. But if you
hear the good Lord call out you name, then you
get on board, brother, you take your seat, sister,
cause you in for a gospel feast for all eternity
sure as you been born."

And with that the rumbling words they stop,
and the peoples they up from they benches they
shouting halleloo halleloo halleloo, sound like a
couple hundred bell ringing round and around,
and some of the people they laughing out loud,
and some they clapping they hands, and some
they burst out singing a heaven-train coming
song, and then everybody dancing, they dancing
on the floor, they dancing on they benches,
they dancing up the aisle to the reading desk,

and the Preacher Barnes he dancing just the
same, he waving his black bible book in the air,
look like he dancing with that book, and then
the Preacher Barnes he start up shouting and
singing, and then the peoples they shouting and
singing to match the preacher, and he shouting
and singing some more and they match him
some more, look like the whole church been set
on fire by the hand of God, and before I know
what what Im is shouting and singing and
dancing with all the rest,

and then the next thing happen Im is back on
that platform and staring into the white of all that
steam, and the conductor he standing on a black
block step out front of that train, and he calling out
names from a book and nodding his head at the old
man in the black cap to let them through, and the
rest aint been called they all hoping so hard look like
the gate go break, only it dont, and some they take
to praying, only no sound coming out, and some
it look like they ready to kick something, only they
just wait and see, and then the conductor he done
calling out names and he close up his book, and then
he step up into the train and then he gone, and with
that the peoples been left they rushing the gate try
to force they way through, only the old man in the
black overalls he working to shut that gate fast as
he can and beating back arms and legs all the while
with his cap, and then the gate it lock up tight and
the blueblack train give a sharp blast of its whistle
and then it pulling out, and some of the peoples they

reaching they arms through the crossstitch like they trying to catch hold of that train, and some they trying to climb over, only it too high, and some they mule- kicking anything get in they way, and with that a couple three fight break out and people losing teeth, and some like me, they aint saying a word, they just staring after that blueblack train, and then it give another sharp sharp whistle blast and it round the bend and then it gone, there nothing but a blueblack shadow hang dead in the air . . .

And with that Im is standing in the middle of the church, and aint nobody dancing and singing no more, look like they all turn face me instead, and some they falling to the floor right there it like they dead, and some they crouching down by they benches they holding they breath, aint nothing move except they black beetle eyes rattle round in they heads, and some they talking to the Lord like he hiding up in they hats, and some they just angry and take a couple three step closer, like they done miss that heaven-bound train wanna take it out on somebody, and then from out the black gold gloom of the church come a black beetle voice, and it rattling like some of them eyes.

"What it . . . what it is you want?"

The voice it coming from the Preacher Barnes, he leaning out from the shadow of his reading desk, and I aint know just what to say cause aint nothing I want, and then it come to me how it aint Jonas Lee suppose to been dead,

only where he at I still don't know, it was me all
along, I is the one been dead, only I don't know
what to say about that neither, so I dont say a
word, and the preacher he pause and bite his
lip, then he rattle loose some more words.

"We done . . . we done everything we could.
You been dead three whole day. What you . .
. what you wanna come bother us for?   Aint
nothing help you now you but the sweet Lord
Jesus."

The preacher then he pull his head back
into the turtle- shell dark, and some of the rest
they pulling they heads in the same, but aint
everyone scare of a three day dead naked island
boy suppose to been dead but aint, and some
they stepping closer almost crowd around to
find out, look like they thinking on make me a
ghost ifn I aint one already, and with that Im
is looking to the reading desk and all around
maybe find somebody help a poor naked boy
aint wanna be a ghost, only aint nobody want
to bother, even my mama she see me looking
she duck her head, and I saying say mama what
the matter with you I aint no ghost, and mama
she saying say course you aint child you just go
right on with what you is, and then she ducking
her head some more she wait and see what
happen next, and them stepping-closer faces
they just about staring me eye to eye, here go,
only just then everybody suck in they breath,
and them stepping-closer faces move over to

one side, and up step Willie, and the next thing
happen his voice it come hissing out through
the gaps in his teeth, and he asking me what I
is ifn I aint no ghost then why I running around
without any clothes it sure do have the feeling
like I one of the devils own, and Willie now
he standing tall in the gold black gloom of the
church, and he shaking his arm in the air along
with his words, there just a glint of gold dance
from his teeth, and he saying say it dont matter
you dead or not cause either way you been
seen with the devil you been seen following his
hand I seen you we all seen you but he been
using you boy try to turn you against you own
people, and the peoples they all rising up, they
eyes glowing with the gold black glint of them
Willie words they move to hear some more,
and Willie he saying say it about time we done
rid us of that old man devil, he been bringing
fire and storm to this here island long enough,
burn my store and warehouse down, been turn
our children against us then eat they bones, the
old man he been after this here boy for eat him
up, try to eat the other one too, but he done
got away, only cost him two broke legs too, but
them boys they only recent, aint none of we
forget what the old man done he get a hold of
a teenage girl, even it a hundred year ago, we a
long memory of that time, and most the peoples
they closing up around Willie they looking up
to him too cause Willie he look to be standing

twenty foot tall, and some they saying they aint
never heard it told that way before, and some
they saying well it the truth any way it told he
must of turn fifty girl against they own, and
some they aint saying a word they just waiting
for Willie tell them what to do, and then all of
a sudden Willie he grab hold of someone black
bible book, and he standing up front by the
reading desk now, and he saying say all we
need is the word of God to chase that devil man
off of this island, like we chasing him with fire,
and then Willie he open up the fire of one of the
church lamps and he dip his black bible book
in the flame till it catch, and then he raise it up
above his head he saying say this here fire this
the ticket we go burn that old man out, and then
he waving his black bible torch in the air for
everybody to be doing the same, this here the
ticket, this here the ticket, and most they eyes
they glowing with the bright red of that Willie
torch it cut like a switch through the deep deep
dark, and then they taking they own books and
they leaping to lamps, and before long there
burning books anywhere you look so many the
church it full up with smoke, and from out of
that smoke come Willie chanting some more he
saying say this is it this is it, and then the rest
they all chanting the same and waving they
black bible torches in the air, and it looking like
some wild hoodoo dance, only it aint no dance,
and then it like everybody been caught up in a

picture and there a voice up inside my head it
saying say *aint I enough sense know what to do the
old man waiting on me now this very minute this
here what suppose to happen so you go do what you
have to do what you suppose to do aint nothing be
afraid of just go,* and then the voice it gone, and
everybody dancing and chanting and waving
they torches some more, and they heading for
the door now they saying say burn him out
burn him out, and the next thing I know I is
through the church doors and running for the
old man's cabin, fast as I can go.

-3-

Is like death itself when I get there. Aint
even the sound of the wind. There a yellow
ballglass lantern hang from a porch hook up
by the door, and the old man he sitting in the
soft shadows on the far side of the porch, only
he aint sitting, he laying back in a cane-back
chair like he done fall asleep, his feet prop
up on a crate, and then Im is up by the door,
and the hot of that yellow lantern light it burn
against the back of my head. Willie he always
been after the old man, and now he coming
with a pack of black bible revengement, but
maybe the old man know what to do, and then
we go see. But its then I see Thaddeus he aint
been sleeping, he been dead, and except for the

lantern been lit just a little while, look like he
been dead a couple three day cause aint nothing
been clean up after the storm. The next thing
I do I is reaching over turn the old man chair
around face the light, only somehow he still
in the shadow, and Im is thinking say what
that mean and staring into two black eye look
like holes the way they sunk in, and then all of
sudden I hears the old man voice, sound like it
coming from everywhere, and the old man he
saying say *it about time you done got here what
been keeping you boy it sure as hell been getting
cold sitting up in this here chair I wunt gonna last
much longer,* and then it seem like the old man
he blink them black, black eyes of his and then
he sitting up and then he saying say *this is yours
now you keep it maybe you see me again maybe you
dont you go on now go on they almost here,* and
then he hanging a chain around my neck, it the
one with that alligator tooth he been talk about,
and then it like he aint move at all, and the last
words he saying say he sure go miss the devils
daughter, and he laughing some, and then the
old mans voice it gone and I is thinking about
that alligator tooth around my neck and how
the old man done said when it was his time he
want to go up just like old Elijah, and before I
know what what Im is lifting the old man from
out that chair and bring him inside the cabin
lay him down on his bed, it almost look like he
smiling, and then Im is down under the sink

lay hold of a kerosene can and empty it out on
the floor and some on the bed and then all over,
and then Im is grabbing hold of that yellowglass lantern off the porch, aint much light left
but it enough, and it almost like the old man
he laughing again, and then I done throw that
lantern through the door watch it bust up under
the old mans bed, and with that there fire everywhere, it roll through the cabin like a stormwater flood, and Im is standing by the door
watch the tide of that fire roll up and over the
shadow of the old man, and all the while Im is
thinking say what everybody go do now the old
man dead, well theres one thing for sure, aint
nobody go blame they troubles on the devil and
look the old mans way, and then Im is thinking
on why the old man he give me his alligator
tooth, and I is sure I dont know, but all the
same it have the feeling like maybe I suppose to
take over where he leave off, only what exactly
that go mean, well I aint know that neither, and
then from out the fire the old man he laughing
some more, and then the laughing it gone, and
the shadow it gone the same, aint nothing left
but the smoke of burning wood, and then Im
is turning from the cabin I go leave it burn,
only there is Willie and the rest of them book
burning people, they faces rising up slow from
the black of the hill and the grass, they eyes
glowing bright with the red of the cabin fire,
and what happen next Im is saying say the old

man he dead already you all just be putting up
them books aint nothing more to do you all just
head on home, but aint nobody move, at least
not at first, and some of them wild-eye people
they looking up to the fire maybe wish they
had a part in it, and some they looking to they
black bible books, only them books they aint
nothing but charred black paper now, and most
everybody they looking to Willie they aint know
what to do, only Willie he aint know what to
do neither, and then a second time Im is saying
say the old man he already dead aint nothing
more for them to do, and with that the people
they shaking they heads they saying say if that
dont beat all, and then they turning one by one
from Willie and the fire and they walking to
the black of the hill and the grass and the sky,
and some they tossing they black bible books to
the ground, they aint hardly worth reading no
more, and then they all gone except for Willie,
and Willie his eyes they still burning bright with
the red of the old mans fire, and he looking at
me like he has to burn something even it me,
but that Willie-look it dont bother me none at
all, and then one more time Im is saying say the
old man he dead he already dead, and with that
the fire from Willie eyes it gone, and then Willie
he turn away a slow slow turning, and then he
walking into the black shadows of the hill and
the sky, and he holding a charred black book in
his hand. . .

. . . and with that the third man he was walking from the swamp and the log and the animals up in them trees, he was walking into the bluegreen haze of the wood, and the animals they was all laughing to theyself, and some was saying say it wunt the alligator world no more that for sure, and then they was all climbing down from they trees and going about they business.

February 21, 2010 Peter Damian Bellis

Made in United States
Orlando, FL
21 May 2024

47096648R00192